Acclaim for the authors of

'Tis

SU...
"Like a sorceres... ...enchants her readers
and carries them on a magical journey into the past."
—*Rendezvous*

SHARI ANTON
"Shari Anton weaves a wonderful tale of chivalry,
honor and love that overcomes the odds!"
—*Affaire de Coeur*

TORI PHILLIPS
"Ms. Phillips weaves an adventurous story…
a good, fast-paced read."
—*Romantic Times Magazine*

Dear Reader,

Happy holidays! Harlequin Historicals is thrilled to bring you *'Tis the Season*, a charming collection of short stories set in Merrie Olde England, written by three of our best-loved authors, Susan Spencer Paul, Shari Anton and Tori Phillips.

Susan Spencer Paul transports us to Regency England in *A Promise To Keep*. A soldier returns home from the Peninsular War determined to make a lovely young woman his bride. Despite his meddling parents, the couple somehow finds a way to be together in time for Christmas.

In *Christmas at Wayfarer Inn,* a medieval tale by Shari Anton, a nobleman disguised as a troubadour takes shelter at a local inn during the holidays, and woos the innkeeper's beautiful daughter with his magical songs. But will he ever reveal his true heritage?

Continuing her popular series THE CAVENDISH CHRONICLES, Tori Phillips brings us *Twelfth Knight,* the spirited tale of a shrewish young noblewoman and the handsome knight who vows to make the lady fall in love with him by Twelfth Night.

We hope you enjoy all three stories of Yuletide romance in enchanting England as much as we did! In December 2001 be sure to look for *The Prisoner Bride,* Susan Spencer Paul's latest book, and Tori Phillips's latest CAVENDISH CHRONICLES, *Dark Knight,* coming in June 2002.

From our family to yours, have a very happy holiday season!

Sincerely,

Tracy Farrell

'Tis The Season

SUSAN SPENCER PAUL

SHARI ANTON

TORI PHILLIPS

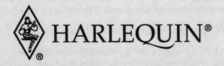

HARLEQUIN®

TORONTO • NEW YORK • LONDON
AMSTERDAM • PARIS • SYDNEY • HAMBURG
STOCKHOLM • ATHENS • TOKYO • MILAN • MADRID
PRAGUE • WARSAW • BUDAPEST • AUCKLAND

ISBN 0-373-29183-3

'TIS THE SEASON

Copyright © 2001 by Harlequin Books S.A.

The publisher acknowledges the copyright holders of the individual works as follows:

A PROMISE TO KEEP
Copyright © 2001 by Mary Liming

CHRISTMAS AT WAYFARER INN
Copyright © 2001 by Sharon Antoniewicz

TWELFTH KNIGHT
Copyright © 2001 by Mary W. Schaller

This edition published by arrangement with Harlequin Books S.A.

® and TM are trademarks of the publisher. Trademarks indicated with ® are registered in the United States Patent and Trademark Office, the Canadian Trade Marks Office and in other countries.

Visit us at www.eHarlequin.com

Printed in U.S.A.

CONTENTS

SUSAN SPENCER PAUL

who also writes as Mary Spencer, lives in Monrovia, California, with her husband, Paul, an R.N., and their three daughters, Carolyn, Kelly and Katharine. She is the author of twelve historical novels set in a variety of time periods, and especially loves writing about the Medieval and Regency eras.

Please address questions and book requests to:
Harlequin Reader Service
U.S.: 3010 Walden Ave., P.O. Box 1325, Buffalo, NY 14269
Canadian: P.O. Box 609, Fort Erie, Ont. L2A 5X3

A PROMISE TO KEEP

Susan Spencer Paul

Dedicated with love to my three beautiful daughters, Carolyn, Kelly and Katharine, who make Christmas Day, and every day, so special.

Chapter One

London, December, 1815

He was glad to be back in London after so many years. Despite the chill and fog and the pervasive wet, it was England, the soil of his homeland, and far preferable to those places where he'd spent his past six Christmases: Portugal, Spain and France. They had been as merry as Christmas might be when observed among soldiers, and Collin had celebrated each one with gratitude. He'd been alive, while many of his friends had not, and even in the midst of war and the daunting misery that accompanied it there had been a song and a cup of wine to share, and the fellowship of his comrades to bring a measure of cheer.

Yes, he'd had reason to be glad…yet even during those moments of gladness he had still dreamed of returning to England, of finding Rose, of being with her on Christmas Day and every day for the rest of their lives.

The street was nearly empty of pedestrians, though a few carriages rolled slowly by through the thick, chilly fog. Their drivers must have wondered, when they saw Collin standing beneath the lamppost, why any sane man would be out in such miserable weather, especially when a warm, dry, cozy inn sat so invitingly nearby. The Lamb and Wig had a reputation in this part of London for hospitality, well-cooked food and fine ale. The coffee room served as a meeting place for many of the lawyers who plied their trade in Holborn, while the inn itself provided comfortable rooms for genteel travelers.

It was a clean, cheerful, pleasant place to stay, and Collin knew the truth of that firsthand. More than six years ago, he'd spent the happiest month of his life at The Lamb and Wig. The memories of that time, and of Rose, had kept him sane during the war, and had drawn him back to stand in the fog on this street, gazing at the building across the way.

He would find Rose. It was impossible to think otherwise. Years ago he'd made his promise to return, to come back to her, and he intended to keep that promise—regardless of the letter she'd sent releasing him of it. He could yet remember the pain he'd felt upon reading the brief, coolly worded missive, so different from the warm and affectionate letters she'd sent him before.

She'd given no reasons for turning him away, but had only said that she thought it best for him to forget her and the promises they'd made. She would not be at The Lamb and Wig if he should try to find her there, she'd said, but was going away forever. All she desired was that he put every thought of her aside and find happiness with another. The letter had ended with a two-word apology, "I'm sorry," and a prayer that he remain safe throughout the war so that he could return to his family in Northamptonshire alive and whole.

He'd been stunned at first, then angry, and then, as he reread the words, filled with despair. He couldn't forget Rose. It wasn't possible. He had loved her almost from the first moment he'd seen her in the coffee room at The Lamb and Wig, where she'd been serving a party of lawyers, smiling and laughing with good nature as they strove to dally with her. Collin hadn't blamed them, for she was the prettiest girl he'd ever seen, with long, black curls framing a delicate face, ivory skin tinged with youthful pink, and eyes so blue they could make sapphires weep with envy.

The lawyers hadn't dared to do more than tease, for Rose was the innkeeper's daughter, and even at the age of seventeen had a talent for keeping men from becoming unruly or ill-mannered. She'd even treated Collin to a dose of reproof, at first, when he tried to engage her in conversation. It took a full week of persistence on his part before she at last gave way, and after that they were together as often as possible.

Collin's father had sent him to London to enjoy a month of pleasure before he and his regiment boarded a ship for Portugal. Being a strict and proper parent, Sir John Mattison had insisted upon his youngest son being lodged in an establishment of good reputation, and had thus made arrangements at The Lamb and Wig.

Collin, however, had protested loudly, wanting to reside in a more exciting part of Town where he might find other young men who could introduce him to the kinds of entertainments that the young bucks in London enjoyed. But after meeting Rose, he had good cause to be thankful to his wise and prudent father for placing him at such a respectable inn.

They had, under the chaperonage of Rose's older brother, Carl, done and seen as much as they possibly could during Collin's three remaining weeks. Vauxhall, the Tower, Madame Tussauds, and every possible museum had been visited. There had been picnics by the Thames and long walks through Hyde Park during the hour when the *ton* paraded themselves.

Collin remembered each moment vividly, especially the private ones, stolen at the inn, when he and Rose had touched, kissed and pressed hard against each other. There had been a deep longing to do more, but Collin hadn't dared to let either himself or Rose lose their heads. She was far too precious to him to treat so lightly, and he doubted that her father would let his only daughter wed a man who'd taken such liberties.

They'd made promises. Collin had vowed to return and marry Rose just as soon as the war was over, and she had promised to wait. They'd agreed to write faithfully, and Collin had extracted one last pledge: that if anything should happen to him, Rose would forget him completely and find another to love. He wouldn't have her alone and pining for a dead man when she deserved so much more.

Leaving her had been harder than he'd believed possible; receiving her first missive in Portugal had been almost equally potent. His fingers had trembled as he'd broken the wax seal and unfolded the thick paper, seeing within her neat, tiny writing. It was the same with each successive letter, the excitement and anticipation never waning. His men teased him about his constancy to a faraway English sweetheart, for Collin never joined them in partaking of the many women who made themselves available to the soldiers. But he knew they envied him, as well, especially when one of Rose's missives arrived.

It cost no small fortune for her to send him so many letters, some of which had likely been lost trying to find him as his division wandered over Spain. He was fortunate that his father had been able to purchase him a lieutenancy, else he might not have received anything from home at all. His quick rise to captain hadn't done him any harm, either, and he'd felt special pride in Rose's glowing congratulations.

That had been in one of her last letters, he reflected now, when she had still written to him with love and longing. He'd kept it, along with the others, and had brought them home from the war as his most precious possessions. All but the last one, which he'd burned in a drunken fit of misery.

Weeks had passed following the arrival of that final letter before Collin began to think that there was more to Rose's cool dismissal than a simple lack of love. She had said that she was leaving The Lamb and Wig, and she would never do such a thing unless she'd found another love…or had been given no choice save to leave.

That she might have given her heart to another was a thought that gnawed at him, but he believed, in truth, that Rose was honorable enough to have told him if that was so. Instead, she'd given no reasons for releasing him of his promise, and that caused him to think that whatever those reasons might be were somehow shameful to her. If Rose and her family had been forced to leave the inn, then he must find out why, and where they'd been made to go and whether Rose was happy and well. Until he saw her and told her that he yet loved her, and heard from her own lips that she no longer felt the same, he could not rest.

Another carriage rattled down the damp street, appearing and disappearing in the fog as it passed in front of him. Collin held the collar of his greatcoat more tightly about his neck and made his way toward the inn, pushing his way out of the wet and cold and into a familiar warmth and cheerfulness that he had longed for and dreamed of for six years.

He had often envisioned what it would be like, strolling back into The Lamb and Wig, shouting out for Rose and seeing the surprise and joy and love in her eyes. He'd imagined her running toward him, arms outstretched, with his own the same to grab her up and hold her tight as he kissed her again and again. All those who'd known him in those earlier days—Rose's father and brother, Jarvis the barkeep, and all of the serving maids—would hail him with affection while the ale flowed and he told his tales and gazed into Rose's lovely face, her hand in his for now and forevermore. It would be the happiest night of his life, he'd believed.

But there were no familiar faces now that he could see, though the place itself was much the same. Warm, friendly, welcoming to any who entered, yet absent of the booming greeting that Rose's father called out to newcomers, or of Carl's smiling face somewhere in the tavern as he served the customers, or of Rose in that quieter part of the inn where the more respectable patrons sat to enjoy conversation or a hot meal.

Aye, they were all gone, and their unique qualities with them, but Collin hadn't spent the past six years commanding unruly fighting men for naught. Someone here would be able to set him toward finding Rose and her family, and Collin would have the information he needed before the night was done.

Determined, he removed his greatcoat with care and set it on a peg to dry, took a brief moment to send up a silent prayer for a Christmas miracle, and resolutely made his way into the tavern to find out what he needed to know.

Chapter Two

Lady Dilbeck's hands were hurting again. Just as they always did at this time of year. Along with her knees, shoulders, elbows and ankles. Cold weather did its worst on elderly joints, which was a fact Rose knew full well, having nursed her father through several painful winters. The trouble was that the remedies which had worked on her father did little to alleviate Lady Dilbeck's suffering, and Rose was at her wit's end. Heated wax, camphor and mint, stewed eucalyptus leaves mixed into a paste with sea salt—all had failed to do more than provide fleeting relief. But Rose knew, in her heart, that nothing could truly ease her employer's misery at this time of year.

Christmas was a torment to Lady Dilbeck, and not merely because of the cold. She'd lost her only child, a son, following Christmas fifteen years earlier, and hadn't celebrated the season since, nor allowed anyone at Dilbeck Manor to celebrate, either. Rather than being one of the happiest times of the year, Christmas at the manor was by far the darkest and least pleasant. Lady Dilbeck was a demanding mistress at the best of times, but during the month of December she was truly hard to bear. Each day was filled with irritation, complaints and angry demands; nothing anyone did could please her.

"Are you warm enough?" Rose asked as she set a steaming bowl on the table near Lady Dilbeck's elbow. "Shall I have Jacob bring more wood?"

"No, no, it's hot as Samhein's dwelling already. You must mean to sweat me to death." Lady Dilbeck examined the contents of the bowl with distaste. "What have you got now? One of your useless concoctions?"

"More of the camphor and mint," Rose replied calmly. "It helped a little last time."

"It didn't help at all," Lady Dilbeck countered irately, though she didn't resist as Rose took one of her hands and slathered it with the warm mixture. "Smells terrible," she added when Rose wrapped her hand in clean, soft linen. "Makes my stomach turn."

Rose smiled and went to work on the other hand. "Last time you thought it smelled too pleasant, and therefore wouldn't be of any use. Perhaps this time it will be more effective."

Lady Dilbeck cast a steely-eyed glare at Rose, then looked away, muttering beneath her breath until Rose had finished her ministrations.

"There," she said, gently patting Lady Dilbeck's wrappings before rising to put the unused cloths into the bowl. "I'll leave you now and ask Miss Carpenter to come and read to you. Those wrappings must stay on for half an hour at least." She took up the bowl and cradled it in one arm. "Once I've removed them I'll bring your tea. Is there anything else I can get for you now, my lady?"

Lady Dilbeck frowned at her wrapped hands, which Rose had arranged carefully atop a pillow in her lap.

"Send Jacob in to stoke the fire," she said shortly, giving a disdainful sniff. "It's cold as a snowstorm in here."

"Yes, I will." Rose drew in a slow breath and gathered her courage. "Lady Dilbeck, there's something I'd like to speak with you about, something the rest of the staff has asked me to—"

"Not now." Lady Dilbeck closed her eyes and rested her head on the back of the chair. "Send Jacob in at once. Sometimes I think you mean to freeze me into the grave."

"Yes, my lady." Rose made a brief curtsy and quit the room, stopping just outside the door to release a frustrated sigh.

A few moments later she pushed her way into the kitchen to find the entire staff of Dilbeck Manor assembled there, clearly waiting for her. Their faces, from Camhort the butler to Janny the cook, reflected a mixture of anxiety and hope.

"How is she?" asked Jacob, the lone footman and general manservant, pushing away from the table against which he'd been reclining. "Did you speak to her?"

"I tried." Rose set the bowl on a counter and wiped her hands on a clean cloth. "Her ladyship didn't wish to discuss anything at the moment," she said more apologetically, adding, "Her hands are giving her pain."

Janny gave a shake of her head. "They always do at this time of year. And if not her hands then it's her shoulders or legs or head. She has enough strength to complain heartily of all her aches, but seldom enough to listen to what anyone else has to say."

"If she doesn't give us permission for the dinner," said Emily, the downstairs maid, "then we'll not have enough time to prepare for it. Especially the pudding."

"We'll not *have* a pudding," Ralf, the stable boy, put in bitterly, kicking the toe of one shoe against the floor. "We never do and never will."

His mother, Hester, the upstairs maid, put an arm about his thin shoulders. "Don't give up hope, Ralf. Miss Rose will ask Lady Dilbeck, won't you, miss? You'll talk her ladyship about, if anyone can."

"We can't put such a burden on Miss Rose," Camhort said, casting a sympathetic glance at Rose. "It's not fair to ask her to get in her ladyship's black graces. We all know how unpleasant it is to make Lady Dilbeck angry.''

"I don't mind, Camhort," Rose assured him. "It's just so difficult to get her to listen. And I'm afraid that no matter how gently or firmly I put the matter before her, she'll refuse to let us have a Christmas dinner.''

"Of course she'll refuse," Janny said angrily. "She won't care that it's only for us, and that she needn't be a party to a moment of it. She'll make Christmas miserable for everyone, just as she always does.''

Emily took a step forward, pressing both hands flat against her white apron. "But surely if you tell her that it's just for us, Miss Rose, and that we'll be very quiet and keep everything in the servants quarters...surely she'll agree. We don't need to have any singing or games.''

Rose smiled at the younger girl, at her youthful hopefulness and enthusiasm.

"I'll do my best to convince her, I promise.''

"When?" Ralf demanded, to be hushed by his mother.

"Very soon," Rose said. "Perhaps this evening, while I'm helping her to bed. She'll have had her wine by then, and will be in a better mood. For now, there is the house to tend to and dinner to cook and accounts to be gone over. Let's be about our chores. Jacob,'' she added as the others began to move away, "Lady Dilbeck wants the fire hotter in the parlor. Please go at once.'' Rose herself turned in the direction of the main stairway, climbing up to the third floor, where she knocked upon a certain door, waiting until she was bid to enter before opening it.

Miss Nancy Carpenter was a thin, nervous young woman who always seemed, to Rose, as if she meant to bolt out of any room she was in at the moment. She hid in her bedroom whenever possible, scribbling endless letters, as she appeared to be doing now, and coming out only when necessary, generally for meals. Her aunt, Lady Dilbeck, frightened her terribly and though Rose had tried endlessly to teach the girl how to manage her difficult relative, nothing seemed to help.

She was a pretty enough creature, with blond hair that she kept swept into a bun at the back of her head, and large blue eyes. But she was dreadfully thin and sallow and, Rose suspected, much in need of fresh air and some outdoor activity. Miss Carpenter had arrived at Dilbeck Manor a year ago to live as a companion with her rich, distantly related aunt, having been sent by her parents with the intention of securing a place in Lady Dilbeck's affections.

But her days here had been far different from the social pleasure that her parents had promised. Lady Dilbeck rarely went out, and had never made any effort to put Miss Carpenter in the way of society. She seemed to find her niece's company as uncomfortable as Miss Carpenter found hers, though it certainly couldn't be said that Lady Dilbeck didn't at least try to make a friend of the girl. Years of loneliness had made her crave the company of those in her household.

"Lady Dilbeck is ready for you to read to her now, Miss Carpenter," Rose said, watching the younger woman's eternally wide eyes widen even more. "She's waiting for you in the parlor." It was one of Miss Carpenter's daily chores, which Rose knew she disliked.

Miss Carpenter's face, if possible, grew even paler. "Thank you, Miss Benham, I'll come right down."

Rose smiled and nodded and moved to close the door.

"Miss Benham?"

Rose stopped and looked inquiringly at her employer's niece. "Yes?"

Miss Carpenter had stood, her hands clutched tightly before her. She looked as if she was trembling.

"Miss Benham, I'm...I'm leaving Dilbeck Manor. J-just as soon as p-possible. Tomorrow."

Rose stood in the open doorway and gazed into Miss

Carpenter's pale face. "I see. I hadn't realized. Lady Dilbeck didn't say anything to me about it."

"She d-doesn't know," Miss Carpenter replied in faltering tones. "I've just had a letter from my father." She indicated an unfolded missive on her writing desk. "He s-says that I can come home for Christmas. And so I'm going. And I won't be c-coming back." She lifted her chin, clearly determined on this course.

"Have you told Lady Dilbeck?" Rose asked quietly. "I fear she'll be very lonely without your company."

Miss Carpenter uttered a humorless laugh. "She hates me, and I can never please her. She'll be happy to see me go, save for the loss of one more person to disparage in her every waking moment. I'm sorry to leave you and the other servants to receive the brunt of her displeasure, but I can't bear it any longer."

"Lady Dilbeck isn't always a pleasant person," Rose conceded, "but she certainly doesn't hate you, Miss Carpenter. If you would but learn to take a firmer hand when she speaks out of turn, she'd treat you in a far different manner. She dislikes weakness, as you know."

"Yes, I know," Miss Carpenter said with a miserable nod. "She treats you well enough, usually, for you seldom let her do otherwise. But I can't stand up to her. It's impossible." She began to look as if she'd start weeping. "I only want to leave and go home. Please help me, Miss Benham. I'm so afraid she won't let me leave if she finds out what I'm planning."

"She can't stop you, Miss Carpenter," Rose told her calmly, stepping inside and closing the door. "But it's clear that you must, indeed, go home. Now, please, sit down and calm yourself and tell me what you wish to do. I promise that I'll do whatever I can to help."

Two hours later Rose finally found a few moments to rest. She pushed her way into her own bedchamber, relieved to have a few quiet minutes to collect her thoughts.

She had managed to calm Miss Carpenter enough to elicit the girl's plans, then had tried, without success, to make her change them. When Miss Carpenter had begun to look as if she would truly be ill, Rose relented. But she couldn't be happy with the plan, which involved keeping Lady Dilbeck in the dark about her niece's departure until the girl was actually gone.

It was unnecessarily cruel to her employer who, despite her seemingly unfeeling behavior, harbored a heart that was easily bruised. Rose had learned long ago that Lady Dilbeck hid that heart behind all her aggravation and complaining, but that was impossible for Miss Carpenter to believe, just as she found it impossible to think that her aunt would truly miss her.

But Rose knew otherwise. Lady Dilbeck probably would have made a pet out of Miss Carpenter if the girl hadn't been so flighty. She might have found someone upon whom to lavish her love and fortune, which had certainly been the wish of Miss Carpenter's parents. If only the younger woman had been able to see beyond the crankiness to what lay beneath, to see how her aunt's expression lit whenever her niece entered the room, how she tried to draw the girl into conversation during their shared meals, though usually without success.

Now Lady Dilbeck would be eating her meals alone once more, as she had for years, with only her unhappiness for company. It had been that way before Miss Carpenter had come, and would be that way now. Perhaps for the remainder of Lady Dilbeck's life, for she had no close family ties, and little discourse with her distant relations. The thought grieved Rose's heart no small measure.

Despite all of Lady Dilbeck's difficult ways, Rose felt an abiding affection for the elderly woman. When Rose had been alone and so very afraid, Lady Dilbeck had taken her in and given her a home and work to do. She'd never once asked Rose for gratitude, or made her feel as if she must be constantly aware of what had been done for her. She simply demanded that Rose do her work well and, better still, had the faith that she could.

And now Rose would repay her employer by helping her unhappy niece sneak out of Dilbeck Manor unnoticed. The pain Lady Dilbeck would suffer upon the discovery would be bad enough, but once the young woman was gone and Lady Dilbeck discovered Rose's part in the deception, there would certainly be no chance of talking her into letting the servants hold a Christmas dinner for themselves at Dilbeck Manor. No chance at all. If anything, quite the opposite. Christmas would be more dismal than usual, and Rose would be fortunate simply to keep her position.

Rose sat on the window seat beneath the largest window in her room and gazed out at the darkening sky. There would be snow soon, perhaps even tonight. That had always been such an exciting time when she was a child, waiting for the first snow of the year to fall. Her father and mother had been hard-pressed to keep her and Carl from staying up night after night, gazing out the window for any sign of falling white flakes.

It hadn't been quite the same when Rose had grown older, for then all wet weather had meant never-ending mud tracked into the inn. Yet there had still been the excitement of the coming holidays, and a pleasant joviality had crept into the demeanor of the inn's patrons. There had been the merry singing of carols in the tavern and much use made of the kissing bough that was hung each year in the entryway of the coffee room. The moods of all those who made The Lamb and Wig their home were considerably lightened, and even the added work of preparing the inn's famous Christmas dinner couldn't dampen them.

With a sigh, Rose smiled and closed her eyes, remembering it all just as clearly as if she was there again. She shouldn't allow herself such a luxury, she knew, for it could do nothing but make her wretched in the end. Yet it was so hard at this time of year not to remember, not to think upon all that her life had once been. Worse, it was impossible not to think of Collin.

She thought of him all during the year, especially in late summer, when they'd spent their few precious weeks together. But, somehow, she'd gotten into the habit of worrying about him most during the winter months, wondering not only if he was safe and well, as she ever did, but also if he was cold and suffering, if he had enough blankets and food and a dry, warm place to sleep.

He would be home by now, she thought, opening her eyes to gaze out at the dark sky. Safe at home in Northampton, received there with joy by his family and recovering from the experiences he had endured during the war. She knew that he had survived, for she had faithfully followed the postings of dead and wounded officers and had only once seen his name, Captain Collin Mattison, wounded at Salamanca, non-fatal.

She'd been stricken with fear, for so many of the wounded eventually died, but Collin's name had never again been on the lists. She had read of him in other papers, especially those that described various battles and the officers who led the troops. Collin had merited mention in nearly every major engagement, and had been notably mentioned in the discourses about the final battle that had taken place only months ago in Belgium.

The war had been over for several months now, and Collin and his family would be preparing to celebrate not only Christmas, but his safe return to England, as well.

There had been a time when she'd envisioned herself being a part of that celebration, when she and Collin had shared their dreams of that wonderful day, both in spoken words, while he'd yet been in London, and in letter, once he'd gone away. She had lived off such dreams for nearly three years, had set all her thoughts and plans on that moment when Collin would cross the threshold of The Lamb and Wig to take her into his arms.

Love had made her so foolish, she thought now, sighing and standing, moving to her closet to pull out a warm knitted shawl, which she set about her shoulders. Love had made her believe that nothing could touch her or her future. But it wasn't true. Love wasn't able to stop life from intruding on dreams, or of destroying them altogether.

Chapter Three

Despite the recent snowfall, the carriage leaving Dilbeck Manor moved at an alarmingly brisk pace. Collin led his horse to the side of the road in order to keep from being run down, and watched with a measure of concern as the vehicle continued on its rapid way. It would be a miracle if there wasn't an accident, but perhaps there was a compelling reason for such urgency. He glimpsed, as the carriage drove past him, the face of a young woman staring wide-eyed at him from out of the window. She looked panicked, though whether that was because of the vehicle's pace or some other reason, he couldn't discern.

In but moments the carriage was gone and the sound of its horses fading, leaving Collin with a much quieter prospect before him.

Dilbeck Manor and its lands had clearly fallen into a state of disrepair. Even the newly fallen snow couldn't hide the fact of that. The manor house, which at one time must have been quite grand, was dilapidated and in much need of care. The manor grounds were unkempt. And the fields that Collin had been riding through hadn't seen a plow or scythe in many a year. Even most of the tenant farms appeared to be left empty and without care, which to Collin's mind was an outright sin.

He knew dozens of men—no, hundreds—who would give anything to have a roof over their heads and a field to till for honest gain. Most of the common soldiers from his own company were now desperate for a way to make a living, having returned to an England that held neither welcome nor further use for them. Dilbeck Manor, as ill managed as it clearly was, would seem a golden haven to each and every one of them.

He wondered if it was that for Rose—a haven—or if it was something altogether different. He knew little of her employer, Lady Dilbeck, save that she was a famous crotchet, and that since the death of her only son some years ago she'd become a recluse. How Rose had even met the woman was a mystery, but somehow she'd done so, for every word he'd heard of her led here, to this place.

She was so near to him now. His heart quickened at the simple thought. And soon, if all went well, and if she was truly there, he would see her, speak to her—perhaps even touch her, if she was as glad to see him as he hoped she would be. A great many things had happened in the past few years, and he knew now, in part, why she'd written him that final letter. But knowing the truth didn't necessarily make everything right.

Not that it mattered. He loved her now as he had ever loved her, and refused to believe that the love she'd held for him had so readily died. Rose was made of far sterner stuff, and Collin was here to find out just what she did feel. He would know when he saw her, for her blue eyes had a tendency to reveal her thoughts.

Soon enough, he would know.

Setting his heels into the flanks of his horse, Collin moved back onto the snow-covered road and headed toward the great, decaying manor house, and Rose.

The stable was equal to the house in condition, and, save for a young boy who came sauntering out to glare at him suspiciously, empty of any formal servants.

"Good day," Collin said to the boy, waiting for him to take hold of his horse's head before he dismounted.

"We don't take in travelers, not even for snow," the boy announced. "There's an inn in the village, but two miles down the road."

"What?" Collin asked with a frown. "Not in any weather? Your mistress would send gentlefolk away without even offering the little comfort of her barn?"

The boy nodded. "That's right," he said, slowly eyeing Collin up and down. "'Specially not soldiers. Her very words. Not that you'd want to bed down here." He motioned to the stable behind him. "The roof only covers part of it, and that's where her ladyship's own horses are kept, warm as I can make 'em in weather like this. You wouldn't *want* to use it for shelter, mister."

"Captain Collin Mattison," Collin corrected affably, offering the boy his gloved hand. "Or just Collin, if you like. And you are…?"

"Ralf." The boy warily took his hand, gave it a brief shake and then immediately let go. He tilted his head to one side. "How did you know that I've got a mistress, but not a master?"

"Because it is your mistress, Lady Dilbeck, and another lady who I pray lives here, who I have come to see. I hope, at least, that you're relieved to know that I'm not here to sleep in your stable."

"Which lady?" Ralf asked, the wariness in his eyes increasing.

"Miss Rose Benham."

"Miss Rose?" Ralf took a step back, his eyes narrowed now. "What do you want with her?"

Collin's heart leaped in his chest. "She's here, then? Thank God." Reaching up, he pulled the hat from his head. "I'd been told she was, but I was afraid she might have gone elsewhere. Is she well? Happy?" He uttered a laugh at the boy's confused expression. "But I shouldn't bother you with such things, Ralf. I apologize."

Ralf took another step away. "You know Miss Rose?"

"Very well," Collin assured him. "We were promised to marry some years ago."

Ralf's eyes widened, and his gaze traveled Collin's length once more, this time with a new appreciation.

"You and Miss Rose?"

Collin nodded. "Yes, just so. And I've come all the way from London with the hope of seeing her."

He said nothing more, but Ralf seemed to understand. He stepped forward to take the horse's head again.

"She's inside, with her ladyship ringing a peal over her just now. Did you see a carriage pass as you rode in?"

"Aye, and like to turn over at the speed of it."

Ralf nodded once. "That was her ladyship's niece taking her leave, with no thought of coming back to Dilbeck Manor for any cause. Miss Rose helped her to go without her ladyship knowing, but her ladyship knows now, and she's not happy 'bout it."

Collin cast a glance toward the aging manor. "Then I'd best go in and see what I can do."

Ralf uttered a humorless laugh. "You don't know her ladyship," he said bitterly. "You won't be able to do nothing. And we won't have Christmas. Again."

Collin smiled at him. "Christmas can't be stopped, Ralf. It comes whether we wish it or not. As to your mistress, I've no doubt that she's a daunting woman, but she can't be worse than a battalion of French infantry bearing down on the field with all their drums and noise." He looked at the stable, then back at the manor. "Is there a steward who manages this estate, Ralf, even if poorly?"

"Nah." Ralf shook his head. "Her ladyship won't pay for a proper steward. There's just enough of us here to take care of her, and hardly that."

"Perfect," Collin murmured, quickly untying the lone

bag that hung from his saddle, which contained all his simple belongings. "Then take care of my horse, if you will, Ralf," he said, slinging the bag over his shoulder and winking at the boy, "and leave Lady Dilbeck to me."

Rose wasn't sure which was worse—Lady Dilbeck's accusations or Lady Dilbeck's long silences. At the moment she was being treated to both, alternately.

She deserved such censure, of course. She had expected and known it would come. But none of that made it any easier.

"You should have come to me," Lady Dilbeck said, not looking at Rose. She sat in her favorite chair by the fire, her hands swathed in warm woolen wraps, her gaze held fast upon them. "I trusted you to always be honest with me. Completely honest."

Rose could hear the pain in Lady Dilbeck's voice, which was a far worse punishment than anything else might have been. Or perhaps not. If the frail, elderly woman began to weep, Rose would start to cry, too.

"I should have told you," she admitted softly, her hands so tightly folded together that her fingers ached. "But Miss Carpenter was determined to go with or without my help. I didn't wish for her to upset the household any more than possible." *Or you,* Rose left unsaid, imagining the awful scene that would have taken place if Lady Dilbeck had tried to stop her niece. The girl had been almost out of her mind with panic, and Rose had truly feared that if Lady Dilbeck suddenly appeared Miss Carpenter would have uttered something desperate and cruel. She was just foolish—and spoiled—enough to do so. And knowing what her niece thought of her would have hurt Lady Dilbeck far, far more than simple abandonment.

"She was homesick," Rose lied, hoping that her ladyship would accept the excuse, "and wished to be home for Christmas. I tried to persuade her to stay, and meant to speak to you about making the manor more cheerful...not only for her but for all of us. But she didn't wish to listen—'' Rose spread her hands wide "—and in the end I gave her my promise not to say anything. But that was wrong of me, and there is no excusing such duplicity. I can only say that I'm deeply sorry, and ask you to forgive me, even if you wish me to leave Dilbeck Manor. Please, my lady, I pray you will at least forgive me before I go.''

"I've said nothing of your going," Lady Dilbeck retorted sharply, looking at Rose with angry blue eyes. "But you should have told me what Nancy had in her mind. She was but a girl, and girls are foolish creatures with little brains and ridiculous notions. I would have gotten to the bottom of what was bothering her and talked her around. The silly little chit," Lady Dilbeck said more tightly, her voice shaking with what Rose knew was deeply concealed hurt. "I would have let her make merry on Christmas Day, if she'd wanted it so much. I would have," she said more sternly, as if to convince herself, "if only she had asked it of me. Surely I could have found a way to keep her happy if I'd known. But *you* didn't tell me."

"No, I didn't," Rose murmured, "and I'm sorry for it."

"Sorry," Lady Dilbeck muttered, giving a shake of her head. They were silent for a long moment, and when Lady Dilbeck spoke again, her tone was less angry but not less sad. "No, it's not your fault, Rose. I know why Nancy left." Her gaze lowered to her hands once more. "I know. She was unhappy here, living so far from society, in the company of an ill-tempered old woman."

"Oh, no, that isn't what she thought, my lady," Rose said quickly.

"Don't lie to me, Rose," Lady Dilbeck said sternly. "And don't cosset me, either. I may be a fool, but I won't be treated like it by my own housekeeper."

"No, my lady," Rose said quietly. "Of course not.

Shall I…would you like me to bring your breakfast to you here?''

"And forgo the pleasure of sitting alone at the dining table?'' Lady Dilbeck asked, her voice tinged with bitterness. "Nay, I must make myself used to it once more, for I don't believe my niece means to return to Dilbeck Manor.'' She looked at Rose. "Does she?''

Rose let out a breath. "No, my lady. Miss Carpenter won't be returning to Dilbeck Manor.''

Lady Dilbeck's already pale cheeks seemed to pale even further. "I see.'' The hands on her lap moved restlessly beneath their wrappings. "I'm feeling tired this morning,'' she murmured. "Help me back to my room, Rose. I'll have some tea there, perhaps.''

"Yes, my lady.''

Rose moved toward her mistress, but a scratching at the door made her stop. The next moment Camhort entered the parlor, his expression filled with consternation.

"Forgive me, my lady, but a young man has arrived and insists that he must speak to you at once.''

"Well, send him away,'' Lady Dilbeck told him irritably. "I never receive at this time of day.''

"I've told him, my lady,'' Camhort assured her, "but he refuses to go. He is very determined.''

"Indeed he is,'' someone behind Camhort agreed, and the parlor doors were pushed wide, revealing that someone.

Rose's first thought was that he hadn't changed very much since she'd last seen him, save that he was perhaps a bit taller and more muscular. Her second thought, as the buzzing cleared in her brain, was *God save me, he's here.*

Collin.

She'd never thought to see him again, but there he stood in the doorway, as handsome and attractive as he'd ever been, smiling at her in the way she remembered so well. His blond hair was overlong and badly in need of a cut, but it still shone with the touch of gold that she'd found so alluring, and his blue eyes sparkled with the same light that they'd held so many years ago.

There was a thin scar beneath his left eye, and another that ran the length of his chin, but neither marred the masculine beauty of his face. Women had always looked twice at Collin upon meeting him, the second look lingering with appreciation. Rose had been both jealous and proud to be the object of such a man's affections, but now, seeing him again, she simply felt faint.

Her vision blurred and darkened: for one awful moment she was certain that she would make a complete fool of herself and swoon. Collin seemed to realize it, too, and his smile faded. He took a step toward her, and Rose took a step back. The movement helped to clear her head, and she drew in a much-needed breath.

"Who are you?" Lady Dilbeck demanded. "How dare you barge into my home without invitation."

Collin's gaze lingered on Rose for a moment longer, then he turned to Lady Dilbeck with that charming smile back in place.

"Forgive me, my lady, but my need to speak with you is pressing, and I feared you might not see me if I didn't set my case before you. Let me introduce myself. I'm Captain Collin Mattison, originally of Northamptonshire, lately of Spain, France and Belgium." He removed his hat and made a bow.

"Mattison?" Lady Dilbeck repeated, considering him more carefully. "Of Northamptonshire? Are you related to Sir John Mattison of that county?"

"Indeed I am, my lady." The charming smile widened. "Sir John is my father."

"Is he, now," Lady Dilbeck said, sitting forward. "I find that difficult to believe, for it's not likely that Sir John, who is as well-behaved a gentleman as I've ever met, would raise a son so entirely without manners. And it's certain he'd allow no child of his to enter a house without invitation.''

"No, he would not," Collin agreed, "but I am his son, all the same, and know that he would be full angered should I give way in any undertaking so easily. Especially one so important." He glanced at Rose, who felt as if she'd gone completely dumb. What was he doing here? Was he going to tell Lady Dilbeck that they knew each other? What would she say if he did? How could she possibly explain this away as a coincidence, if coincidence it was. But it couldn't be. Collin had come to Dilbeck Manor because of her. That had to be so. He'd come to demand what she hadn't been able to give him in that last letter she'd written. An explanation.

She should have expected that of Collin. If she'd learned anything about him during their few short weeks together, it was that Collin Mattison pursued what he wanted with unflagging persistence, just as he'd pursued a career in the army, despite his father's objections. Just as he'd pursued her, regardless of how coolly she had treated him when first they'd met. Just as he'd pursue an explanation until he got one, whether Rose wished to give it or not.

"And what could be so pressing that it cannot wait for manners?" Lady Dilbeck asked.

"A favor," he replied. "A very great favor. I've come to ask for a position as your steward, to begin immediately. Today, in fact."

Everyone in the room, including Camhort, gaped at him. Rose's mouth dropped open, and it took an effort for her to close it.

"What?" she said, and was shocked to realize that she'd said it.

Collin turned his smile on her. "Yes, miss?"

She wordlessly shook her head at him.

"I can see that I've taken you by surprise," he said to

Lady Dilbeck. "But, please, I pray you, give me leave to explain."

Lady Dilbeck, as bereft of speech as Rose, nodded.

Collin took a step forward, holding his somewhat battered hat in both hands. For the first time, Rose noted the forlorn condition of his greatcoat and the bit of uniform she could see beneath. Both had clearly seen a great deal of travel and duty, just as Collin had.

"I've only just returned to England, having finished my duty in Brussels. I had hoped to be with my family by now, but something occurred...or, rather, didn't occur. I can't explain to you what it was, save to say that because of it, I cannot yet go home. And so I've come to you, remembering you as my father's friend, in the hope that you'll make some use of me in return for food and lodging. I'll be glad to be housed wherever you deem fit, even in the stable, for I've been a soldier and know well how to sleep in every weather.

"And, if you'll forgive me," he added more firmly, "it seems that Dilbeck Manor could use a steward. I would be a good one, I vow. My father taught me well in the ways of managing an estate."

Lady Dilbeck stared at him. "You want to be my steward," she said slowly. "For food and lodging, only?"

"To begin with, yes," he replied. "Let me be your steward until Christmas, without pay. Then, if you're pleased with my work, we'll discuss a reasonable recompense, which needn't be made in money."

"You'll get no land out of me," Lady Dilbeck warned.

"I wouldn't ask it of you," he said with slight offense. "My father would take a whip to me should I do anything so dishonorable, and I'd never shame either him or my mother by doing so. Whatever terms we agree upon, my lady, would have to be wholly agreeable to you."

Lady Dilbeck considered him for a long moment. "There's not much that you, or any man, could do to this estate in but three weeks, Captain Mattison. You saw the condition of it as you rode in, I'm sure.''

"Yes, my lady, I did. But I believe I can prove my worth to you—to everyone—at Dilbeck Manor in that time." He glanced at Rose again, then returned his attention to Lady Dilbeck. "Will you give me the chance?"

"I should press you to explain yourself better," her ladyship said. "Your father was much better known to my husband than to me, but we are acquaintances of long-standing, and I don't want to get caught in a quarrel between a father and his son. I don't like to question a man in matters that he wishes to keep private, but I want to be assured that I'll not be angering Sir John."

Collin set his hat over his heart. "There is no quarrel, my lady, and my father would not be angered. I give you my word of honor upon it."

Rose was shaking her head, astonished that Lady Dilbeck would consider allowing a complete stranger to manage her lands for even a minute, despite her acquaintance with his father. She'd ever been the kind of woman who'd looked for a bargain, but she'd also been equally wary of the unknown. It was impossible that she should contemplate such a pact with a total unknown.

"This is my housekeeper, Miss Benham." Lady Dilbeck motioned toward Rose with one wrapped hand.

"Miss Benham—" Collin turned to Rose with all formality and bowed low "—I'm pleased to make your acquaintance."

Rose tried to make her lips work, to murmur his name, but in the end all she could manage was a brief curtsy.

"I rely upon Miss Benham's advice a great deal, Captain," Lady Dilbeck said, eyeing him. "I shall leave it to her to decide your fate. What do you say, Rose? Shall we give Captain Mattison the chance he desires?"

They were both looking at her, Collin and Lady Dilbeck,

and with the same expectant expression upon their faces. Rose looked from one to the other, utterly lost.

"I...my lady, surely you don't wish me to decide anything so important."

"Of course I do," Lady Dilbeck returned irritably. "I just said as much, didn't I?"

"I should be honored to have your consideration, Miss Benham," Collin said. "And I'll abide by your decision. If you tell me to go, I'll go, and will give you no further trouble."

He took a single step nearer, gazing directly into her eyes, so achingly familiar, her own much-loved Collin.

"But if you say that I shall stay, then I'll stay, and strive every moment to prove myself to you."

But she didn't want him to stay and prove himself. She had prayed never to see him again, to never know the pain of seeing that beloved face once more. Letting him go had been the hardest but most necessary thing she'd ever done. How could she bear to be near him, to speak to him and feel the warmth of his nearness, to smell the scent that was uniquely Collin, and then let go of him again?

She couldn't do it...she knew she couldn't...and, yet, looking into that dear face, into those eyes, she could do nothing else.

"Stay," she murmured. "If that's what you truly wish."

"It is," he said. "Very much. Thank you, Miss Benham." He turned back to Lady Dilbeck. "Shall I begin now, my lady? I've left my horse in Ralf's care, and my only belongings are in a bag outside the door. I'm ready to start my duties at once, if it pleases you."

"Yes, start now, Captain," Lady Dilbeck said with the wave of a hand, looking weary. "Rose—Miss Benham—will show you to a suitable chamber, and will then introduce you to Jacob. He's my footman, and can show you the grounds. Make no changes to the estate without first consulting me, else you'll be on your way to Northampton the next hour without a kind word to warm your way."

"I'll do nothing without speaking to you first, my lady," Collin promised. "If you approve, I'll ride over the estate this afternoon and offer my first thoughts and recommendations to you this evening."

"By this evening?" Lady Dilbeck said with an approving nod. "You are indeed a fast starter, Captain. I like that. Rose, take Captain Mattison to the east wing and see that he's settled. You'll be alone, sir, for no one else is housed there, but the rooms are comfortable enough."

"Thank you, my lady. I'm content to be placed anywhere." Collin gave her one last bow, then looked expectantly at Rose.

She drew in a deep breath and pulled the shawl she wore tight about her shoulders.

"If you would collect your things, Captain, and follow me," she said, moving toward the door, "I'll show you to your room."

Chapter Four

She had changed in the past six years. Her glorious black hair, which she used to wear loose about her shoulders, was pulled back in a ruthlessly tight and unforgiving bun. Her face, which had then been alive with youth and health, was now thin and pale, almost completely absent of color. Her body was thinner, too, and quite different from her former figure with the lush, delightfully plump curves that had filled him with endless desire and, more often, outright lust.

Yet for all that had changed, Collin couldn't help but look at Rose and still find her to be the most beautiful, desirable woman on God's earth. He'd seen innumerable women during his years in the army, many of them quite alluring. But none could set his heart to beating as Rose could; none apart from her could make him feel as if she held his entire world in her two hands.

He'd walked into Lady Dilbeck's parlor, taken one look at Rose, and felt as if his head would explode from the amazement of simply being near her again. That her own response in seeing him had been one of distress had dampened his joy, but only momentarily. They were together again, despite the difficulties that lay between them, and nothing could change the wonder of that.

She moved ahead of him, climbing the stairs with her back held rigidly straight, appearing completely untouchable and unapproachable. Her voice, too, when she spoke, was chilly and distant.

"You'll stay here," she said as they reached the second landing, pushing open the first door they came to. "It hasn't been occupied for some time, but the fireplace works, and I'll have Jacob bring coal up at once. There is only one upstairs maid, and her duties will be somewhat increased by your presence on this side of the house."

Rose crossed the room to the first of two high windows, pulling the heavy curtains back with a sharp tug before moving to the next window. Winter light flooded the rather gloomy, dust-ridden room. "Her name is Hester, and I would appreciate it if you'd do what you can to lighten her load as much as possible by being careful in your demands." She turned to face him, her features tight with unspoken emotion. "I'll instruct her to bring you towels and fresh water in the evenings and hot water each morning."

"Rose," Collin began, "I..."

She walked to the high bed in the middle of the room, where she began to remove the dusty counterpane with stiff, jerky movements.

"If you could have any laundry ready for Hester to take away in the mornings, I'll make certain that it's cleaned and returned to you by evening."

"Rose," he said again, letting the bag on his shoulder slide to the floor. "I didn't mean to take you so much by surprise, but I had to seek you out. Surely you knew that I would, once I returned to England."

She didn't look at him, didn't even acknowledge him, but began to move about the room, pulling dustcovers from the few pieces of furniture. It would be a handsome chamber, Collin thought dimly, watching her, once the fire and several candles were lit.

"I know about your father and brother," he said, moving a bit closer to where she uncovered a particularly large chair that was set near the fire. "And about the cousin who inherited the inn. I'm so sorry for all of it."

"Meals for servants are eaten in the kitchen," she stated, folding the heavy white cover and placing it on a nearby table. "We keep country hours, and Janny, our cook, is up early every morning. If your work requires that you be out in the estate before breakfast is served, she'll be glad to feed you when necessary."

Collin stepped even nearer, close enough to touch her. "Why didn't you tell me the truth when you wrote to me? I would have managed a leave of absence to come to you. Or I would have sent you to my parents in Northampton, to stay with them until I could come home. You would have been welcomed there with all gladness," he told her.

"You know that they were eager for you to stay with them while I was gone from England, though they understood that you were needed at the inn. My father remembered you so well from his visits at The Lamb and Wig, and my mother had hoped to know you better than simply by letters." Reaching out, he touched her arm. "Rose, only listen to me a moment."

She jerked away, her body rigid, and walked to another chair.

"The midday meal is come as you can. Janny will have a pot of soup warming throughout the day and you can fill a bowl as you like. If you're to be out during the day she'll pack some bread and cheese for you to take along. The evening meal is served at seven, after her ladyship has supped." The dustcover slipped from the chair, sending dust flying everywhere. Rose paid it little mind as she handled the cloth, rapidly folding it into a small, neat square.

"If you miss it, you'll be obliged to talk Janny into feeding you, which she won't like to do, for she's done with cooking by then. But I have no doubt that you could charm her into dragging out every freshly cleaned pot in the kitchen and putting it to use. You have a gift for charming women. Lady Dilbeck is clearly no exception.''

She didn't say it bitterly, but stated it as simple fact. The familiarity made Collin's heart take a hopeful leap.

"I had to exert myself to do so," Collin said. "I've not had much practice since leaving England—and you—six years ago.''

She made a sound halfway between a laugh and a snort of disbelief.

"I was faithful to you, Rose, just as I promised I would be. It wasn't a hardship. Not even after that final letter.''

Saying nothing, not looking at him, she crossed the room once more to collect the folded covers. Collin determinedly followed.

"I wish you'd told me the truth, Rose, when you wrote that letter. I didn't know that Carl had any idea of joining up. You never mentioned it in any of your other missives. If I'd known—and if he'd arrived in Spain alive—I would have tracked him down and done everything possible to send him home again. He never should have left you and your father alone. It was a foolish thing to do. Rose, won't you even look at me?''

She turned, the pile of cloths in her hands, looked at him very directly and said, "If you require anything further, Captain Mattison, please make your requests known to me rather than Camhort or either of the maids. I'll make certain that you have everything you need. While you're out looking at the estate this afternoon, Hester and Emily, our downstairs maid, will come in and freshen the room.'' She started for the door. "And, now, please excuse me. I have a great many duties to attend to.''

Collin stepped in front of her, barring her way.

"This is foolish," he said tightly. "You can't pretend that you don't know me, Rose. Not after all we've shared.''

"I'm not the one who began this farce," she retorted, glaring at him. "You pretended to be a stranger to me when we were with Lady Dilbeck. I'm merely playing along."

"I did that for your benefit, not mine. I have little doubt that you've not told Lady Dilbeck you were once promised to marry a soldier. Or have you?"

Her cheeks pinked and her tone was less strident.

"There was no need to do so. Just as there was no need for you to come here." She closed her eyes briefly. "I should have told you about my father and Carl, but I feared what you've said, that you would try to do something for me." She looked away. "And so I wrote as I did, hoping you'd leave well enough alone."

"Of course I would have done something for you," he said, unable to keep the hurt her words wrought out of his voice. "I loved you. I lived every moment until your final letter believing that you were to be my wife. I would have done anything and everything for you."

"I know," she said shakily, lifting her eyes to his once more. "But it wouldn't have been right. If Carl had only stayed in London, so that when Papa died I wouldn't have been left alone, or if he hadn't fallen ill on his way to Spain, everything would have been all right. It would have been difficult to run the inn by myself, but I believe I could have done it. Jarvis would have stayed with me to tend the customers, and Anna and Mary would have stayed, too, I'm certain. But once Carl died, so quickly after Papa, everything was lost to Papa's distant cousin, Mister Klivans, a man I'd never even met."

"And he sent you away with nothing," Collin said softly, remarking the look of surprise in her eyes. "Jarvis told me about it. Mister Klivans at least had the sense to keep one faithful servant on in the tavern, though he dismissed Anna and Mary. I know as much as Jarvis was able to tell me."

"I see." She turned, walked back to the table and set the cloths on it again, making a neat, careful pile. "I thought, when I first saw you below, that you must have discovered a great deal, though I hoped you'd not learned the worst of it. But perhaps it's for the best, for now you understand why I had to write as I did. Why I had to release you from our understanding."

Collin shook his head. "I don't understand it at all. It changes *nothing* between us."

Her eyes were wide when she turned to him. "How can you say that? It was difficult enough for us to consider being wed when my father and brother were alive, but at least the inn was of good repute and I could lay claim to being the daughter of a respectable man of trade. Even so, it was a miracle that your parents had no objection when you wrote to them about me."

"No objection?" he repeated. "How can you use such cold words for their response? They were pleased beyond measure to know that my heart had at last been taken by a properly raised girl. They'd given up hope that I'd ever be serious enough to find a wife."

"Yes, they did seem pleased," she agreed, "though there was reserve, as well. That you must admit." She gave a sigh. "It would have been strange if there had not been, for your father knew me only briefly, and your mother not at all. But despite that, they were very kind, especially your mother, when she wrote to assure me of their assent. It was a measure of their love and trust in you that they didn't question your attachment to a girl with so little to recommend her, whom you'd only known a short time."

"You have everything to recommend you," he stated angrily. "Everything that I desire in a wife, leastwise, and that's all that matters. Both your mother and father came from good families, and your father saw that you were educated as well as any highborn lady."

"My parents were innkeepers," she said softly, "and I've labored in the way of a servant—cooking, cleaning and serving customers. That is not what well-born girls do, Collin. But for the fourth son of a landed gentleman, I might have been considered suitable. But that's all changed." The smile died. "Now I am a servant, and not the daughter of an innkeeper. But worse—" she drew in a steadying breath "—before Lady Dilbeck took mercy on me, I was much less than a servant." She folded her hands against her stomach.

"Much less, Collin. Mister Klivans sent me away with only those few belongings that I could carry, and I...I lived as best I could, where I could. I don't wish to tell you the full of that time, save to say that I was fortunate enough not to have to sell myself for...for the pleasure of men." Her cheeks burned, and she looked away. "But the manner in which I did live was little better. There were others who were as desperate as I was, and I lived with them. Together we found ways to survive. I think you understand me well enough."

Collin's heart lurched painfully at what he believed she was trying to tell him. Thieves. A family of thieves. They were common on the streets of London, and elsewhere, but it was difficult to think of Rose living among them.

"It doesn't matter," he murmured, shaking off the surprise her words had given him. "Many suffer during these difficult days, and do what they must to survive. Even good people. Soldiers who served under my command in the war—men of pride and honor—have turned to the same manner of life, having come home to England to find nothing else waiting for them."

"Yes, I know." A smile ghosted on her lips, both faint and sad. "There were former soldiers among those whom I lived with. Wounded men, mainly, and some without an arm or a leg or both. They chose stealing above begging." She shook her head at the memory. "Just as I chose stealing over whoring. It seemed more honorable, somehow, but it wasn't an easy choice.'' Lowering her head, Rose moved toward the door. He didn't bar her way this time. ''And so you see, Collin, that it would be impossible for you to wed me now. Your family would rightly not allow it—''

''That doesn't matter.''

''—and I'd not let you do anything so foolish as to wed without their consent,'' she finished. ''No matter how much I might love you, or how greatly I might wish to wed you.''

Collin gazed at her from where he stood.

''Do you love me, Rose?''

She stared at him for a long, silent moment, then said, ''I shall always love you.'' She set her hand upon the doorknob. ''I'll send Jacob to bring coal, and will ask him to collect the dust cloths before he goes.''

''I'm not leaving Dilbeck Manor,'' Collin warned. ''Not until I've found the way to convince you to be my wife. For I love you, too, Rose. And always will. I won't give way on anything so important, as you know full well.''

For the first time, tears began to fill her eyes, and she was obliged to blink them back.

''Don't be foolish, Collin. There's nothing left between us now, and you only make it harder by not letting go. I'll write to your parents, if I must, and tell them the full of it, the truth of all that I've done and how I've lived. They will make you see sense, even if I can't.''

''Write them,'' he replied, lifting a hand in invitation, ''and see if it makes any difference.''

A tear trickled down her cheek. Collin longed to wipe it away, to take her in his arms and hold her, to kiss every misery and sadness away. But she was unapproachable, gazing at him with a mixture of anger and frustration that left him in no doubt as to how unwelcome such an advance would be. She needed time and reassurance, and the kind of love such as only he could give her. All three he had in good measure now, and meant to make full use of them, if only he could make himself patient enough to do so.

She paused as she opened the door and looked back at him. "I want you to know one thing." Lifting a hand, she wiped the moisture from her face. "I did try to find honest employment after leaving the inn. I searched everywhere, and was willing to do any kind of work. But there was nothing."

"I never believed that you had done otherwise," he said. "It's inconceivable that you would have. And it would have been a miracle if you'd been able to find work in London, even as a scullery maid. All of England is desolate of employment, Rose. That you found work here, even with someone like Lady Dilbeck, is beyond fortunate."

"Yes," she whispered. "More than you know, Collin. Far more than you could ever know. Please don't make me give that up in order to be away from you."

He opened his mouth to speak, to deny that he would ever do such a thing, but she opened the door more widely and slid out of the room without sound, leaving him alone with only his rattled thoughts for company.

Chapter Five

"Well, well." Collin stepped back and wiped the back of one gloved hand across his damp forehead. "What's this? It almost looks as if we might make some use of it."

"The sleigh?" Jacob asked, looking over Collin's shoulder. "It's in fine condition. Needs some cleaning and a bit of grease and paint, but we could hitch the horses up this very minute and be on our way without trouble."

"It was buried under all this pile of blankets and old furniture," Collin remarked. "Which tells me that it's not been made use of in some years."

"Nay, not for the past ten years, at least, even when the snow was too deep for the carriage. But her ladyship doesn't go out when there's snow. Not anymore, leastwise. I ride into the village on old Robbie when anything is needed, or the merchants come here to us. But it's a fine sleigh," Jacob repeated, wiping his dirty hands on the heavy leather apron he wore, "even if it's not used."

"Lady Dilbeck never goes out in the winter?" Collin asked. "Not even for church services?"

Jacob shook his head. "The vicar comes for tea each Sunday to read the Bible and pray with her, but she'll not step foot in the church until Lent—and then only if the snow has melted. Do we move this, then?" He nodded toward the sled. "We can work easier with it out of the way."

It was late afternoon, but Collin was determined to at least make a start on repairing the stable roof. He'd ridden out to speak to each of Lady Dilbeck's few remaining tenants earlier in the day, and had secured agreement from some of the men to come in the morning and lend their aid in the work, with the hope that the weather held.

Laboring in the winter chill would be unpleasant as it was, but trying to roof a stable in falling snow would be miserable work. One way or another, it had to be done, and whatever he and Jacob could do to prepare for the coming task, the quicker and easier the work would be.

"Let's put it over there for now, by the horses. We'll move it outside tomorrow—God willing that the weather should be clear—and let Ralf have a go at cleaning it." Collin moved to the far side of the once-elegant sleigh and set his shoulder against it. Jacob went to the other side and did likewise. With no small effort they slid it across the hay-strewn floor to the other end of the stable.

"That's grand." Jacob smiled, removing his hat and running one hand through his dark, curly hair. "I don't say her ladyship will like it, but it'll be good to see this old beauty look as it used to. Or as close to it as Ralf can make it look." He walked about the large vehicle, sliding a hand along the wood.

Jacob was a handsome, good-natured fellow, of an age with Collin, strong and tall and fit for the great variety of work required of him at Dilbeck Manor. He was also, unless Collin was much mistaken, deeply smitten with the pretty downstairs maid, Emily. He'd caught the two of them eyeing each other when Camhort had formally introduced him to the entire staff.

"I remember how his lordship, may God bless him, used to drive out in this sleigh as soon as he could each year, polished and shining it was, and decked with greenery.

And her ladyship and Master Bruce beside him, laughing and merry. They were all so merry, then,'' Jacob said, sighing at the memory. ''You never saw any family so happy as that, especially among the Quality.

''His lordship was never afraid to laugh out loud, nor was his son, who was as game as he could be. And her ladyship—'' he gave a shake of his head ''—she was so different from what she is now. Beautiful, even.'' He looked at Collin as if to convince him of it. ''And a sweet, pleasant lady in every way. She loved Christmas in those days. Loved everything about it.''

''Did she?'' Collin regarded the other man curiously. ''Was it her son's death that caused her to stop celebrating the holiday?''

''That, mostly,'' Jacob replied somberly, ''though the change began when Lord Dilbeck died. He'd been the one who'd brought all the cheer into the manor. The whole household was decorated with holly and berries—even the portraits in the dining hall. There were kissing boughs and mistletoe and many pretty maids to kiss beneath them. My eldest sister was among them, before she married and left the manor.''

''Is that how you came to be here?'' Collin asked as they walked back to the roofless side of the stable. ''Because your sister worked here?''

''Aye. I was raised at the manor, since I was but a young lad. Lady Dilbeck was good enough to keep me as a stable boy after letting so many of the others go. Time was, years back, that Dilbeck Manor was properly staffed, with maids and footmen and gardeners and stable hands aplenty, all in uniform. And the tenant farms were all occupied and in good condition. Lord Dilbeck kept the estate proudly, though you'd never think it to see the place now.''

They were clearing the area beneath the open roof, pushing the remaining refuse aside.

''Lady Dilbeck's son died some years ago, did he not?''

"Fifteen years past, when he had only just taken on the title following his father's death. Master Bruce was but twenty-five years of age, and a fine lord he would have been, just like his father, had he not caught the chill. That was just before Christmas, and he died the next month, January. All those days Lady Dilbeck nursed him, sitting by his side nearly every hour, watching him worsen and then die. It's why she doesn't like the time of year, you see," Jacob said, glancing at Collin. "She can't stand to think of those days, which had always been such glad ones before."

"It must have been a very hard time," Collin said with sympathy, "to have lost both her husband and son within but months of each other."

"Aye, and that being nearly all the family she had in the world," Jacob said with a nod, accepting one of the two brooms Collin had lifted from where they'd leaned against a stall door.

"She has some family, though?" Collin asked, setting his own broom into motion, clearing away the considerable straw, rocks and filth on the ground. It looked as if this part of the stable hadn't had a proper cleaning in years. "Distant family?"

"All distant," Jacob said with a grunt. "Vultures, I call them, after her ladyship's money and nothing else. Like that Miss Carpenter," he said with blunt distaste. "God save me, she wasn't the worst of the lot, but she was bad enough. Flighty, ill-mannered bit of a female she was, and so fearful that she leaped at the sight of her own shadow."

He stopped sweeping and looked up at Collin. "I won't say I'm sorry that she's gone, for I'm not, save that her going hurt Lady Dilbeck and got Miss Rose into trouble. And," he added more dolefully, starting to sweep again, "ruined our chance of having a proper Christmas. Her ladyship will never agree to it now, no matter how Miss Rose puts the matter before her."

"Had she promised to speak to her ladyship about it? You don't think Lady Dilbeck would listen to one of the rest of you? Perhaps Camhort?"

"Nah." Jacob shook her head. "Her ladyship don't listen to no one but Miss Rose, and then only now and again, or when Miss Rose insists it's something for her ladyship's health. Then she puts her foot down and there's no arguing," he said with a laugh. "It always puts Lady Dilbeck into a bit of a spin, if you know what I mean."

"I know very well," Collin replied, remembering how stubborn Rose could be. It had been one of the things he'd found so delightful about her.

"Ralf told me that you knew Miss Rose a long time ago," Jacob said, glancing up at Collin. "Knew her well."

"We were promised to wed, before I went away to war," Collin told him, certain that the entire staff knew of it by now. "And sometime during the war that changed, though I very much wish it hadn't. However, Lady Dilbeck doesn't know about my past relationship with Miss Rose, and Miss Rose doesn't wish her to…at least not yet. If you'd be so good as to keep that secret to yourself, and to ask the others to do so—for Miss Rose's sake—I'd appreciate it."

Jacob straightened and gazed at Collin very directly, his gloved hands folded on the top of the broom handle.

"You don't mean to upset Miss Rose, do you?"

The warning in the man's voice and eyes was unmistakable, and made Collin smile. It was clear that all the people at Dilbeck Manor, including Lady Dilbeck, held Rose in great affection.

"I love Miss Rose," he replied simply, "and would never bring her harm. I give you my word as both an officer in His Majesty's army and as a gentleman on that."

Jacob's cheeks pinked at the tips, and he began to sweep once more.

"I didn't mean to say that you were a bad sort, Captain," he said.

"I never thought you did," Collin said affably, setting his broom aside and glancing about. "This looks ready. We should be able to get most of the roof on before tomorrow night, God willing. If you'll finish up here, I'll go speak to Janny about food and drink for the men."

Jacob gave him a curious look. "Food and drink? Her ladyship won't see any reason for giving them any. Or she'll expect them to bring their own."

Collin took up his coat and began to shrug into it.

"I promised them food and drink in exchange for their labor, and food and drink they'll have. I thought a hot rum punch would make the work lighter, if I can talk Janny into mixing one up."

Jacob uttered a disbelieving laugh. "Rum punch? You're mad, Captain, if you think her ladyship will ever allow such as that."

"And why not?" Collin asked, buttoning his collar. "It's nearly Christmas, after all, and what could be more appropriate than a hot rum punch?"

"Better have Camhort mix it," Jacob advised as Collin moved for the stable doors. "Janny'll stint on the rum."

Rose couldn't bear to look at her reflection in the mirror. She was ugly. Ugly and thin and colorless. There had been a time in her life when she'd perhaps been a bit vain. Men had admired her thick, curling hair and her healthy figure, and she'd been assured, not infrequently, that she was a "very pretty gel."

But no longer. No matter how long or hard she gazed at herself in that mirror, she couldn't deny what she saw. She'd lost so much of herself in the past few years. So much of what she'd once been. Her hair, if she let it loose, was still long and curling, but it was dull, without shine or luster. Her skin was pale and her eyes shadowed. And her body—that was the worst of all. She had the figure of a young girl, all thin and reedy. What Collin must think when he looked at her made Rose want to burst into tears. She'd been struggling since she'd left him to not do just that.

He was even more handsome than he'd been six years past, if such a thing was possible. He'd been still much of a boy, then, but he was a man now, with the face and body of a man, strong and powerful and so self-assured. Though he'd always been self-assured, she thought, turning from the mirror. There had been a time when she, too, had felt that way, as if nothing in the world could defeat her.

She had learned, to her sorrow, that she'd been wrong. And now she must help Collin to learn it, too, whether he wished it or not.

She crossed the room to her dressing table and picked up the letter she'd written, casting an appraising eye over the words on the single page. They were few and to the point; Collin's parents wouldn't need more than that to set them toward rescuing their stubborn son from a ruinous alliance. They would demand that he leave Dilbeck Manor at once, hopefully before Rose wavered and gave way to the foolishness of her heart.

She wanted to let herself believe that there was a chance…that a miracle might happen…that they might be together. But she couldn't. It was too painful to hope for what could never be. She'd spent so many years striving to find peace after giving Collin up; now she would have to begin all over again, just as soon as he left Dilbeck Manor.

And he would leave. His parents would make certain of it, if Collin didn't come to his senses before then and depart on his own. Though somehow she doubted he'd come to that, for his determination was full amazing. That he'd come all this way to find her, and had lowered himself to taking a position as a steward on such a poor estate, was evidence of just how stubborn he could be.

Collin had gone out to ride about the grounds almost immediately after Camhort had formally introduced him to the rest of the staff, and returned some hours later to charm a late afternoon meal of bread and ale out of Janny. Then he'd appropriated Jacob and made use of him in clearing out the stable, having informed the household staff—but not Lady Dilbeck—that some of the tenants were coming to repair the roof on the morrow.

Rose had warned him that her ladyship wouldn't like it, but Collin had only smiled and assured her that all would be well. Then he and Jacob had departed to make the stable ready. Rose had spent the following two hours avoiding Lady Dilbeck's questions about what Captain Mattison was up to, praying that Collin would find a way to tell his new employer before the day was done.

It was getting late, and darkness fell quickly these days. She had best be on her way to the village if she didn't wish to walk back to Dilbeck Manor in the dark.

She passed the kitchen as she made her way to the servant's door and, hearing laughter, paused just long enough to hear Janny offering "Captain Mattison" a freshly made cup of tea.

Janny never made fresh tea at this time of day, unless it was for Lady Dilbeck. But her ladyship was fast asleep—Rose had helped to put her to bed but half an hour past.

The deep rumble of Collin's voice filtered into the hall, and then there was more laughter—mostly Janny's. Rose nearly rolled her eyes at the sound. She'd been at Dilbeck Manor for almost three years now, and in all that time had only seen Janny smile half a dozen times, and had never heard her laugh. Collin had only been at the manor for half a day, and he already had the usually temperamental cook filled with merriment.

* * *

She'd walked but half an hour—briskly and through ankle-deep snow—when she heard horse hooves behind her.

"Rose!" Collin called out, nearing her and slowing his handsome mount to a walk. "What are you doing walking in this weather? If you'd needed a ride into the village, I would have made the carriage ready for you."

Rose kept walking, her gaze straight ahead.

"Her ladyship prefers that the carriage is kept for her sole use," she said. "It's not far to the village. I don't mind walking."

"Your feet must be frozen near to ice," he chided, "and your shoes will be hours drying. Come, let me give you a ride." He pulled a little ahead of her, reaching down and extending a hand.

"I'm fine, thank you." Though he was right, she thought with aggravation. Her feet did feel like ice.

"Rose," he said in a warning tone, his hand yet extended, "I'll not go away until you come up here and ride with me into the village. Do you want me to follow you the rest of the way, pestering you?"

She cast an angry glance at him.

"I wish to be left alone."

He smiled beguilingly. "But I won't do so. I can hardly leave you to walk another mile in this snow and yet call myself a gentleman. Don't be so stubborn."

Rose stopped and turned to look up at him.

"You dare to call *me* stubborn?" she asked with disbelief. "You're the most stubborn man who ever walked God's earth, Collin Mattison."

"Yes, that's true," he admitted. "And now that we're agreed, you'll realize that it's no good to stand there and argue with me, for I'll not give way. Here, put your foot on top of my boot and I'll pull you up." He reached his hand down even farther.

Resigned, Rose put her own in it and let him pull her

up before him. With one arm about her waist, he settled her more securely and set the horse into motion.

"There," he said cheerfully, "we've plenty of room. You're comfortable, aren't you?"

No, she wasn't. Not in the very least. His body was hard against her back, and she felt enveloped by his strength and heat. Memories of being held in his arms like this flooded her. Memories of being kissed and caressed, of kissing and caressing him in return, running her hands over his shoulders and arms and...

"Rose?"

"Yes, I'm comfortable," she answered quickly, drawing in a shaking breath. "What are you doing out so late in the afternoon?" She strove to sound more herself. "I thought you'd finished riding about the estate before you and Jacob went out to the stable."

"Yes, but I need supplies for tomorrow. Janny has promised a fine repast for the tenants and Camhort has agreed to mix a hot rum punch—save that he hasn't any rum, and Janny insists that her ladyship won't spare one of the hams from the larder."

"Do you mean to say that you're going to buy rum and a ham out of your own funds?" Rose asked, squirming to look back at him. "That will cost a small fortune, Collin. You mustn't do it. I'll speak with Lady Dilbeck."

"I don't mind," he assured her. "The money is of little consequence to me."

"But you're not even being paid for your labors," Rose protested. "You shouldn't spend money from your own pocket for what Lady Dilbeck should rightly be paying for."

"Rose, I don't mind," he said again, squeezing her lightly about the waist. He smiled into her upturned face, so close to his own, and was hard-pressed not to kiss her. He hadn't been prepared for how it would feel to have her in his arms again, to be touching her, holding her, once more. After so many years and so many dreams, Rose was right there with him, warm against his body. And looking up at him with an expression of irate frustration that he found fully adorable.

Her cheeks were a healthy pink from her walking and the cold, and her blue eyes sparkled with the old fire he knew so well. "I promise you, it's not a burden for me to do some small thing for the men who are coming tomorrow. It gives me pleasure to give them a bit of holiday cheer, even if Christmas is some days off."

Rose paled. "Collin, you mustn't mention Christmas to her ladyship. She doesn't celebrate it, and becomes very unhappy if anyone speaks of it in the household. And you mustn't make any show of celebrating the holiday, even with the tenants. If Lady Dilbeck should learn of it..."

"Never fear, I'll make all right with her ladyship."

"Collin..."

"Trust me," he said gently. "I know all about why her ladyship dislikes Christmas, and I'll act with every care. Why are you going to the village at such a late hour?" he asked when she opened her mouth to argue the matter further. "You might have been obliged to walk home in the dark, and her ladyship would have begun to worry for you." And all the rest of us, he left unsaid.

She turned forward and was silent a moment, then finally replied, "I've written to your parents, and mean to post the letter at once."

"I'm glad," he said. "They'll be pleased to have word from you."

"Collin," she said chidingly, giving a shake of her head. "You've ever been determined to see black as white. They'll be angered that you've come to Dilbeck Manor in search of me, and they'll talk sense into you at once."

"I'm my own man, Rose, and, though I respect them deeply, my parents hold little sway over me in matters of such import as love. And being a fourth son affords me a greater measure of freedom. I'm by no means wealthy, of course, but I've saved enough from my years in the army to buy a farm and set up my own household. It will be a simple life, but respectable, and my wife will never have need to be ashamed. Nor will she want for anything.''

''I'm certain that's true,'' Rose murmured, ''but your parents will yet insist that you wed suitably, regardless of what your life may be.''

''I'll choose my own wife, Rose,'' he said, ''and pray that she'll choose me, as well. My parents will have very little say in the matter. Now, here's the village, coming fast upon us.'' He pulled his horse to a slower pace. ''Tell me where you wish to post your letter, and then lead me in the direction of the butchery. We'll finish our purchases and be on our way back before the sun has gone.''

They were on their way back well before the sun had gone, Collin's horse laden with packages. He'd not only paid for her letter to be sent to his family—deaf to her protestations—but he'd also gone mad in making purchases throughout the village. Tied to his saddle were a small ham, a sizable roast, a wrapped bundle of suet, a small casket of fine rum, a cloth-covered bottle of brandy, five loaves of bread, two whole cheeses, a variety of fruits and nuts and some pieces of toffee for Ralf.

Rose knew what he was trying to do, and didn't approve in the least—even if, secretly, she hoped his attempts would work. Still, she commented primly as they left the village, ''Your horse will grow weary with so many unnecessary burdens. Lady Dilbeck will never let us have a Christmas pudding, and the money you've spent will have gone for nothing. And you should have let me walk back to the manor,'' she added less convincingly, for he felt even warmer and more comfortable as the late afternoon chilled. ''Your horse shouldn't have to carry so much.''

''My horse,'' Collin replied, ''has carried a great deal more under far more difficult circumstances. We had occasion to carry wounded men from the field of battle, sometimes two at a time, if there was no other choice. He will be thinking you a sweet burden by comparison. And as to our Christmas pudding, which Janny assures me will be glorious, don't trouble yourself over it. Just enjoy the coming days and this beautiful time of year.

"During the war I used to dream of being in England, just to see the snow upon the ground untainted by blood or fighting. This is what I dreamed of," he said, his arm about her tightening. "Exactly this. I don't intend to take it for granted for even one day, ever again."

Rose could imagine what winters had been like during the war, compared to this one. Despite the cold and wet, the countryside was blanketed in white beauty, clean and fresh for as far as the eye could see. Riding atop Collin's horse, and held within the shelter of his arms, Rose was warm and content. For just this time, then, she would do as he advised and enjoy what was, and worry about tomorrow when it arrived.

Chapter Six

They were greeted at the manor by a mild uproar. Her ladyship, it seemed, had woken in a foul mood a half hour past, and had demanded Rose's immediate attention. Upon learning that Rose wasn't present, her ladyship's mood had grown worse. She was now in full fury, and her staff was desperately trying to please her. Hester had helped her ladyship dress and make her way to the downstairs parlor, where she was now waiting—impatiently—for dinner to be announced.

"Is that for Lady Dilbeck?" Collin asked, setting the bundle of fruits and nuts on a large table before going to the stove to lift the lid off a simmering pot and sniff the contents. "God save me, it smells like pure heaven." He cast a smile at Janny, who was kneading bread a short distance away. "What I wouldn't have given for a bowl of oxtail soup during the war. My men and I would have called ourselves blessed if we'd had someone like you to cook for us, Janny."

Janny lit up like a candle and, much to Rose's surprise, even blushed.

"It's just a simple recipe," she said. "One of m'mother's. But I do think it turns out well. It's among her ladyship's favorites."

"I think it must be among anyone's favorite, once it's been tasted." Collin set the lid back on the pot and turned to contemplate Rose, who was setting the bottle of brandy carefully next to the rest of the bounty they'd brought back from the village. "Is there enough for three at her ladyship's table tonight, Janny?" he asked.

Everyone looked up, including Emily, who was busy polishing wineglasses, and Camhort, who was laying out the silverware her ladyship would use during her dinner.

"Her ladyship doesn't have company this evening," Rose said, praying that the gleam in his eyes didn't mean what she thought.

"I think," he replied, "that she will."

It went far more smoothly than Collin had dared to hope. The confidence he strove to show the others when speaking of handling Lady Dilbeck consisted far more of smoke than reality. But smoke, as he'd discovered during the war, could be a helpful ally. Still, it wasn't his intention to harm or mislead Lady Dilbeck, and he knew that he must act with real care.

But he was certain that she'd rather not eat alone, despite her insistence otherwise. Miss Carpenter's defection had stung deeply, though her ladyship would never reveal that to him. Still, she didn't argue very long or hard, or make reference to his impertinence too many times, before giving way. She even agreed when Collin suggested that both he and Rose join her at the formal dining table, for then he would be able to discuss his plans for the estate with both of them at once.

Discussion, however, was far from a simple matter with Lady Dilbeck. She liked to argue, and found fault with all of Collin's ideas—starting with the repair of the stable roof.

"I'll not have it," she declared, setting her soupspoon beside her empty bowl. "Strange men on my property, wandering where they will and getting into my things. No,

I will *not* allow it,'' she said with as much finality as a general deciding the course of a battle.

Collin had had a great deal of experience in dealing with generals.

"They are not strangers. They're your own tenants, and they'll arrive early in the morning and, with good fortune and hard work, be done before the sun sets. The stable roof is but the first of the repairs that will be done on the estate during the winter months. Your tenants' farms require a great deal of attention, as well, and every man will pitch in his fair share of labor to receive labor in turn for his own house and outbuildings. Once the needs of the existing tenants—and the manor, itself, of course—have been seen to, we'll need to turn our attention to the tenant houses and lands that are going unoccupied and uncared for."

"Dilbeck doesn't require more tenants," Lady Dilbeck said stubbornly, sitting straight in her chair as Camhort set fresh plates before each of them. "They're more trouble than they're worth, always complaining and letting their children run wild. I'll be glad to see those still here leave."

Collin waited until Camhort had served her ladyship the fish course before answering.

"Dilbeck will become unprofitable without tenants, and without some income the entire estate will eventually fall into ruin. The manor house alone requires a great deal more repair than even the men here can provide." He ladled fish onto his own plate as Camhort offered it. The white fish and delicate sauce, laced with herbs, was another of Janny's masterpieces. "Surely you don't wish to see an estate of such historic importance fall into complete disrepair, Lady Dilbeck. Your husband's family has been here for many generations, have they not?"

Rose cleared her throat to gain his attention, but it was too late. He could see, by Lady Dilbeck's expression, that he'd said the wrong thing.

"Yes," she murmured, her head lowering, the fork drooping in her hand. "The Favreaus have been at Dilbeck for more than three hundred years. But no more, once I'm gone. There are no more Favreaus remaining, from the direct line. Dilbeck Manor will go to some unknown relative or, worse, to strangers, for after my son's passing the entailment ended." She seemed to wilt even further, as if the words had leeched the energy out of her body.

"I see," Collin said gently, casting caution to the wind and reaching out to briefly touch her hand. "Then we must at least make certain that the estate is kept whole for your benefit, while you live, as both Lord Dilbeck and your son would have wished. Tell me, had you been to Dilbeck before you were wed to your husband, or did you first see it as a new bride?"

The question, as Rose was certain Collin intended it to, not only changed the subject but also genuinely engaged Lady Dilbeck's interest. There was nothing she loved discussing so much as her early years at Dilbeck Manor, when her son was a child and her life had been so happy. It was difficult for her to speak of the years nearer to the death of her beloved husband and son, but she could talk endlessly of all the days that had come before.

Rose sat in silence, eating her dinner and watching with wonderment as Collin managed the conversation, drawing Lady Dilbeck far away from her sadness and into glowing, enlivened pleasure. Her ladyship began to look almost youthful, and the pain that ever shadowed her eyes eased. It was only later, when they had finished dinner and were in the parlor before the fire, that weariness and pain began to make themselves known.

"Your hands plague you?" Collin asked, setting his cup of tea aside. "I have a balm in my room that I found most helpful during the war. I'm certain it would ease some of the ache. Let me go and fetch it."

"No, don't trouble yourself," her ladyship said as he

rose from his chair. "Nothing helps any longer. Rose will fix one of her usual potions and force it upon me, whether I wish it or not."

But Collin wouldn't be turned aside. He left the parlor and returned a few minutes later bearing a small, battered tin, which he opened to reveal a heavily pungent ointment.

Rose took one sniff and backed away, murmuring, "Oh, dear." Her ladyship covered her nose with one hand and said, "God in heaven, put the lid on again. It smells terrible. Take it away. I won't have it."

Rose was certain that Collin had at last run into a refusal that he couldn't overcome, but she was wrong. Somehow, with almost no difficulty or resistance at all, Collin slathered the foul-smelling ointment over both of Lady Dilbeck's hands and, with some help from Rose, carefully wrapped each of them in linen cloth.

"Why, it doesn't burn at all, as I was sure it would," Lady Dilbeck said approvingly, lifting her wrapped hands and turning them about experimentally. "It's quite a pleasant sensation, just a bit of tingling. And soothing." She looked up at Rose, her expression filled with true amazement. "The pain lessens each moment. What can it be, Rose?"

From the smell of it, Rose wasn't certain she wanted to guess, but if it eased her ladyship's suffering, she would gladly learn to mix the foul-smelling ointment and keep it in great supply.

"I don't know, my lady. Perhaps Captain Mattison could supply me with the receipt?"

"I only wish I could," he replied. "But I fear I don't know what it is. A soldier in my regiment used to mix it up for us when he could find what he needed. He was quite an interesting young fellow, and able to tend almost any wound, even those that might kill a man."

"He was a doctor, then?" Lady Dilbeck asked.

"No," Collin replied, taking up his teacup again. "Elliot Haysbert is a gardener. Or was, before the war, when he was employed on an estate in Sussex. He's in London now, along with a number of other men who served under my command." He held the cup and saucer out to Rose when she offered to refill it. "I'd be pleased to write Elliot," he said to Lady Dilbeck, "and ask him to send me the receipt. Better still, I'll ask him to come to Dilbeck Manor and show Miss Rose how to make the mixture himself. That way there'll be no chance of a mistake being made."

Rose frowned at him. "I'm certain I can follow any directions he writes out."

But Lady Dilbeck, sitting back and closing her eyes in contentment and relief, said, "That would be fine, Captain. Write him tomorrow, if you will, and ask him to come at once. I vow he must be a miracle worker to have made such a useful salve. It's been a long while since I've had such respite from my aches."

"I'm glad," Collin murmured, smiling gently at Rose over the rim of his teacup. "I'll write Elliot in the morning, before going out to oversee the work on the stable roof. It will be good to see him again," he said before her ladyship, whose eyes had opened, could protest the repairs once more. "My men are all that I've missed about the war. Even those who gave me trouble. It's strange to think of how greatly we all longed to be home in England, especially at this time of year, only to return and find so little welcome—and less work—waiting for us."

"A plague of scoundrels and thieves," Lady Dilbeck declared. "That's what has come home to England. Excepting the officers," she amended, "who at least are of birth. But the rest—bah! They've caused nothing but trouble. Rioting in the streets, stealing from decent people. And spreading filth and disease. Wellington would have done better to leave them in Spain and France."

Rose saw anger flash in Collin's blue eyes, but his expression remained as calm and polite as before.

"He left a great many of them in those countries, my lady, where they died to preserve a way of life that those who did not fight continue to enjoy. I do not deny that many of my men were scoundrels and thieves, some of them having chosen the army over a tree and noose. But yet they fought and were ready to die, if not for England, then for each other and for me."

Lady Dilbeck wasn't in the least chagrined, and readily launched into a spirited discussion on the subject. Rose, horrified to hear Collin speak to her ladyship in so open and free a manner, sat through the lengthy argument in stiff silence, refusing to be drawn into the fray. She was certain that her ladyship, at any moment, was going to send Collin away from the manor, and couldn't decide whether she felt relief...or distress. She did want him to go away, after all. Didn't she?

But her ladyship didn't ask Collin to leave. Instead, she was even more pleased with him, once their argument died away, than she'd been before. The matter ended with both of them laughing at their own stubbornness, and agreeing that they were too well matched to argue with the other further.

"What did you miss the most about England, Captain Mattison?" her ladyship asked, settling back into her chair with a relaxed sigh. "Your family? Or perhaps your sweetheart?"

"My sweetheart, most certainly," Collin replied, glancing meaningfully at Rose, who felt her cheeks heat as she looked quickly away. "And my family as well. But after those, I think I would have to say I missed special occasions and holidays. Christmas, most of all."

Rose cleared her throat nervously and murmured, "Would you like more tea, my lady?"

But her ladyship wasn't paying attention to Rose. She was gazing at Collin.

"Christmas?" she repeated. "Not Easter or St. George's Day?"

"I missed those, too," he admitted. "But Christmas more than the rest. We would sit about the fire on a Christmas Eve and think of what our families were doing back home, safe in their houses, we hoped, with good cheer and full bellies and plenty of coal to keep them warm. Talking of such things made our own pitiful surroundings seem less so. Still," he said with a sigh, "winter will never come but that I don't remember the long nights we spent in foreign lands, with the snow hard upon the ground and that same ground our beds. We didn't always have tents on such nights, or food. But we had our small fire and a drink to share along with our memories, and with those we made our Christmas."

Both Rose and Lady Dilbeck had grown silent, listening intently.

"One year," he went on, "one of the soldiers' wives scraped together enough ingredients to make a small pudding, and we all shared it by the fire on Christmas Eve." He uttered a laugh at the memory. "It was a tasteless pudding, I vow, but we were so glad to have it that I think it must ever be considered the best we ever dined upon, little as our portions were." He looked at Lady Dilbeck. "I imagine you've had many grand puddings here at Dilbeck Manor."

"The finest ever to be had, when Lord Dilbeck was alive," her ladyship murmured. "He was so fond of a good pudding, and loved to gather the household to each take their turn at the spoon on the day it was made. The servants' children started first, and everyone else, one by one, until my husband alone was left." She chuckled at the memory. "He was so lordly, making the final stir and declaring that Christmas was now upon us, as if it was a gift he was making to us all. He was quite foolish over the holiday," she said fondly. "I think he would have made it last all year, if he'd had the power to do so."

"He sounds like a wonderful man," Collin said.

"Oh, he was," Lady Dilbeck assured him. "And loved by everyone at Dilbeck Manor, from the tenants to the servants, and all those in the village as well."

"I wish I could have known him. My father and mother always spoke well of Lord Dilbeck, and of you."

Lady Dilbeck smiled and nodded, but then the smile slowly faded.

"You should be at home with your family, Captain Mattison, celebrating the season just as you wished to do during your years in the war. Dilbeck Manor is no place for you to be. We don't celebrate Christmas anymore. Not since my husband and son died."

Collin shrugged lightly. "I don't mind it so much. In truth, I would far rather be here than at home. As I told young Ralf, Christmas comes whether we wish it or not. Even on the battlefield in a foreign land, and even here at Dilbeck Manor."

"You're wrong, Captain," her ladyship countered. "It's just what my husband thought it was, a gift. And if there is no one to give it," she said sadly, "then the gift cannot be given."

"Just as God gave us a gift on a Christmas long ago?" Collin murmured. "Perhaps you're right, my lady. And perhaps all we need at Dilbeck Manor is someone to give gifts again."

"That was very well done," Rose said a half hour later, as she and Collin stood outside Lady Dilbeck's chamber door, "if incautious."

"I could see that you were terrified the whole while," he said teasingly, grinning down at her. "You had absolutely no faith in me, and expected her ladyship to explode with fury at any moment.''

He had joined in helping Lady Dilbeck make her way up the stairs, easily supporting the weary elderly woman with the kind of strong arm that Rose had often wished she possessed. The gentleness and patience with which he treated her ladyship—no matter how terse or irate she was—truly amazed Rose. She felt as if she was learning something altogether new about Collin, something as wonderful as the rest of him was.

''Very well,'' she conceded. ''I was terrified. I've never seen her ladyship so amenable before, certainly not when Christmas is discussed. To ask about her early years at Dilbeck was an inspiration. She loves nothing better than remembering those days when she was so happy.''

''That's true for us all,'' he said. ''Though perhaps more so for the elderly. Let me take the candle, Rose, and I'll escort you to your room.''

Her cheeks heated at the words, and she was grateful for the darkness in the hall.

''It's just here, at this next door,'' she murmured, indicating the place with a nod of her head. ''I stay near her ladyship in case she should need me during the night. She has a bell that I can hear when she rings it.''

''Oh,'' Collin said, sounding, for once, as if he were at a loss. ''I see. Well, then...''

''I'll be happy to escort you to your own bedchamber,'' she offered, wondering, the moment the words were out, whether she'd lost her mind.

''I don't wish to trouble you, Rose.''

''But you'll need the candle to guide your way,'' she said, ''and I haven't yet turned down the lamps in the parlor and dining room.''

''Camhort doesn't take care of them?''

''No, I took over the task two years ago, when I realized how weary he becomes in the evenings. He often seeks his bed before Lady Dilbeck does and, considering his age, that's as it should be.''

''I'll help you with the lights,'' he said quietly as they began to walk toward the stairs. ''I had wondered at Camhort yet tending his duties as a butler. I suppose he's been with Lady Dilbeck for many years.''

''Most of his life.'' Rose set her hand on the smooth banister as they began their descent. ''He shouldn't be working at all, of course, but his duties here are light and Lady Dilbeck could never ask him to go.''

''No, I don't suppose she could.''

They continued in the same manner, speaking in low voices of trivial matters, walking through the empty rooms and tending fires and lamps. The rest of the house was dark and still, the others having sought their own rooms.

Collin walked very close to her, and Rose knew that his thoughts, despite their mundane conversation, were the same as hers. And she knew, too, what was going to happen. It had become inevitable from the moment she'd offered to escort him to his room and, though her mind warned her to turn back, her heart longed to go forward.

''What's this?'' Collin asked as they passed a certain door.

Rose stopped. ''The music room.''

''Music room?'' Collin repeated, sounding faintly amused. ''Lady Dilbeck has a music room.'' His hand lifted, and his fingers curled about her elbow. ''Will you show it to me, Rose?''

Her heart pounded violently in her chest and her breathing was shaky as she whispered, ''Yes.''

She opened the door; he closed it almost silently behind them. Only the single candle illuminated the large, elegant room. Slowly Rose moved toward the far wall, Collin's following footsteps loud in her ears.

''This is a reputable likeness of Lord Dilbeck,'' she said,

lifting the candle to expose a tall portrait of a handsome gentleman. "Or so her ladyship has assured me."

"He looks familiar to me," Collin murmured, standing so close that Rose could feel the heat of his body. "I think I must have met him when I was a child." His hand touched her shoulder, one finger falling on the bare skin of her neck, sending shivers down her back. "Rose?"

She skittered away so quickly that the candle flame flickered and nearly died.

"And th-this is a smaller portrait of Master Bruce Favreau, when he was just twenty."

"Rose," he said again, and she could both hear and feel him coming up behind her. Gently his fingers closed over the brass candleholder and pulled it from her grasp. He moved to the side, setting it on a table where the dim glow did little to dispel the room's darkness. Then he came back, stopping very closely in front of her. His hands came up to frame her face, warm on her skin but trembling, too, just as she was.

"I've dreamed of you for so long," he murmured, his breathing heightened. "You can't begin to know how much I wanted you…just to touch you like this."

He lowered his head and Rose lifted to meet him. Their mouths touched and held, soft and warm and familiar. So wonderfully familiar, everything about him. The scent and feel of him, the touch of his hands. Rose had dreamed of him, too, and of this. She felt, for a moment, as if she were spinning, as if she and Collin had stepped into a fantasy world where only touch and feeling existed.

His hands were in her hair; hers slid up to grip his shoulders. When his mouth opened over hers, she groaned and eagerly met his seeking tongue with her own. The heated kiss was sleek and moist, ardent with desire and love. Rose pressed closer until their bodies were fully met and heard, gladly, his murmuring response of need.

He broke the kiss only briefly, to lift her up against the

nearest wall and pin her there with his body. His mouth came down again, kissing her more feverishly, while Rose's arms lashed hard about him, pulling him even closer, tighter.

Collin's hands slid back into her hair, where his clever fingers began to undo her arrangement until her curls tumbled free.

"Oh, Rose," he whispered breathlessly, pulling back to gaze down at her. "I love you. Every moment, I loved you. I never stopped. I need you."

"I love you," she told him, her chest rising and falling with each breath. "I need you, too, Collin."

She meant the words, and said them without regret. Giving herself to Collin would be a gift to both of them, something to remember and treasure for the rest of her life. She loved him and only him, and would never love another. She would never regret lying with him.

Even in the darkness she could see his brilliant smile. "Then you'll marry me, Rose? Will you? Just as soon as I can get a license?"

Her heart sank. Rose slid her hands to his chest, pushing until he backed up enough to release her. When her feet touched the floor, she gazed up at him and said, "No, Collin. Not that." She swallowed hard. "I'll go with you now…to your room. I'll stay the night with you because I love you, and because I wish to. But there can be no more than that between us."

His smile died. "But I want more, Rose. Much more. I want all of you, as my wife, and I want to give you all of me, as your husband. Tell me that you'll marry me and I'll carry you to my bed this moment, faster than you can begin to imagine."

Tears filled her eyes. "I cannot wed you, Collin. I've told you how and why, but you won't listen. I've been a *thief*. I've played a part in stealing from others, for nothing more than my own good, and it was only by the grace of

God and the help of friends that I didn't go to prison for it. But, even so, it cannot be forgiven, except in secret by God. How could you ever take such a wife?''

"If God can forgive, then who am I to hold past sins against you. If sins they are. You stole because you were hungry and desperate, Rose, not for profit. You survived, just as I did what I had to do to survive the war. Why should you be judged more harshly for keeping yourself safe and alive by the only means you could find?''

"The law cares little for why a thief steals, only that she does, and the law is what brands me a thief. You cannot take a thief to wife, Collin. I'll not let you.''

He took her face in his hands once more, gazing at her intently. "I don't care what the law may do or say. I love you, and none of what came before means a whit to me. Give me every happiness and be my wife. Marry me, Rose.''

Her voice was a trembling whisper. "No.''

He dropped his hands and stepped back. "Then let me take you back to your room. I won't need the candle to find my way afterward.'' He turned to fetch the flickering light. "I'm not so blind as you seem to be.''

Chapter Seven

Christmas was a gift, Lady Dilbeck had said, while in Collin's opinion it came whether one wished it to or not—or, as he had amended, perhaps it was a bit of both. Rose couldn't say which of them was right, but one thing became perfectly clear the next day: Collin intended to make a gift of Christmas to everyone at Dilbeck Manor regardless of what any of them thought, wished *or* wanted.

The pudding was the first step toward celebrating a holiday that Lady Dilbeck had dismissed for so many years. With Collin's encouragement, Janny had begun preparing the rich concoction, right after she'd finished feeding the tenants who'd come to work on the stable roof an ample breakfast of bread, fried ham and ale. With the sounds of the repairs faint in the background, she chopped and grated and pounded with glee, her happiness only marred every few minutes when she complained that the pudding should have been made a week earlier, so that it could more properly "sit."

"It'll not taste as well as it should with only twenty days to ripen, but at least we'll have a pudding for Christmas, and made with all the best that could be had from the village." She stopped and looked up at Rose, who was finishing a cup of tea. "Her ladyship will allow it, won't she, Miss Rose? Captain Mattison said she would, but she's never done so before.''

"I don't know," Rose replied honestly. "We shall have to pray and see what happens."

"It would be a great waste," Janny said, gazing at the various ingredients before her. "And it will be a fine pudding, even if it only has twenty days to sit."

"Let's leave the matter to Captain Mattison," Rose said reassuringly, "and say nothing to Lady Dilbeck of it until he's been able to do so." She rose and swept a few bread-crumbs—all that remained of her breakfast—from her apron. "Tell me when the pudding is ready for stirring, and if the captain hasn't yet spoken to her ladyship, I'll remind him. Now, if Lady Dilbeck's breakfast is ready, I'll take it up to her."

Her ladyship was already awake and sitting up when Rose entered her chamber, her gaze fixed on the room's far window.

"Good morning, my lady." Rose set the tray she carried upon a table near the bed. "You look very well."

"What's all that noise I hear coming from outside?" her ladyship asked. "Are they working on the stable?"

"Yes, my lady. Would you like chocolate this morning, or some tea?"

Lady Dilbeck pushed her covers aside. "Come and help me to the window, Rose. I wish to see what they're doing."

"Very well. Let me fetch your warmest wrap and slippers, first. It's a chilly morning."

Duly wrapped and slippered, her ladyship stood by the window for a long while, gazing silently at the men below.

"Captain Mattison works beside them," she murmured, watching his tall, hatless figure as he strode from one side of the stable to the other. "Just as if he were one of them. His father surely taught him better."

Rose smiled, her own gaze fixed on Collin's handsome

face and form. She could hear his cheerful voice through the thick-paned window, could see the flash of his smile and the gleam of his golden hair. All the men appeared to be working happily, despite the early hour and the coldness of the day. Off to one side, a small fire was blazing, and over that hung one of Janny's large black pots, bubbling with what Rose supposed was Camhort's special rum punch.

"I think his father taught him very well, if you'll forgive me for saying so, my lady."

Lady Dilbeck sighed. "I suppose I must go down and speak to them. It's my duty as the lady of the manor."

Rose was surprised to hear Lady Dilbeck say such a thing. She'd never before embraced duties owed her tenants. Indeed, she had usually ignored their existence.

"They'll not expect it of you," she murmured.

"But my husband would," Lady Dilbeck said. "Help me to dress, Rose, and then I'll break my fast and go down."

If Rose thought she was surprised by Lady Dilbeck's determination to speak to her tenants, the tenants were much more so. The sight of Lady Dilbeck tottering out of the mansion, supported by Rose, drew their attention at once, and by the time her ladyship reached them, the men had all stopped their work and lined up respectfully to greet her, their caps pulled from their heads. Collin, Rose noted, didn't seem surprised at all.

"Good morning, my lady," he greeted cheerfully as she and Rose neared the group, and made an elegant bow. "And Miss Benham." He gave her a particularly beguiling smile. He had dressed in plain working clothes, rather than his uniform, but managed to look just as dashing and handsome.

"I've come to see your work, Captain," Lady Dilbeck said, her tone stiffly formal, "and to thank my tenants."

The tenants shuffled and murmured, clearly pleased and embarrassed.

"We've a good hot punch here, my lady." Collin gestured to the bubbling pot, which smelled, in Rose's opinion, heavenly in the cold winter air. "Will you honor us by sharing a cup?"

"I'd be pleased," said her ladyship, and the men about her visibly relaxed.

It was an enlightening half hour for Rose, watching Lady Dilbeck as she stood among her tenants, speaking to them in a refined, lady-of-the-manor voice. She'd never seen her ladyship behave so, had never guessed that she could. Though she should have known. Lady Dilbeck hadn't always been a recluse; there must have been a time when she was much more like this...gracious and self-assured.

Collin watched the gathering with satisfaction. It was clear that Lady Dilbeck was enjoying herself. She drank two cups of rum punch and looked ready for more. And the tenants were quite obviously proud to be in company with their mistress. He'd never seen so many grown men blush and stammer simply because an elderly woman smiled and thanked them. They looked, to a man, as if they'd be willing to rebuild the entire estate just to make Lady Dilbeck happy.

And Rose, well, she was more beautiful than ever, though she stood off to one side, not looking at him. She wore her hair in a softer style today, with a few inky curls drifting loose, framing her chill-pinkened cheeks.

He hadn't been certain, after they'd parted ways the night before, whether she'd be able to easily forgive him. He'd spent much of the remaining night hours lying awake in his bed, missing and wanting her and telling himself that he was a fool to have turned her aside. He might have persuaded her to accept him as a husband once he'd taken her to his bed. There were ways to manage such a thing.

Especially if he'd told Lady Dilbeck, or his father and mother. All three of them would have produced a vicar and a license within hours, and Rose would've found herself Mrs. Collin Mattison before she had a chance to object.

But he didn't want her forced into being his wife. He wanted her to come to him freely, as she had done once before.

"Captain Mattison?" Lady Dilbeck was suddenly before him. "A word in private, if you will?"

She looked weary, he thought. Cheerful and relaxed, but weary. He took her hand and tucked it through his arm. "Certainly, my lady." They walked a few steps away.

"It's been a long while since I've smelled a Christmas pudding, Captain," Lady Dilbeck said without preamble, "but I think that I would yet know the scent of one being made. Especially in my own home. Tell me if I mistook what I smelled as Rose and I made our way out of doors."

"I fear you didn't mistake it, my lady. But you mustn't blame Janny. I asked her to make a pudding for Christmas, and gave her the ingredients. Some small part may have come from your own pantry, but these I will be happy to repay."

"No, no," she said irritably. "I'm not such a pennythrift as that."

Collin stopped and turned to face her.

"I meant no insult by asking for the pudding to be made, though I was aware you might not be pleased. I had hoped, just as we spoke of last night, to make a gift of it to you, perhaps to bring some pleasant memory of your husband and son back to you. I thought you might wish to take your husband's place at the spoon, and give the household your blessing, as the lady of Dilbeck Manor."

"No." The word was hard and cold. Final. "I do not celebrate Christmas, Captain Mattison. Not anymore."

Collin reached down and gently took hold of both her

hands. He gazed directly into her face, and said, "I know. But, please, consider doing this one small thing. It would mean much to all of us, and I truly believe—if you will forgive me the impertinence—that it's what your husband would have desired you to do."

She pulled her hands free and glared at him angrily. "You *are* impertinent," she declared. "Beyond all reason!"

"Forgive me," he said again. "But I believe I speak the truth. Lord Dilbeck loved Christmas—you told me that yourself. He would have been grieved to know that it's become so unhappy a time for you."

She said nothing more, but stared at him for a long, silent moment with furious eyes. Then she turned on her heel and called for Rose to take her back into the manor.

Collin returned to the repairs on the stables, feeling somewhat more glum than he had before. He began forming some sort of speech to give Janny and the others when her ladyship refused to attend the stirring, or if her ladyship refused to even allow the pudding to exist. All Janny's hard work would come to nothing, and Collin's already slim chances of managing any kind of Christmas celebration at Dilbeck Manor would become even slimmer.

But her ladyship surprised him—all of them—when the time for the stirring came. Supported by Rose, she made her way into the kitchen, where the other members of the household had gathered around the steaming pot, each ready to take his or her turn at the spoon. When they saw Lady Dilbeck come through the kitchen doors, they all stiffened and moved away, fully expecting the worst.

Collin stepped forward. "My lady," he began, only to be silenced by an imperious wave of her hand.

Reaching the pot, Lady Dilbeck pushed free of Rose's helping hand and lifted her chin. "Lord Dilbeck, may God rest his soul, stood as master each year over the stirring of the pudding. Now I will do so, in his memory."

The stunned silence was complete, as everyone stared in disbelief at Lady Dilbeck, who stared defiantly back.

"Well?" she asked. "Why do we wait? The pudding is ready to stir. Ralf, you're the youngest. You'll come first. Captain Mattison, where are the men who were here this morning? My tenants?"

"They're still working on the stable roof, my lady. I didn't think you'd wish them to—"

"Go and fetch them," she commanded. "All of them. And bring the rum punch if there's any left. We'll have a cup once the stirring is done, and bless my late husband's name, as is right."

Collin bowed. "Yes, my lady." He left at once to do her bidding.

"Come, then, Ralf," Lady Dilbeck said more kindly to the boy. "Make your Christmas wish and stir the pudding. You must do it as hard as you can, to make certain your wish comes true."

By the time the stirring was nearly done, her ladyship's eyes had brightened, and her laughter was as loud and merry as that of all the others in the kitchen, including the tenants. Collin knew that it had been hard for Lady Dilbeck to face her conflicting feelings about Christmas, and his admiration for her had, at the sight of her walking through the kitchen doors, increased tenfold. When she stood at the pot to take her place as the last one to stir, his admiration knew no bounds.

"Lord Dilbeck," she said, "as some of you will remember, was given to making a grand speech each year when he took his turn at the spoon. He would say 'God grant us a full and pleasant Christmas,' and 'Let us be forgiving and loving in all things,' and 'God bless each one here, and also those in our village and county, in our country, and His world, so much as it pleases Him.'" Her voice grew softer, gentler.

"I wish that I could remember in entirety every word

that he uttered, for I fear I'm not a speech maker, as Lord Dilbeck was. But this I will say, and know that it's what he would want me to say. Thank you for your efforts at Dilbeck Manor, and may God bless you for them. And here is my wish,'' she said as she began to stir, ''that each of you would have a merry Christmas and a new year filled with health, goodness and prosperity.''

A cheer went up in the kitchen, and cups were lifted both to the name of the late Lord Dilbeck and to the present Lady Dilbeck.

If the doors to letting Christmas into the manor hadn't been precisely flung wide, they had at least been cracked open.

Collin and the others tried to be circumspect, but Lady Dilbeck was fully aware of the greenery that was being sneaked into her house, bit by bit. The portraits in the entryway were the first to sprout festive holly at their corners, followed by those in the various hallways. The dining room was next, where the fireplaces were decked with ropes of holly and berries. The parlor, Lady Dilbeck suspected, was left untouched for the sake of her own feelings, for that was where she spent most of each day.

She was grateful for the consideration shown by her staff, and bemused by their strong desire to celebrate Christmas, even at the risk of rousing her wrath. There was a time, only days before, when she would have been angry, but now...now, as she walked about the mansion, noting the changes, she wasn't certain quite how she felt.

She had thought it would hurt to feel the effects of Christmas and remember her husband and son, but it wasn't really painful at all. It was more like an ache or, still yet, a longing, partly sweet and partly mournful. She knew that she couldn't bring back the brilliant joyfulness of her husband's Christmases, nor could she forever linger over the harsh sorrow and loss of her son's final Christmas, but she could perhaps find a dimmer joy and a much lessened sorrow, and somewhere among the two discover a way to enjoy the holiday once more.

Five days after the stirring of the pudding, Lady Dilbeck stopped Rose as she was leaving the parlor, having just served tea.

"Yes, my lady?" Rose asked, standing in the open doorway with the tea tray in her hands.

"I want to speak to you about the decorations in the manor. You may think me blind, but I've seen them."

Rose paled, and the tray lowered slightly.

"Shall I speak with the others, my lady?"

"Indeed you will," Lady Dilbeck replied with all the crustiness she could manage. "You'll tell them that I'm deeply offended."

"Yes, my lady," Rose replied mournfully. "At once."

"Very well," Lady Dilbeck said. "Make certain to instruct them, as well, that I expect this parlor to be attended to right away, but not before the portraits of my husband and son in the music room have been decorated."

Rose nearly dropped the tea tray altogether.

"My lady?"

Lady Dilbeck picked up her teacup, careful of her hand wrappings. "What is it, Rose? Didn't you understand me?"

Rose stared at her. "I think so."

"You think so? I don't believe I misspoke, or mumbled, or made my instructions too difficult to understand. I want this room and my husband's and son's portraits decorated. As soon as possible, and before another inch of this manor is hung with mistletoe and holly."

The smile on Rose's face grew slowly, filling with excitement. "Yes, my lady. I'll tell them at once. Thank you. Thank you so very much."

"Don't be foolish," Lady Dilbeck admonished. "Go

along, now. And tell Captain Mattison that I expect him to be timely at dinner this evening,'' she added before the door closed altogether.

She sighed and sipped her tea once Rose had gone, and contemplated the state of her feelings. No, it hadn't been painful. It had been...pleasant, just as the thought of the manor being filled with greenery was pleasant. And the smile on Rose's face had been worth any brief discomfort she'd suffered. Rose didn't smile enough, had never done so, though Lady Dilbeck thought that there'd been a change for the better in her since Captain Mattison had arrived. That her new steward was smitten with her housekeeper hadn't escaped Lady Dilbeck's attention, either.

She rather liked the idea of Captain Mattison setting his heart on Rose, even if his parents might be somewhat dismayed. If the two married, he'd be much more likely to remain at Dilbeck Manor, and she did so want him to stay. He was such a pleasant, intelligent young man, much like his father. Each night at dinner he told her of his plans for Dilbeck, some foolish, some quite sensible, and each night she went away from their conversations—and their arguments—with a renewed outlook about the estate.

For so long she'd believed that, alone, she could do nothing to keep the land and properties from wasting away, and had accepted with resignation that there would be nothing left worth having once she died. She'd been quite ready, had even hoped, that it would be so. Without someone to love the estate as she did, who would continue to care for it once she'd gone?

But Captain Mattison might stay, if he had an incentive to do so, and if he stayed he would take good care of the estate. Lady Dilbeck could think of no one she'd rather have to oversee her lands and properties—or to leave them to following her death—and felt certain that her husband would have agreed.

Perhaps, she thought as she sipped her tea, she would do well to write his parents and invite them to come to Dilbeck Manor for a visit. And if they could come sooner than later, then so much the better.

Chapter Eight

The snow that had fallen overnight lay smooth and thick across the countryside, covering shrubs and trees so well that Collin wondered if the task set before Rose and him wouldn't be impossible. Lady Dilbeck wanted a kissing bough hung in the manor's entryway, and had insisted that her housekeeper and steward go in search of the proper foliage. The weather had cleared and, she said, was ideal for such an activity. Of course, they must take the sleigh, which Ralf had done such a fine job with.

It wasn't the first time in the past few days that her ladyship had contrived to throw Rose in Collin's path, and he was beginning to wonder if Lady Dilbeck wasn't trying to play matchmaker. Not that he minded; far from it. He was grateful for any opportunity to be alone with Rose. Unfortunately, he couldn't say that Rose felt the same. She was polite but distant, and had been since that night in the music room. If it had been in his nature, Collin would have given way to discouragement, but Rose loved him—she'd told him so—and as long as that remained true, he couldn't give up hope. *Wouldn't* give up.

"I can't think we'll find any mistletoe left anywhere on the estate," Rose said, pulling her warm cloak more closely about her neck. "Jacob and Emily have spent hours gathering as much as they could find this past week."

Collin uttered a laugh. "Jacob and Emily have spent hours making good use of the mistletoe they've found. I've never seen two people run into each other so frequently, directly under a sprig of mistletoe."

Rose laughed, too. The sound sent the most delightful shivers tingling along the length of Collin's spine.

"I told myself it was coincidence at first," she said, "but gave that up after catching them for the fifth time in one afternoon. I won't be surprised if there isn't a wedding at Dilbeck Manor come spring. Or sooner."

"They make a fine couple," Collin said, slowing the horses as they swung about a curve in the snow-covered road. "Will Lady Dilbeck object, do you think?"

"I don't know," Rose replied thoughtfully. "She's ever been displeased by unions among the servants, or so I've been told. I haven't been with her long enough to know firsthand. Before Emily came to the manor two years ago, we didn't have any dallying among the staff."

"You didn't have enough staff to make it possible," Collin replied, casting a grin at her. "But we're adding on almost daily now, what with Elliot and Jimmy finding employment with her ladyship. And me, as well."

"Too many men," Rose said. "Not enough ladies."

"Not with Emily and Jacob out of the running. And if we exclude Camhort. That leaves three and three…and since I've already staked my claim to you—"

"Collin," she said chidingly. "Don't."

"Well, I'll certainly not let Elliot or Jimmy set their sights on you, Miss Benham. I was their captain during the war, and I'll not be outmaneuvered by my own men, especially when it comes to winning a lady's hand."

The answer amused her, as he had hoped it would. Elliot Haysbert had arrived in summons to Collin's urgent missive three days earlier, with another of Collin's former soldiers, Jimmy Steele, in tow. Jimmy had tagged along in the hope that Dilbeck Manor might need a good man with horses. Since Dilbeck Manor didn't have such a man, and as Jimmy was a master at managing four-legged creatures of all kinds, it was a fortunate decision. Lady Dilbeck hired him on the spot or, rather, just as soon as Elliot had mixed up a fresh batch of his special ointment and charmed Lady Dilbeck into hiring Jimmy.

Elliot, too, had quickly become a member of the household. He had discovered a kindred spirit in Lady Dilbeck, who once had a great passion for gardening, long ago, when the gardens at Dilbeck had been part of her making. The day after Elliot arrived, Collin found him and Lady Dilbeck in the parlor, their heads together as Elliot massaged her ladyships hands, deep in discussion over what flowers might be planted in the spring.

Since then Elliot had been Lady Dilbeck's almost constant companion, happily taking over her care from Rose in as many ways as he could. Her ladyship seemed pleased by it, and pronounced the young man both delightful and competent. The pain she suffered in her hands and limbs, too, had lessened beneath Elliot's ministrations, and for that alone Lady Dilbeck wished him to remain at the manor.

"I'm glad they've come, though," Rose said. "Camhort and Janny and Jacob speak of the old days, when Dilbeck Manor was fully staffed and there was so much activity, especially during holidays. But my own experience has been one of loneliness, as if the few of us here are isolated from the rest of the world. We so seldom have visitors, apart from the vicar when he comes on Sundays during winter. It's nice to have more company in the manor." She smiled at him. "It makes it seem more like Christmas."

"It's a bit more like what you were used to at the inn,"

Collin admitted. "I wish I'd spent a Christmas with you there, though I'd not change the time we did have."

"We did have such a wonderful time at The Lamb and Wig during the holidays," she said with a sigh. "I wish you could have been there, too. You would have thought my father and brother quite mad."

"More than usual, you mean?" he retorted, and was glad to hear her laugh even more. She had laughed a great deal when they were younger.

"Look, Collin." She pointed to a group of oak trees covered in snow. "That's mistletoe, isn't it?"

Collin slowed the carriage. "Yes, I believe it is. And more than enough for a kissing bough, if I can reach it."

He was obliged to climb up to the second lowest branch in order to reach the cluster of leaves, with Rose dancing nervously beneath him.

"Be careful," she begged, gazing up with apprehension. "I won't be able to carry you to the sleigh if you fall and break your neck."

"God forbid," Collin muttered, stretching out a hand to reach his goal while clinging mightily to the branch with his other hand and both legs. "You'd have to leave me lying in the snow and go for help. I'd be frozen solid by the time you—"

"Collin!"

The mistletoe came off with a snap, just as Collin, with a shout, slipped off the branch and fell into the snow at Rose's feet, landing faceup, flat on his back.

"Oh, God," Rose uttered with horror. "Are you all right? Collin?" She knelt and leaned over him, peering closely into his wide-open eyes.

He shuddered and coughed once, then drew in a long breath. "I'm fine," he croaked out in a small, stunned voice. "The snow broke my fall." One hand lifted out of the snow. "I got the mistletoe."

She set her gloved hands on either side of his face, her

eyes filled with concern. "Can you move? No, wait, don't move. You might hurt yourself more." His hat had fallen off, and she began to pat all about the top of his head, as if she would find half of it suddenly missing.

"I'm fine, Rose. Nothing's broken."

"Are you certain?" She kept patting.

"Absolutely certain." To prove it, he dropped the mistletoe and set his arms about her, pulling her nearly on top of him. "But if you kiss me I'll feel even better."

"Collin, don't tease!" She struggled until he freed her, sitting up once more. "Can you move or not?"

"I can," he said, and proved it by sitting up, putting his arms about her again and kissing her. He only meant it to be a brief embrace, but, despite Rose's initial gasp of surprise, the kiss gentled, then lingered. Within moments Collin found that he was lying on the ground again, Rose twined tightly in his arms. Her lips were soft and warm against his own, and parted beneath his murmured encouragement, allowing the kiss to deepen.

Just as Collin's hands were trying to find their way beneath her heavy cloak, Rose abruptly pushed away, scrambling quickly out of his reach and to her feet. She stood, turned away from him, striving to catch her breath.

"I admit that it's not the most comfortable place to make love," Collin said as he slowly rose, brushing snow off his coat. "But hopefully it wasn't entirely unpleasant. I feel certain it wasn't unwanted, given your participation, brief as it was."

"I shouldn't have participated at all."

"There's no need to hurt my feelings."

"You don't have a right to hurt feelings," she replied tartly, reaching up to tug her bonnet back into place. "I did offer to share a bed with you, if you'll remember aright, and you turned me aside."

"Don't think I haven't wished since—almost constantly—that I hadn't," he assured her.

She turned to look at him. "Don't make a jest of it."

"I'm not." He took a step forward. "I don't make jest of my love for you. Or of how greatly I want you. I've longed to lie with you almost since the day I met you. But I won't share a bed with you until you're mine—completely mine—and until I'm completely yours. As husband and wife."

"You torment me, Collin," she murmured. "How can I make you understand that it will never be?" She looked at him very directly, pleading with him. "Soon you'll be gone from Dilbeck Manor, and we'll likely never even see each other again. Please, don't give me reason to hope and dream when I know nothing can make our union possible. Miracles like that just don't happen." She shook her head sadly. "Not even at Christmas."

"They do this Christmas," he countered firmly, striding close enough to take both her hands in his. "I'll *make* them happen, if I must. One thing I promise you, Rose, and vow it before God—we'll not be parted again. Ever. I'll not leave Dilbeck Manor without you, and if you leave, I'll follow wherever you go. Six years was far too long to be absent from each other, and I'll not spend another day of my life without you."

"You'll have to," she told him. "Collin, listen to me. Your parents are coming to Dilbeck Manor. Lady Dilbeck had a message from them just this morning. They'll be here perhaps as early as tomorrow if the weather holds and there isn't any more snow. They're coming to talk sense into you, and to take you home with them."

Collin was momentarily struck speechless, not by the idea of his parents coming, but by Rose's belief that they could bend him to do that which he didn't wish to do.

"I know that my parents are coming," he said at last. "And though you may not have noticed it, I'm a man full grown, and I make my own decisions."

Now it was Rose's turn to be felled into silence.

"You *know* they're coming?" she managed at last.

"Of course. I wrote and asked them to come. The letter was posted in the village before I even started for Dilbeck Manor."

"Oh, no," she murmured with dismay, shaking her head and pulling her hands free. "Oh, no, Collin. When I wrote them I asked them to come, in order to make you go away. Good heavens, what will they think of us?"

"Probably that we're both half-mad," he said, then laughed. "I would have liked to see their faces when they had your letter. They probably felt sorry for you, having to deal with me without any warning."

He laughed again and Rose, striving to look fully disapproving, couldn't help but smile. He looked so much like a mischievous boy, his blond hair free of its hat, tousled and shining in the midday sun. His blue eyes were filled with humor, and his entire face lit up by amusement. Before she knew it, Rose was laughing, too, though whether because she felt so foolish or because Collin's laughter was infectious, she didn't know.

At last she sobered and sighed, noting that, as usual, it had little effect on Collin. "It really isn't funny," she told him. "For whatever reason your parents are coming, they'll never give us their blessing. I told them everything in my letter, about the months I spent living among thieves, and about taking part in thievery, too."

Collin's smile died away. "I told you that I don't care about any of that, Rose. You did what you could to survive, and chose the lesser evil of thieving over the other choices before you. In truth, I honor you for that. And if it will make you feel better, we'll make whatever recompense we can to those who suffered any loss at your hands, once we're wed."

Her cold cheeks burned with embarrassment. "That's kind of you, Collin, but...recompense has already been made. At least, much of it has. The worst of it."

Collin looked at her quizzically and, hesitating at first, Rose went on. "I never truly stole anything by my own hands. I was the distraction…the decoy. I would approach a well-dressed gentleman and engage his attention by various means—" at this, she blushed more hotly and turned away "—and some of the better thieves would pick his pockets. I wasn't very good at it, but the others always chose me to play the part."

"I imagine they would," Collin said gently from close behind her. "You're very beautiful, Rose, as well as distracting. I imagine you weren't very good because you disliked doing it."

"I hated it!" she said vehemently. "I hated having any part of such deception. But, in truth, if I'd been better at it I might never have gotten caught. So it was a blessing, really."

He touched her arm. "You were caught? By the authorities?"

"No, by a man called the Black Earl. That's not his real name, of course." She let him turn her back to face him. "He's really the Earl of Cardemore. Do you know him? Or of him?"

He nodded slowly, his expression filled with concern. "Cardemore has a reputation for having dealings in some of London's darker alleyways. There were rumors that he lived as a pirate before his brother, the former earl, died. He didn't harm you, did he? Or threaten you?"

"Oh, no, not in the least," she assured him quickly. "In truth, he was incredibly kind to me. Well, after he was done being quite angry, of course. I had helped in the robbing of one of the earl's acquaintances one night, and the earl, coming upon us, grabbed and held me. My friends all ran away, but I expected no less of them, especially once I understood how greatly they feared the Black Earl. But he was a godsend, because he recognized me.

"He'd been to The Lamb and Wig twice in recent years

to speak to his man of business, and remembered me from there. He demanded to know how I had come to be in the company of thieves. I was trembling so greatly that I scarce know how I answered him, but once the tale was told, he became very kind and gentle. He understood everything, and even offered to make my cousin disappear.'' She uttered a weak laugh at the remembrance. ''Then, he took me to his home.''

''To his home!'' Collin repeated, his hands fisting. ''Alone, with him?''

''No, we weren't alone in the least,'' she assured him quickly. ''He has a house filled with servants, and attached one of them to me as both maid and companion while I was with him. And he helped me to make things right with anyone who had brought a complaint before the authorities regarding a young woman of my coloring and description. He even took me to stand before a judge, to settle any disputes openly and completely, though no one knew who I was or could likely ever have found me. But if there had been a chance of it, Lord Cardemore made certain it would not happen, and I wanted to make everything right. I can never repay him for such magnanimity. He must have parted with a small fortune for my sake.''

''I'll repay him every ha'penny,'' Collin said tightly, clearly angered by the idea of a strange man caring for Rose in such an intimate way.

''You would insult him by making such an offer,'' she told him, ''and he wouldn't accept it, regardless. I merely tried to give him my thanks, but he'd have none of it. He…he seemed to find pleasure in spiting my cousin by helping me. He thought it very cruel, you see, that a relative would do something like that to another. He never told me why, but I think it must have had something to do with his own family and his relationship to them.

''And then, having done so much already, he found me employment with Lady Dilbeck, and convinced her to give

me a chance, though I had no letters of recommendation
or even any experience as a housekeeper.'' She laid a hand
on Collin's sleeve, seeing that he yet looked disgruntled.
''I would still have been living on London's streets if it
hadn't been for the earl. Or I might have already died
somewhere among them. He saved me from so much.''

Collin's muscles relaxed, and he set a hand over hers,
pressing lightly. ''Yes, he did, and I'm ashamed for being
jealous. I just wish that I'd been the one to take care of
you, as would have been right. If I'd only known.''

''We've been through all that,'' she said, relieved to at
last have the entire truth out in the open. ''But now, surely,
you must understand why I can never marry you, or anyone, for that matter. I've stood before a judge and a record
has been made of my crimes.''

''They're *not* crimes,'' he stated harshly. ''You haven't
committed any murders. You haven't truly been a thief.''

''There have been records made of my confessions to
helping thieves,'' she said, spreading her hands out, ''and
records made by those who accused, and then forgave me,
of such things. Anyone could find those records, if they
looked, and you would be shamed beyond measure if any
of your friends and acquaintances knew the truth.''

Anger possessed his features. He took Rose by the
shoulders and gave her a furious shake.

''How can you say such a thing? I don't care if the
whole world learns of it. I *love* you and want you for my
wife, no matter what any man or woman may think of it.''

''Collin, think of your family,'' she pleaded. ''Think of
your parents and the scandal that would ensue if it should
be known that their son had married a woman who'd once
lived among thieves.'' She set her hands over those he held
on her shoulders. ''*Think* of that, Collin.''

For the first time, she saw shadows of doubt in his eyes.
His expression grew somber, serious.

''Think of the gossip they would have to endure,'' she

pressed. "The stares and laughter and the whispering behind fans whenever they went out into society. Could you marry me, knowing that your parents and brothers and sisters and all their families might suffer for it?"

"Yes," he whispered. "Even for that, I'd gladly and thankfully take you for my wife."

"Oh, Collin." Setting her gloved hands on either side of his beloved face, she reached up to kiss him. "You wouldn't. You love them all too well. And I'd not bind you in a union that you'd come to regret. Do you think I could ever do such a thing to you, loving you as I do?"

Her words had clearly taken him aback for a moment, but now he rallied, the familiar smile growing on his lips and in his eyes.

"Rose, let us make a bargain. Shall we?"

With distrust, Rose dropped her hands from his face.

"What is it?"

"Let my parents make the final decision. If they don't mind our union, then we'll be wed at once. If they express any hesitation at all, I'll leave you in peace."

"You'd talk them into accepting the union," she charged, "even if they didn't truly wish it."

Collin straightened and set one hand over his heart. "I promise you, upon my honor and the love I bear you, that I'll do nothing to sway their decision, either by word or deed."

Rose was yet suspicious, but she was convinced that whether she agreed or not, the outcome would be the same. His parents would never relent toward such a match for their son. Perhaps, by making the bargain, Collin would accept the finality of their parting more easily.

"Very well, then," she said slowly. "I'll agree to let your parents decide the matter. If you'll truly promise to abide by their decision. With no argument."

"Agreed," he said, his smile wide as he reached out to pull her into his arms again.

"Collin!" Rose protested, though she gave no struggle.

"We have to seal our bargain with a kiss, Rose," he told her. "Else it won't be a true bargain."

"We might shake hands."

"Not at Christmas," he said, lowering his head. "At this happy time of year, only a kiss will do."

Chapter Nine

Christmas had come to Dilbeck Manor for the first time in many a year and, perhaps because it had been a stranger for far too long, it was embraced with undaunted enthusiasm by one and all. Ralf, especially, was overjoyed by the turn of events, and spent much of each day sneaking into the kitchen to sample the treats that Janny was preparing for the Christmas Day feast.

Lady Dilbeck, with sudden largesse, had sent to the village for a treasure trove of foods and goods such as Ralf had never before seen at Dilbeck Manor. As a consequence, Janny had made candies and cakes and sweets enough to make any twelve-year-old boy feel quite overcome with excitement and anticipation. If she hadn't let him sneak a taste every now and then, Ralf was certain that he would have expired long before Christmas officially arrived.

The house, too, had undergone a transformation. All of the rooms had been opened and cleaned and decorated, even the music room, which had been closed for as long as Ralf, or anyone in the household, could remember. And, what was more, there was music. Miss Rose, as it turned out, could play the pianoforte, and did so each night, after some prodding by Captain Mattison, with reluctant but admirable skill. She could sing, too, and, with Captain Mattison joining in, sang all of the old carols that had everyone who could hear them smiling in memory. Even Lady Dilbeck, who had taken to sitting in the music room after dinner, with Mr. Haysbert at her side, would smile mistily and nod her head in time to the music.

By Lady Dilbeck's command, candles were lit each evening in every corner of the manor, and a hot punch mixed by Camhort was served to mistress and servants alike. In anticipation of the coming celebrations, a magnificent Yule log had been prepared by Captain Mattison and his men, Elliot Haysbert and Jimmy Steele, and lay even now in the large fireplace in the music room, where it would be lit to officially begin Christmas.

News that Captain Mattison's parents were coming to spend Christmas at Dilbeck Manor added to the happy uproar, and the finest guest rooms were prepared for them and their servants. Exactly when Sir John and Lady Mattison would come, no one was certain, but all would be ready for them when they at last arrived.

Camhort, especially, was pleased by the thought of such fine guests coming once more to Dilbeck Manor. Apart from Miss Carpenter, who hadn't truly behaved as a proper guest should, he'd not had anyone other than her ladyship upon whom to utilize his skills and services. He was in his element now, working day in and day out with Miss Rose to make the manor perfect, and to ensure that Sir John and Lady Mattison enjoyed their stay at Dilbeck thoroughly. His finest uniform had been meticulously mended, cleaned and pressed, and his shoes polished until they gleamed. At the age of seventy, Camhort was looking forward to Christmas as he never had before.

Two days before Christmas, a large delivery came from the village, and the residents of Dilbeck Manor found themselves, at their lady's instructions, putting together baskets for all of the tenants, as had been the custom in years past. There were hams for each basket, as well as a loaf of bread, sweets and cakes, and a bottle of her ladyship's own favorite wine.

The next morning, which was Christmas Eve, Jacob and Captain Mattison loaded the baskets into the sleigh, and then, with the entire household sneaking to watch through the windows, Captain Mattison, with some help from Elliot Haysbert, handed Lady Dilbeck up into the sleigh.

Tentatively her ladyship settled into the seat, letting Mr. Haysbert arrange a variety of thick blankets about her. When he climbed up beside her and Captain Mattison gave Jimmy Steele permission to release the horses' heads, those assembled inside the manor gave a collective sigh of relief.

"After all these years," Janny said, sniffling and wiping her eyes with her apron as the sleigh pulled out of sight, "she's finally done it. God bless dear Captain Mattison. He's given her back all the things she loved best."

"She did look so happy, didn't she?" Emily murmured, smiling shyly up at Jacob, who smiled back.

"Just as she did in the old days," he said. "Lord Dilbeck would have been pleased, God bless him."

"I think he *is* pleased," Camhort put in, wiping his own eyes. "He's looking down from heaven and rejoicing. He did love Christmas so."

"Come along, everyone," Rose said, pushing away from her place at the window. "There's a great deal to do before tonight, especially if we're to have any dancing, as her ladyship said we might. And don't forget that Sir John and Lady Mattison will most likely be here at any time, since the main roads have been cleared enough to make travel so easy."

With that reminder, they returned to their various chores. But even work couldn't dispel the excitement of the coming night and day. Janny could be heard singing aloud in the kitchen, and Emily and Jacob could be found kissing at almost any moment beneath one of the several sprigs of mistletoe hung about the manor. Camhort hummed as he went from room to room, arranging and rearranging everything to his exacting taste. Hester had her hands full trying to keep Ralf from constantly being underfoot as she made the upstairs rooms ready for their occupants.

The cheerfulness that possessed the others, however, eluded Rose as she went about her own duties. For her, this was one of the saddest Christmases she'd known, far worse than the one that had followed the deaths of her mother or her father and brother. This Christmas, rather than bringing peace and joy, would only bring the final end to all her dreams.

But it was foolish to let herself feel such sorrow and pity, she told herself firmly. She had known for a long, long time that she couldn't have Collin. It was seeing him again, being with him, loving him so desperately, that had made her heart vulnerable once more. When his parents made him leave Dilbeck, she would find the way to let him go at last. Forever. Even if she did keep loving him for the rest of her days.

Lady Dilbeck returned to the manor in a weary but happy state. Her cheeks were pinked by the cold wind, and her hands, she admitted, ached badly, but she had clearly enjoyed every moment of her outing.

"Oh, Rose, we're so very fortunate to have such goodly tenants," her ladyship declared as Rose and Elliot Haysbert helped her up the stairs. "I've invited them all to come on Epiphany for a small assembly. We'll have dancing and punch and a light supper and little gifts for the children. Will Janny make a bean cake for us, do you think?"

"Of a certainty, my lady," Rose replied. "She'll be most pleased."

"Then we'll have a bean king, or perhaps a queen. I

vow it's been years since I've anticipated anything so grand. Have Sir John and Lady Mattison arrived yet? I didn't see their carriage.''

"Not yet, my lady, but I'm sure they'll be here soon.''

"Yes, yes,'' her ladyship agreed, yawning as they reached the landing. "You must wake me when they arrive. I want to greet them properly, you understand.''

"Yes, my lady.''

"I do hope they'll arrive in time for church services. Captain Mattison said that he would take us in good time. I'm looking forward to it. And then we'll have our lovely supper and dancing and music...'' She trailed off, yawning again as they reached her door.

"I'll fetch the ointment tin,'' Elliot offered, earning Rose's grateful nod before he bowed and hurried away.

Rose helped Lady Dilbeck into bed, then rubbed her hands with the ointment after Elliot delivered it. She smiled as Lady Dilbeck chatted on, her eyes closed but her voice as excited as any child's. She'd never heard such pleasure and happiness in her ladyship's voice, and that in itself was a gift. She left Lady Dilbeck's room, with her ladyship sleeping soundly, in a much happier mood.

Sir John and Lady Mattison arrived late in the afternoon, just after Lady Dilbeck had risen and refreshed herself and well before they were to sit down for a light dinner.

They arrived with three carriages in all: one for them to travel in, one for Sir John's valet and Lady Mattison's maid and one for all their things. Camhort, seeing this, was speechless with joy.

Rose watched from just inside the mansion door, lined up with the other servants, as Collin rushed out to greet his parents. She'd been unsettled by the fact that he had come directly after her, rather than go home, when he'd finished his army duties. This was the first moment that his parents had seen him in over six years, and for her part in delaying their reunion, Rose thought his parents would surely hate her. It must have been an agony for them to know that he was back in England, yet hadn't come to them.

She prepared herself for the worst as Collin led them indoors, stopping first to greet Lady Dilbeck, with whom they exchanged the kinds of embraces and kisses reserved for acquaintances so long unseen, and then toward her.

"This is Rose," he said proudly, "though I needn't tell you, I'm sure."

Rose began to sink into a deep curtsy, only to find herself stopped and embraced by Lady Mattison.

"No, of course you needn't tell us," Collin's mother said, hugging the breath out of Rose. "I should have known her at once. Dear Rose."

She sounded as if she was crying, and Rose felt tears prick at her own eyes.

"Thank you, my lady," she murmured.

Lady Mattison pulled away and gazed at Rose. She was extraordinarily beautiful, a shorter, daintier version of Collin, with the same gleaming wheat-gold hair and dazzling blue eyes. She was hardly touched by age, with but a few lines that showed when she smiled, and a hint of gray here and there. Otherwise, she might very well have been mistaken for Collin's sister.

"There's no need to thank me, my dear. Indeed, Sir John and I are the ones who are thankful to you. Isn't that so, my lord?" She pulled her husband forward.

Sir John was a tall, very refined gentleman, handsome in a quiet way, with dark hair peppered liberally with gray and sober green eyes. He took Rose's hand in his and bent to place a light kiss upon it.

Straightening, he said, "Miss Benham, I'm pleased to see you once again. I doubt that you'll remember me, but I was fortunate enough to lodge at The Lamb and Wig during certain brief visits to London, and couldn't help but be struck by your beauty. When Collin told me who it was he'd set his heart upon, I knew at once who you were. The knowledge pleased me greatly. My hope is that, very soon, I shall have the honor of naming you as my daughter.''

"What is this you say, John?'' Lady Dilbeck demanded from behind him. "A marriage, between Rose and Captain Mattison?''

"You didn't know, Eunice?'' Sir John said, looking at his hostess with bemusement. "Miss Benham and Collin have been betrothed for some years, since before he went away to the war.''

Lady Dilbeck was thunderstruck. She stared at Rose in disbelief, while Rose furiously shook her head.

"Not during all of those years, my lady. Not when I came into your service. Lady Mattison—'' she held a pleading hand out to Collin's mother "—surely you had my letter, explaining everything?''

"Sir John and I received a number of letters,'' Lady Mattison said with a touch of amusement. "From you, from Collin and from dear Lady Dilbeck. And all of them asking us to come to Dilbeck Manor as soon as we possibly could. With so much encouragement, how could we fail to respond?''

Now it was Rose's turn to stare at Lady Dilbeck. "You wrote to Sir John and Lady Mattison, as well, my lady?''

Lady Dilbeck's cheeks pinked, and she covered her embarrassment with consternation.

"This isn't at all the time to discuss such matters. Especially not when Sir John and Lady Mattison must be terribly fatigued from so much travel, and desirous of continuing their reunion with their son in a more private setting. Come John, Madeline. We'll go into the parlor where a fire is waiting.''

"But Rose must come with us.'' Lady Mattison reached for Rose's hand. "As much as I long to be with Collin again, I wish so much to know her better.''

"Oh, no, I couldn't," Rose said at once, very aware of the close scrutiny of all those present, including the rest of Lady Dilbeck's staff. "I have to make certain dinner is ready soon, so that everyone will be able to leave for church in good time. And your maid and valet will wish to be settled before then, as well. Please, go into the parlor with Lady Dilbeck and Captain Mattison, and I'll have tea sent in at once."

"I'll help Rose," Collin offered, "and will bring the tea in with her so that we can all sit together."

"No, please," Rose pleaded, embarrassed by the fuss, even more embarrassed by the situation. She was dressed in her uniform and apron, so clearly a servant, and yet she was being treated as if she were someone far more important. "I've so much to do, and will finish it more quickly on my own. Please, go into the parlor and be warmed. Camhort will see to your immediate needs."

Lady Mattison patted Rose's hand and gave her a sympathetic smile.

"I understand fully, my dear. Chores are always more demanding with so many people underfoot. We'll leave you to do as you will, but later, you must promise me quite faithfully, we'll have a nice, long coze together, just you and I." She leaned forward to kiss Rose's cheek. "I've looked forward these many years to coming to know you better, and can only check my impatience for so much longer."

"Yes, my lady," Rose murmured, casting an uneasy glance at Collin, who responded with a smile and a nod. "I'd be pleased."

She curtsied and watched as Camhort escorted Lady Dilbeck and her visitors away, a flurry of conversation starting as they all began to speak at once, Lady Dilbeck to Sir John, and Collin to his mother.

When she turned around to greet Sir John's valet and Lady Mattison's maid, it was to find the rest of the household staff, and Ralf, as well, grinning at her from ear to ear.

"This doesn't mean anything," she told them sternly.

"No, of course it doesn't," Hester replied with a small laugh, which was immediately echoed by the rest.

"I believe that her ladyship has just had guests arrive," Rose said, lifting her chin. "And unless we wish to shame her, we had best make certain that all is as it should be. Jacob and Elliot, be pleased to help Sir John's coachmen and footmen with the luggage. Hester, make certain the rooms are ready, and I'll bring the valet and maid up presently. Janny and Emily, hurry with the tea tray, if you will. I'll ask Camhort to take it into the parlor as soon as it's ready. And Ralf, you help Jimmy with the horses. Hurry, everyone!" She clapped her hands, setting them all into motion.

Getting the newly arrived servants, luggage, horses and carriages settled kept Rose occupied until it was almost time for dinner to be served. She asked Camhort to inform all those in the parlor of the approaching meal, giving them plenty of time to retire to their rooms and prepare themselves. But he returned, having made this announcement, to say that Lady Dilbeck and her guests intended to go straight into the dining room when dinner was announced, and afterward retire to their rooms to dress for the Christmas Eve church service.

However, Sir John and Lady Mattison had specifically requested that Rose join them for dinner, and Lady Dilbeck had consented. She had asked Camhort to convey this message to Rose, so that she might have time to make herself suitable for the occasion.

"They want me to join them for dinner?" Rose repeated, amazed. It had been one thing for her to join Collin and Lady Dilbeck, because the situation had been so relaxed and informal, and her ladyship had been lonely for company following Miss Carpenter's departure. But for a mere housekeeper to be asked to sit with formal company—it was beyond comprehension.

Camhort nodded. "Her ladyship was in full agreement. And I need not add that Captain Mattison was, as well." His usually grave eyes twinkled with amusement. "You're to join them in twenty minutes, so that you may all walk into dinner together."

"I see," Rose said with resignation. "Then I had better hurry to change my clothes. Thank you, Camhort."

She entered the parlor in perfect time, dressed in the only truly pretty outfit she had, a simple but elegant gown of blue muslin that Lord Cardemore had insisted she must have, just in case there was a dance or assembly that she might attend. She had assured him, at the time, that her position as housekeeper in Lady Dilbeck's home would not be likely to afford her such opportunities, but now she silently thanked him for such kindness and foresight.

Collin's gaze was appreciative as it traveled the length of her form, and Rose's only regret, as he came forward to take her hand, was that she'd not been able to do anything more with her hair than brush it out and tie the unruly black curls back from her face with a ribbon.

"You look beautiful," he murmured in her ear as he led her to a chair. "This will be one of the happiest nights of our lives, I promise you." He gave her hand a squeeze before moving away to his own chair.

She had thought it would be uncomfortable, making conversation with Collin's family, knowing that they were aware of her past, as she had related it to them in her letter. But it wasn't. They were charming and friendly, and Collin's mother especially put Rose at ease with her gentle smile and easy manner. Lady Mattison chatted throughout dinner and during the ride to the church and, following the service, all the way back to Dilbeck Manor.

But her merriment came to a halt once they went indoors. Lady Mattison detached her son's hand from Rose's arm, and said, "Now, Rose, will you come up to my room with me for a moment? We can have our chat, and perhaps you'd be so good as to help me change into something more suitable for the dancing that I understand we're to have."

Rose looked at Collin, her heart hammering in her chest with a mixture of confusion and anticipation. He gave her a reassuring nod, then said, "Don't keep Rose away too long, Mother."

"Knowing your impatience," she replied, "I'll be certain not to."

Lady Mattison dismissed her maid the moment she and Rose gained her room, preferring to remove her own cloak and gloves, which she lay across her dressing table.

"Please be comfortable, Rose," she said, motioning her toward a chair near the fire. "I know you're anxious about a number of matters, but I want to set your mind at ease."

"That will be difficult, I fear," Rose replied honestly, sitting in the chair across from the one her ladyship had taken. "You said that you'd had my letter, and if you've read it completely, then you know the truth. I'm sorry if Collin has led you to believe that I intend to make him honor the agreement we once had. You've been so kind to me, for his sake, but I can't believe you would truly wish for him to wed me."

"What I wish," said Lady Mattison, sitting forward to gaze into Rose's face, "and my husband with me, is for our children to be happy. Collin especially, after what he's endured during the war. I admit that I had reservations at first when he wrote to tell us of having so quickly fallen in love with a girl whom we didn't know, but his letters, and yours, as well as my husband's memories of you, eased my mind. And, too, I knew my son well enough to believe that if he hadn't formed a lasting regard for you, he would reveal the fact of it soon enough. Such inconstancy was ever his way as a boy," she said with a smile.

"But that moment never came in regard to you, Rose. Now, having met you at last, I can understand why Collin loved you at once and has continued to do so. I believe in my heart that he will never stop, regardless of what either you or his parents or anyone may do or say."

Lady Mattison reached out to touch Rose's hand, which rested upon her knee.

"When I read your letter, my dear, I realized that your love for Collin must be equally fierce, else you never would have revealed such painful memories in order to do what you thought best for him."

Rose gave a mournful shake of her head. "I do love him, my lady, but that can have nothing to say in the matter. You can't wish for your son to take a thief as a wife. I refuse to believe it of you or Sir John."

"If you had been a willing thief, or had shown no remorse for what was, in all truth, forced upon you by circumstances, we might feel differently. But I confess that when I look at you, Rose, and hear what both my husband and my son, let alone Lady Dilbeck, who praises you to the skies, have to say of you, I can't set you in so unflattering a light.

"What I see," she said, tilting her head in contemplation of Rose, "is a lovely, intelligent young woman of excellent manner and breeding who has a pleasing personality and good conversation. I'm sure that neither Sir John nor I could have asked for a better wife for our son. And, as fortune would have it, you and Collin love each other, which makes the entire matter that much easier."

Rose was afraid to let herself believe that Lady Mattison was truly saying such things. It was a dream, and she would wake soon and find herself alone with the truth.

"Lady Mattison, not only have I been a thief and lived upon the streets, but I've become a mere servant. Regardless of what my family and upbringing may have been, nothing can change what I've become."

Lady Mattison squeezed Rose's hand. "Nor can it change what you *will* become," she said with conviction. "I sit before you as example of that. I was not born a lady, Rose, nor even of very good family. And when I met Sir John, I was exactly what you are now…a housekeeper in the home of a titled lord. Sir John came to visit at the estate, and we met and fell in love. You may believe that I was just as convinced that we would never be allowed to marry, especially as John was his parents' eldest son and heir. I had nothing to recommend me, as you do, save the mercy of a good education, which my father, a parson, provided, and the love that I bore John."

"Did his parents accept you?" Rose asked.

"Oh, in time. They didn't want us to marry, and I, like you, was ready to send John away. But he was just as stubborn as his youngest son, and threatened to abduct and force me to wed him if his parents and I didn't agree. They gave way with little grace, as you might imagine, but in time we came to love and accept each other. And once I began to give them grandchildren, they actually began to dote upon me." She laughed, causing Rose to smile for the first time since they'd entered the chamber.

"It wasn't easy, of course," Lady Mattison went on, "for I had no formal training to be a lady. But my mother-in-law took me beneath her guiding hand and taught me how to be a proper wife to John, and to be able to meet the duties required of me. I like to flatter myself that I've done well enough to silence some of the rumors and gossip that are still said about me."

"I can't imagine anyone speaking ill of you, my lady," Rose said truthfully. "You are as fine a lady as I've ever seen."

"Then you must believe that you will find the task of being a gentleman's wife a far simpler thing than I, for you have all the advantages that I did not, and the one advantage I did—that of having managed a large household. The experience comes in remarkably useful," she said, "especially after one has children."

Rose's cheeks bloomed at the thought of bearing Collin's children.

"It all seems so impossible," she murmured. "I simply can't believe that it can happen. Just as I once dreamed it would."

"I'm living proof," said her ladyship. "And, in truth, my dear, do you honestly believe that Collin will ever give way, loving you as he does? The poor boy has waited six years to make you his wife—almost as long as the biblical Jacob—and I think that's long enough, don't you?"

"Yes," Rose whispered.

"You've waited for far too long, as well," Lady Mattison said kindly, giving Rose's hand one last pat before sitting back. "And suffered far more than any young lady should ever have to suffer, though I pray, and believe, that these past few years with Lady Dilbeck have been safe for you. But it's time for you to go forward now and claim the chance that's been set before you. A life with Collin, filled with the same joys and difficulties that those who truly love meet with. I needn't tell you, of course, that he's just as stubborn as he is charming?"

"No," Rose answered with a laugh. "You needn't say a word, for I know very well." Moving forward, she knelt before Lady Mattison, taking both her hands and gazing up into her face. "Are you quite sure, my lady, that it's what you want?" Her voice trembled with hope.

"Yes, my dear," Lady Mattison said. "Quite sure, for both my husband and I, and especially for Collin. Now, here, don't begin to cry, or your eyes will be red and swollen when you go downstairs to speak with Collin. He'll be waiting anxiously for us to return, you know, and as my dear late mother-in-law would say, it's never appropriate for a lady to greet a man with tears."

Tears filled Rose's eyes despite the teasing admonition, and she flung herself forward to hug Lady Mattison tightly. "Thank you," she murmured. "Thank you so very much. I promise that you'll never have cause to be sorry."

Lady Mattison chuckled and returned the embrace with affection. "My dear, I'm the one who gives you my thanks. I know you'll make Collin happy, and that's all that his father and I ask of you. Come." She lifted Rose's tear-streaked face and smiled. "Help me to change for tonight's celebration, of both Christmas and your coming union, and then you must hurry downstairs to Collin before he comes up in search of you."

Chapter Ten

Despite his father's admonition to be patient, Collin couldn't keep from pacing at the foot of the stairs, counting the minutes since his mother and Rose had climbed them. He was on the verge of following after and pounding on his mother's door, demanding to know what was going on, when the sight of Rose on the next landing stopped him.

She looked as if she'd been crying, but the smile on her face told him all that he wanted to know. He uttered her name and started upward to meet her, picking her up in a ferocious embrace and hugging the breath out of her.

"Is it all right, then?" he heard himself asking, and wondered how anyone could say anything so foolish in such a moment.

But she said, "Yes," and then took his face in her hands and kissed him. In that moment, every misery he'd suffered in the past six years melted away, and the world was right. She was *his,* fully and completely, and he would never let her go.

"You won't be sorry." He turned with her still in his arms and made his way down the stairs. "Everything will be just as you wish. If you want to stay at Dilbeck Manor, then we'll stay, and if you want to go away, we'll go wherever you please. Though my own preference is to stay," he added as they reached the last step, "because I have so many plans and Lady Dilbeck would miss us terribly and—"

She kissed him again, long and hard, until he was too breathless to speak. "We'll stay if Lady Dilbeck wishes it," she told him, "and if your parents wish it. But when we have children, Captain Mattison, we must think of setting up our own home."

"Oh, long before that, I think," he said with a grin, still carrying her in his arms until they stood properly beneath the kissing bough. "As it happens, her ladyship owns a small, unoccupied farm not far from here. The house is of a goodly size and build, perfect for a large family and the land sits waiting to be tilled and planted."

"I think I know the place you speak of," Rose said, gazing at him in wonderment. "But a mile east of Dilbeck Manor. Is that the farm you mean? Her ladyship owns it?"

"The very one." He was encouraged by her tone. "I've already spoken to her ladyship about it, and she's agreed to sell it to us at a shockingly low price, provided that we remain close by her there, and that I continue to manage Dilbeck. As to a housekeeper, she wasn't pleased by the idea, but is resigned to having to find a new one."

"Collin!" Rose pushed at him until he set her upon her feet. "You planned everything without knowing what your parents would say? What I would say?"

"I meant what I said about leaving you in peace should my parents disagree to a marriage between us, but I never intended to be parted from you, even for that. And it seemed as likely a place to live as anywhere else, though without you, it would have been intolerably lonely."

"You were likewise remiss in not telling me that your mother had once been a housekeeper, as I am," she charged. "Why did you say nothing, when it might have changed my mind about what your parents would think of me?"

He gave a light shrug. "I didn't consider it," he replied honestly. "Truly, my love, I never thought of it," he insisted at her look of disbelief. "It never mattered to me. Even when I was teased by friends at school, I was never ashamed of my mother. Though I did dole out a few black eyes," he added cheerfully. "But that was a pleasure, and my friends all came, in short order, to honor my mother just as greatly."

"That I can well believe," Rose said, her arms sliding up about his neck in gentle embrace. "But I'll not have you, or our children, fighting such battles on my behalf. I can't change what I was, but, as your mother told me, what I was can't change what I'm going to become. If there is gossip—and there is certain to be a good deal of it for all of our lives—then we'll counter it with that bit of good sense. Your mother is a very wise woman."

"God bless her, she is," Collin agreed. "As is my soon-to-be wife, Miss Rose, who listened and understood and chose happiness over misery—for the both of us." He gathered her close. "It's not yet the day, but I will greet you with it, anyway. Merry Christmas, Rose."

"Merry Christmas, Collin," she murmured, going on up tiptoe to meet his kiss.

From the parlor, they were watched not only by Lady Dilbeck and Collin's parents, but by the rest of the household, all of whom had assembled for a night of singing and dancing in celebration of Christmas Eve.

"This will be a Christmas to remember," Lady Mattison said happily, exchanging smiles with her husband.

"With good memories," Lady Dilbeck murmured, dabbing her eyes with a handkerchief. "More good memories to replace the bad."

Sir John set a hand on her shoulder in a reassuring gesture. "And many more to come, Eunice, with Rose and Collin staying so near. If I know my son, he'll be here every day, setting his plans for Dilbeck before you and not giving way until you've agreed to each and every one. He's the most stubborn lad on God's earth when it comes to having his way. I can almost pity our new daughter.''

"There's no need," Lady Mattison told him. "Rose will hold her own with Collin. They're perfectly matched.''

Lady Dilbeck nodded, gazing at the couple who yet stood beneath the kissing bough.

"That they are," she said with affection, "and I thank God for bringing them here to me." She gave a tremulous sigh. "I should have been so lonely without them. Without all of you." She looked about at her guests and servants. "But come, let us have a glass of wine, and we will toast ourselves and a marriage that will soon be made, and, most importantly, give each other God's blessings and good cheer for the coming Christmas.''

Her guests and servants agreed with full hearts and loud voice, and left the happy couple yet entwined beneath the kissing bough to celebrate Christmas peacefully and in their own special way for as long as it pleased them to do so.

* * * * *

SHARI ANTON's

husband is convinced she plans vacations around doing historical research, which means visiting every Civil War reenactment, medieval fair and pioneer cemetery she can find. Shari graciously concedes he might be right, while noticing that he doesn't mind when they can take the Harleys to get there!

When not writing, Shari is usually playing with her grandchildren. She lives in southeastern Wisconsin, is a member of RWA and WisRWA, and loves to hear from readers. You can write to her at P.O. Box 510611, New Berlin, WI 53151-0611.

Please address questions and book requests to:
Harlequin Reader Service
U.S.: 3010 Walden Ave., P.O. Box 1325, Buffalo, NY 14269
Canadian: P.O. Box 609, Fort Erie, Ont. L2A 5X3

CHRISTMAS AT WAYFARER INN

Shari Anton

To the composers of love songs,
especially the medieval troubadours,
whose lyrics are quoted in the story.

Happy Holidays!

Chapter One

Grace Brewer detested the odious chore of chopping wood, but hated the option of freezing to death.

She tossed her woolen cloak on the woodpile, scattering a dusting of snowflakes. With the long-handled ax in hand, she hoped this might be the last time she must split large chunks of wood into hearth-sized pieces.

Her white-haired father steadied her first victim on the chopping block, then shuffled back several paces out of harm's way. Though she'd taken over the chore two years ago, her aim still suffered. One never knew where a shard of wood might fly.

Nay, she'd not miss this chore, nor the other back-straining tasks necessary to keep the Wayfarer Inn open. Still, after selling the inn, she'd miss the only home she'd ever known. 'Twas the best home Watt and Nelda Brewer, her aging parents, had known, too. Both loved the inn they'd purchased shortly after their marriage. Unfortunately, their only offspring didn't possess the vigor to keep up with the work. Nor had she summoned the courage to tell her parents they must sell out, having decided they deserved a last Yuletide in their beloved inn before confronting the inevitable changes to come.

Grace swung the blade in a decent arc. The edge bit too

far to the right. A shard shot toward her father, landing at his feet. With his good arm, he picked up the piece fit only for kindling and tossed it into a large basket.

"Your mother ready to go to the ovens yet?" he asked.

Grateful he rarely commented on her poor aim, Grace answered, "Not yet. She was kneading the dough when I came out."

He nodded approval. "Good. We need extra victuals and heat for tonight. Storm coming up. Heavy snow brings guests. Mayhap tonight we will fill all the pallets above stairs."

"Mayhap." Though Grace echoed the sentiment, she knew better than to hope for such a miracle.

She trusted his prediction of snow: the ache in Watt Brewer's knees rarely proved wrong. But she wouldn't bet a copper on filling more than a pallet or two—not, she thought ruefully, that she had a spare coin to wager. Too few travelers stopped these days to sample the fare, quaff a mug of Nelda Brewer's heady ale, or rest weary bones on an upstairs pallet.

Grace knew the lack of patrons was her fault. She simply wasn't the son her parents should have had late in life—instead of the daughter they'd been given—to care for them in their old age. And not a pretty, sweet-tempered daughter, either, capable of attracting a hardworking, pleasantly disposed husband to take over the business.

She'd been betrothed once, to Rob, the youngest of the blacksmith's sons, thinking him a decent choice until realizing he planned to spend his days in the taproom sampling the ale. When informed she expected him to work, he promptly broke the betrothal and ran off with the miller's daughter. Grace knew it mean-spirited, but she wished them the joy of each other.

She ignored the burn in her arms and sweat on her brow. From down the lane in the village square she heard the merry laughter of children at play. Countering the tykes' laughter, angry geese honked in the butcher's yard, making her heart ache. While she yearned to buy the plumpest goose for Christmas supper, Grace shook off the fanciful wish.

Only five days hence, the holiday would be a meager one. She and her parents would attend Mass, visit with the parish priest and the other villagers, then come home to bowls of thin stew and slices of brown bread and yellow cheese. Soon after, the goat would need milking and the mule want feeding, and that most holy of days would succumb to the patter of any other day at the inn.

Her father bent over to pick up a piece of wood. Grace heard the unmistakable sound of ripping cloth. His breeches. This time not in the seam. She withheld a groan.

"Time to don your new breeches, Father."

"Hellfire." He rubbed at his bared rump where the cloth had given way. "I were saving them for when the weather turned cold."

"'Tis cold enough. Go change."

He gathered up what wood he could carry and grumbled all the way to the door of the taproom. Grace sighed and leaned the ax against the woodpile, her arms weary, her conscience burdened.

Sweet heaven, she loved her parents so very much, but no matter how hard or long she worked, she couldn't keep up. Best for all to sell the inn and purchase a retirement for her parents from Glaxton Abbey. They'd be given a small but comfortable hut and the monks would see to their well-being.

As for herself, perhaps the new owner of the Wayfarer Inn would allow her to stay, serve ale and food in exchange for her pallet on the storeroom floor. If not, then she'd need to find work in another inn, hopefully in a nearby village or town.

"Hail, milady! Have you room for a very hungry, much misused traveler."

Grace spun around to the question asked by a deep, rich male voice. A tall, inordinately handsome man led a magnificent but limping white horse across the inn's yard. Out of habit, she assessed this would-be patron who sauntered toward her.

Wrapped against the weather in a knee-length beaver cloak, he held the reins with black leather riding gloves. Boots to match molded to his calves.

A man of means, she judged him, given the quality of both horse and garments. Not a knight, for he wore no chain mail or sword. Not a noble, for he traveled without escort.

He pushed back his hood, revealing shoulder-skimming hair of sable, a high brow and eyes of sparkling amber. His lush mouth curved upward in an enchanting smile. A charmer.

The warm stirring low in her belly brought her up short and made her frown. Over the years she'd dealt with her share of charmers, rebuffed their advances and managed to escape unscathed. Her father hadn't been so fortunate. Grace quickly squelched the flash of guilt over the incident that had robbed her father of full use of his right arm.

Or perhaps she wasn't being fair. This man might prove of a chivalrous bent, possessed of courtly manners and generous with his coin. One could hope. Either way, she couldn't afford to turn away a paying guest. Perhaps a plump goose for Christmas wasn't beyond reach after all.

"Pallet and a meal costs tuppence." She waved toward the stable. "Another copper to shelter and feed your horse."

He stopped a mere pace before her. His smile faltered. "Ah, therein lies my problem. I have no coin."

The sad state of her purse didn't allow for charity.

"Glaxton Abbey is but two leagues east. The monks will grant you a night of hospitality."

"For myself, I would continue on." He reached down

to rub at his horse's leg. "Yseult's injury will not suffer the strain of the walk, I fear. Mayhap we can agree on some other payment."

Against her better judgment, she asked, "Such as?"

His smile returned full force. He bowed low, with a courtly flourish. "I am Alaine, minstrel of some renown. Mayhap you have heard of me."

"Nay." Now she knew why he had no money. Minstrels wandered among the nobles' grand manors and castles, entertaining lords and ladies for the price of a meal and pallet, earning only what coin an appreciative guest might toss his way. A frivolous way to make one's way in the world. Though Alaine must not have done too badly. His horse would bring a fine price.

"Well, then, mayhap you have heard a ballad or two that I wrote. My music is much sung by other minstrels and courtiers."

"Minstrels and courtiers do not often grace our taproom. I fear your renown has not reached our ears."

He stepped forward and leaned toward her, too close, sending shivers down her spine to the tips of her toes. Sweet heaven, those eyes! Pure amber gems, enticing and mesmerizing, luring her into a sweet befuddlement she didn't dare allow.

"Mayhap 'tis time you heard my songs," he said. "What say I entertain you for my bed and bread this night, with tales of knights brave and ladies fair, and the kisses they steal in the moonlight? Truly, I am very skilled at chansons de geste."

He thought to sing her love songs and steal a kiss, perhaps more, in the moonlight, did he? 'Twas galling Alaine thought her so easily swayed with the promise of a love song, and twice over annoying that she briefly considered the offer.

She needed money, not pretty songs.

"Unless your song has the power to lure a goose into my soup pot, then I must decline."

He gave a resigned sigh. "You turn me away then."

"This is a business, not a charity." To her own ears, she sounded a fishwife, but stood firm. Her parents' needs came first, not those of a wandering minstrel, not even during a season of goodwill.

Alaine gave his horse a gentle pat. "Might I beg favor for Yseult? I promise to return for her, coin due in hand, after Twelfth Night."

Grace thought to say nay, then changed her mind. Father wouldn't mind caring for the horse, nor would the expense be great. And if Alaine didn't return for the mare, she could sell it for a goodly sum of money.

"She may stay. Come, we will put her in a stall."

At the gate, he reached for the latch, to find it broken. He took a long look around him and frowned his disapproval.

Grace hurriedly reassured him. "The building is sturdy, and I will fix the latch anon. Your horse will be safe with us."

He didn't look so much convinced as resigned. "Perhaps I might fix the latch before I leave."

She wasn't about to argue. "If you wish."

Grace fetched a bucket of oats. Alaine led Yseult into the stall and removed his packs from the horse's rump. She assumed one pack held his possessions. The other was oddly shaped, rousing her curiosity.

As if he heard her silent question, Alaine opened the pack and pulled out the most beautifully crafted lute she'd ever set eyes on.

"Shall I play you a song?"

Oh, 'twas tempting to listen to the lute's lovely voice! But she had no time for frivolous pleasures.

"My thanks, but nay. You must be on your way and I have wood to chop."

He removed his cloak, revealing a sapphire woolen tunic that draped lovingly from his broad shoulders. A belt of gold links cinched his trim waist. A fine figure of a man, was Alaine.

Grace didn't want to know what his glittering belt was worth. A gift from a noblewoman, perhaps? She'd heard of how minstrels sometimes dedicated songs to wealthy women and were rewarded in return. Surely no song was worth such a prize.

"A few moments more will not matter." He removed his gloves to expose long-fingered hands, which he then wrapped around the lute's neck. "Just one song?"

She shouldn't give in, but when he plucked at the strings to play a melody so soft and sweet, her resistance weakened. "A short song, perhaps?"

He smiled. "As milady wishes."

The lute's voice filled the stable; the bright melody lightened her heart. Then Alaine sang, his deep, clear voice a pleasing contrast to the lute's lilt.

She didn't understand the words. He sang in French, the language of noble courts and the songs of minstrels. Grace knew enough French phrases to serve the needs of the few nobles who stopped at the inn, but no more. Still she closed her eyes to better absorb the music flowing around her, allowed her spirit to rise at the beauty of it all.

When the last note resonated in the stable's beams, Alaine stated, "Mayhap I pleaded my case badly."

The spell broke abruptly. Prepared for another plea for charity, Grace scolded herself for giving him the chance. "Have you found coins in your pack?"

"Nay, but I believe I offered you the wrong bargain." He waved toward the gate. "The latch needs repair. Several boards in here beg a nail or two. Surely, there are other tasks about the place I can do to earn my bed and bread."

So many she couldn't count. If the minstrel was willing

to trade true labor for his supper, she knew exactly the task to give him, which might be worth thinning tonight's stew to stretch for one more person.

"There is wood to chop."

He hesitated for a moment before he said, "Done."

The minstrel propped his lute against the side of the stall before following her outside and over to the woodpile. He picked up the ax, held it out as a knight might test the heft and balance of a sword, then ran a thumb across the blade. The wood on the block yielded easily to his mighty, well-aimed swing. He made it look so easy.

"You have done this before," she commented, unable to hide her chagrin.

He laughed lightly. "Oh, aye, though I admit not for a long time. 'Tis a thing one never forgets how to do."

The wistful note in his voice made her wonder if the chore brought forth some special memory. She'd not ask, though, fearing becoming overly friendly. 'Struth, she'd made too many allowances for him already.

Grace pulled on her cloak and gathered the wood he cut. Within minutes her arms were laden with more than she could cut in an hour.

"Father will come out to help you gather and haul."

Alaine didn't comment, just put another chunk on the block. Grace headed for the taproom.

The mellow odor of ale-soaked oak welcomed her inside. She crossed the dirt floor, winding her way among tables and benches to the far end where her father fed the fire. He tilted his head, listening, confused.

"I hear chopping."

Grace dumped the wood into the hearth-side crate. "We have a guest with no money. He does the chopping in return for bed and bread and to stable his injured horse until after Twelfth Night."

"A fair bargain."

"So I thought. I told him you would come out to help

gather what he cuts.'' She brushed her hands clean. "His name is Alaine, claims to be a minstrel of some renown. He plays a lute and, I must admit, possesses a fair voice.''

Her father's eyes narrowed sharply. "You set a lute player to chopping wood? Hellfire, what if he should harm his hands?''

Father scurried out of the inn before she could comment that Alaine didn't seem worried overmuch about his hands.

Grace headed for the kitchen, where brown flour coated most of the worktable and the floor—and Nelda Brewer, who hummed a bawdy drinking song while shaping mounds of dough into round loaves. A wide streak of flour smudged Mother's prominent cheekbone. Tiny and fragile, her mother wasn't neat, but baked the best bread and brewed the heartiest ale in the village.

Deciding she had time to fetch water before the bread was ready to haul to the communal oven, Grace grabbed a bucket. "I am off to the well, Mother. Need you anything from the village?''

"Nay, dearest. Think you we might hang holly when you return? The taproom sorely lacks for color and 'tis nearly Christmas.''

Mother tended to hang holly from nearly every beam. Grace couldn't begrudge her mother the pleasure, no matter the work.

"After the bread is baked. Will that serve?''

"Bread first, then holly. 'Tis sensible.''

Grace hurried out of the inn. On her way to the village well she glanced toward the woodpile—and stopped.

Alaine and Father engaged in seemingly amused conversation. A few of the village children had gathered to gawk at the stranger. Likely the village maidens would gather, too, when word spread that a handsome barechested minstrel chopped wood in the inn's yard.

Sweet mercy, Alaine was glorious to look upon. Sweat glistened on his smooth, wide chest and sinewy arms. A magnificently sculpted male with an enchanting smile. A danger to females everywhere. If Alaine didn't don his tunic soon, she'd have to beat the innocents off with a broom handle until their fathers came to fetch them.

Of course, if the fathers came, they might shoo their daughters home but stay to visit with Watt. And purchase an ale or two. A good thing.

Water bucket swinging at her side, Grace strode up the lane, pausing long enough to inspect the butcher's geese and hope Alaine shunned his tunic for a little while longer.

Chapter Two

The innkeeper's daughter was named Grace.

While half listening to Watt beg pardon for his daughter's audacity, Alaine watched Grace stroll toward the heart of the village, appreciating the seductive sway of her hips. Always one to mark the finer qualities of a woman's attributes, he freely admitted he'd not seen finer in an age. Lush curves, sapphire eyes, golden hair. The type of woman to whom minstrels paid tribute in the love ballads.

A hard woman, that one, or so she wanted him to believe. But Grace possessed a gentler nature than the straight spine and stoic manner she presented to the world.

In the stable, while he sang, she'd let down her guard. She'd closed her eyes filled with weariness. The thin line of her mouth eased. Beautiful. Exquisitely so.

Then she'd become the inn's caretaker again and set him to chopping wood, a task he hadn't attended to since his days as a squire in his uncle's castle. A squire in need of building muscle and learning discipline.

"Have you a noble house in which to entertain this Christmas?" Watt asked.

Alaine again hefted the ax, determined to cut enough wood so Grace would have no complaint of him when she returned.

"I do. Darby Castle, yet two days north if I must walk, and I suppose I must." A hardship he'd endure to spare his horse. Yseult had proved dependable and loyal, qualities he admired in men as well as horses. "Have you an unguent that might ease the strained muscle in my mare's leg?"

"Nay, but likely the smithy will." Watt waved a hand at the group of lads. "Hail, Thomas! Fetch the smithy for me."

A towheaded boy nodded and sped up the road so rutted that Yseult had misstepped and twisted her leg a few leagues back. If not for the incident, he'd be well along the road to Darby and the comfort of his uncle's grand hall. Instead, he was stranded at the Wayfarer Inn, doing menial work to earn a crust of bread and a likely lice-riddled pallet for the night.

Alaine sliced through a chunk of wood. "I suppose now I must perform some chore for the smithy to pay for the unguent."

Watt scratched his head. "Mayhap not. There be a copper or two in the money box to pay for the unguent."

A copper or two Watt didn't have to spare, judging from the looks of the place. "I wish to cause you no hardship."

Watt smiled brightly. "Lad, you will more than earn your keep tonight with your lute." He glanced at the woodpile where Alaine had tossed his tunic and belt. "How is it you carry no coin? You have done well for yourself. Hellfire, those gold links must be worth a knight's ransom."

Watt overguessed the belt's worth. A knight's ransom cost a suit of chain mail, a horse, a sword and shield. Alaine had both given and received ransom during his tournament days, thankfully now behind him. Of course, if he hadn't fought in the tourneys, then he'd not now have Yseult.

"The belt was a gift of thanks, from a countess whose

guests I entertained last Easter.'' Chagrined, Alaine admitted, "I fear I misjudged upon leaving London. I thought I would have no need of coin, so left my money purse with…a trustworthy friend.''

Alaine was relieved he'd caught his wagging tongue. 'Twould be a mistake to tell Watt that he'd left his money with the king's exchequer, a fine, trustworthy fellow he'd known since childhood. Peasants, even well-to-do peasants, tended to stand off in awe, or revulsion, when they learned of his rank. Best he keep his nobility to himself.

Watt shrugged a shoulder, his left. The man's right arm hung limp, rarely moving. Something had happened to rob Watt of the arm's use. 'Twas why Grace cut wood and mended latches, usually a man's work—because her father couldn't.

"A man should always have a coin or two at hand," Watt mused, "if only to purchase an ale along his journey.''

Alaine chuckled. "Spoken like a true innkeeper.''

"Nearly my whole life. Ah, the smithy comes.''

Watt shuffled across the yard toward the burly man coming up the road, patting a youngster on the head as he passed the children. More of the young ones had gathered. A group of wide-eyed older girls now stood near the gate, females much too young to be of any interest to him. He preferred his female companions older, more worldly and lushly curved.

The lushly curved innkeeper's daughter hadn't returned as yet, so he'd best get back to his chore before she did. Alaine easily swung into the rhythm of placing a log on the chopping block, splitting it in half, knocking the pieces off to the side to begin the process over again.

How much wood need he chop? Were both taproom and upper floor heated? He hoped so, for that's where his pallet would lie, upstairs in a large room with pallets lining the walls.

At Darby Castle, he'd have a room of his own with a large bed and charcoal brazier. He'd not have to worry about bugs in the straw mattress or wonder if the linens were clean. He'd spend his days catching up on the lives of those he loved there, and his nights strumming his lute for his uncle's guests.

'Twas more than an honor to be invited. Though he'd plied his chosen profession at manors and castles throughout England and France, 'twas the first time the man who'd been like a father to him had issued an invitation to sing at Darby for Christmas.

Matthew of Darby hadn't been pleased when Alaine put down the sword and picked up the lute. Mayhap, on this visit, his uncle would show some acceptance of his nephew's choice. Alaine could think of no other reason he'd been asked to provide the entertainment for the castle's many and highborn Christmas guests. Still, he needed to hear Matthew say the words, or see some sign in his manner, to be sure of the conjecture.

His arm and back muscles began to burn. Sweat trickled from his brow down the side of his face. Not in an age had he worked this hard, for this long. He rarely raised a sweat, not even when sparring sword to sword with the knights of the noble households where he entertained. 'Twould be good to be home, to cross swords with old friends.

However, for tonight he'd rest in a village he knew not the name of, at a place called Wayfarer Inn, with a friendly innkeeper and his comely daughter for company. This eve, his lute would lure patrons into the taproom. Ale would flow and coins pass into Grace's hands. Then, mayhap, she'd realize that his songs were worth more to her than a stack of chopped wood.

She liked the way he sang, though 'twould be more enjoyable for her if she understood the words. He knew a few songs he could sing that Grace might wholly under-

stand. The rowdy drinking songs came to mind naturally.
But of ballads, of love songs, there were few which yielded
easily to English.

"The Wish of Aucassin," perhaps? Grace had enjoyed
the music earlier.

He softly hummed a few lines, swiftly replacing French
with English. Settled on the translation, he sang aloud to
test the phrasing.

> "In paradise what would I do?
> Therein I'd fain not enter.
> But let me have my Nicolette,
> my fair sweet friend I love so."

Ah, a good match.

'Twas the silence he heard. Alaine let the ax fall to his
side and glanced about the inn's yard. A full crowd, male
and female, young and old, all stood about quietly listening.

Grace, too. She stood in the inn's shadow, the water
bucket at her feet. Had Grace ever been a man's fair sweet
friend, as Nicolette had been lover to Aucassin?

Alaine pushed aside the irritating thought of Grace
granting favors to any man who might pay the price, as
some innkeeper's daughters or serving wenches were wont
to do. He couldn't imagine Grace doing so, yet he had no
trouble envisioning himself kissing those lips of burgundy,
nuzzling in the silken skin of her neck, enjoying the soft-
ness of her curves and more.

Grace sauntered toward him. An enticing fantasy sprang
full to life and heated his loins, the result of his wayward
thoughts bulging in his breeches.

Her eyes widened slightly; a light blush bloomed on her
cheeks. She looked her fill, leaving Alaine to wonder if
she liked what she saw. Her tongue wetted her lower lip,
sending him into throes of agony.

"You sang the same song for me earlier, did you not?" she asked softly.

"Aye," was all he could answer.

She smiled then, warm and full. "You have cut an abundance of wood, more than I anticipated. Mayhap you should come inside to warm yourself, and rest."

He wasn't cold, basking in her smile.

Resisting the temptation to ask if she'd rest beside him, Alaine measured how much wood lay on the ground against what he'd intended to chop. He'd gone beyond his goal while lost in his thoughts and music. Not unusual. 'Twas easy to lose track of time when the notes and words flowed through his head.

"If you are content that I fulfill my part of our bargain, then I shall be more than pleased to set aside the ax."

"I am content."

He leaned the ax against the woodpile and grabbed his tunic and belt. An audible sigh wafted across the yard. One of the girls near the gate blushed red at the crowd's ensuing laughter.

"You have made an impression," Grace commented, barely containing her amusement.

"'Twas not my intent to impress, at least not this way, and not a willow wisp of a girl." Time to test the waters of Grace's interest. "However, if *you* were to sigh so forthrightly, I might never don the garment again."

She never blinked an eye. "I do not sigh."

"Never?"

"I have not yet found a man worthy of my sighs."

Grace turned her back on him and sauntered toward the inn, leaving Alaine to wonder if she'd just warned him off or issued a challenge.

Under her mother's direction, Grace hung holly branches. The decorations brightened her mood, as did the outcome of this morn's events in the yard.

As she hoped would happen, several of the village men stayed to visit with her father. They had already downed several mugs of ale while conversing around a trestle table.

Not Alaine, though. He'd come into the inn, hauled his packs up the stairs and donned an obviously older tunic of earthen brown. He now sat off by himself with quill and parchment, busily writing.

Grace dearly wanted to peek over his shoulder to see what he wrote. Her curiosity nagged hard, but she stayed far away, too embarrassed to approach him. 'Struth, she'd been shameless in her inspection of him this morn. She may not have sighed, but her thoughts had drifted decidedly wanton when his lust manifested itself.

Men had looked at her with lust before, become aroused in her presence. A couple had become violent when she rebuffed their advances. Ever since the last miscreant so badly wounded her father, the evidence of a man's randy nature evoked either disgust or fear. Not this morn, not with Alaine. Her body responded in kind, female to male, with an urgency that should scare her witless but didn't in the least.

Alaine wanted the same thing all those other men wanted. A romp on her pallet.

Truly, she hadn't known before this morn how compelling the urge to join bodies could be. She hadn't known the call to mate could muddle one's mind, direct one's tongue. Not until she saw Alaine nearly naked and aroused had she understood how swift and sharp her own response could bloom. She'd gone hot and wet within the space of a breath.

Not good at all.

'Twas because she'd never seen so fine a male body before, she was sure. Alaine's handsome face and enchanting smile only made him more appealing. That his pure, deep voice could lure the fish out of their ponds added to the enticement.

Yet here Alaine sat, fully garbed, deep in quiet thought, and she couldn't look at him without feeling the tug on her innards. Her fingers fair itched to skim those broad shoulders, entangle in his hair. She *wanted* to sit on his lap, his face buried in her bosom, his hands roaming to forbidden places.

"What of over here, Gracie?" her mother called. "Shall we hang some holly on these beams?"

Naturally Mother had drifted to the corner where Alaine sat writing. His head came up when she neared his table, those lovely amber eyes aglitter with…what? Excitement? Amusement? She wasn't sure, but whatever made his eyes light up, she wished it would fade. The flutter in her stomach wasn't from lack of food, she knew, because she'd already eaten two pieces of the freshly baked bread in a vain attempt to quell the hunger.

"I believe I have finished," he said. "Care to hear?"

He'd written a song! "Certes."

"I shall get my lute."

Before she could tell him to just sing, he was up and off toward the stairs. She blew out her impatience and tried to concentrate on the task at hand. Hanging greenery. She took the holly from her mother's outstretched hand.

To hang the holly over the beam, she used the bench Alaine had sat on, proud of herself for not looking at the parchment still on the table. She'd rather hear the words sung.

The bench wasn't all that steady, but then none other in the inn would suit better. Mother had tied three branches together to form a vine. Grace draped the vine around her neck and eased her way up, careful of her balance, then tossed an end of the vine over a beam. To her relief, it caught tight and held.

Alaine's footsteps pounded down the stairs. He stopped in the middle of the room and stared at her, so hard she felt naked, markedly uncomfortable in a room where too many people witnessed his regard.

After too long a moment, she had to ask, "Is something amiss?"

He crossed the room slowly, put his lute on the table.

"I was thinking that every man should have the privilege of watching a beautiful woman hang greenery. You appear an enticing gift all wrapped up in the holly."

Stunned, Grace couldn't think of a thing to say. Her mother had no such trouble.

"Ah, ain't you the gallant one, Alaine. Tsk, must come from all those ballads you know."

Alaine smiled at Nelda. "A gallant knight always takes a moment to pay compliments to a lady's beauty, and to offer his assistance should she be in distress."

To Grace's dismay, he wrapped his large, warm hands around her waist. If he leaned forward, and not too far forward at all, his mouth would touch her breast. She shivered, and knew he felt her tremble.

"Finish your chore so you can come down," he said.

"Truly, I am not in distress." Or hadn't been until he'd put his hands on her. "I need no assistance."

He looked so deep into her eyes he touched her core. "Mayhap not, but I intend to hold fast," he stated, then lowered his voice to just above a whisper. "I should hate to see you fall and the lovely package I behold become bloodied."

Why did Alaine affect her so? Why this minstrel who made his home wherever he happened to be, who relied upon the fickle generosity of others to make his way in the world? Why had she never felt this incredible pull toward a man better suited to her needs, one who found enjoyment in cutting wood and fixing latches, in settling into a quiet life of home and family?

How terribly unfair!

She hurriedly tossed the holly over the other beam. "You may let go now."

He didn't. "Put your hands on my shoulders."

He meant to help her down. She hesitated.

"You need not fear, Grace. I would not let any harm come to you."

Too late, a small voice within her cried. She placed her hands on the broad shoulders she'd longed to touch. So strong, so sturdy. His eyes darkened when he lifted her as if she were light as thistledown. By the time her feet touched the floor, she could barely breathe. His hands lingered on her waist.

Grace searched for a way to break the tension sizzling between them. "Your song."

He let go of her then and took up his lute. With one foot planted on the bench, Alaine cradled the instrument firmly against him. 'Twas ridiculous to be jealous of a lute.

Her mother settled onto a nearby bench. The men gathered at the trestle table fell silent.

Alaine played the melody now becoming familiar, heard first in the stable then in the yard. He sang of a knight yearning for the favor of his sweet fair friend, of their disapproving fathers, of escape together to a land of adventure, of a long, forced separation. And at the end, of how Aucassin and his Nicolette returned home to find acceptance and happiness, together and forever, the reward due their true love.

Her mother sighed. The men stomped their feet and banged their ale cups on the table. One of them tossed a copper at Alaine, who caught it and graciously bowed his thanks.

Grace wondered what it might be like to be so deeply and thoroughly loved as had been Nicolette by her gallant Aucassin.

Chapter Three

Alaine sat at the table and listened to the villagers complain about the rents and labor due their overlord. He lightly fingered the lute strings and kept his mouth firmly closed.

He knew well how the system worked. This village was owned by Lord Thorpe, who lived in a manor nearby. From planting time until after harvest, the villagers owed a day or two of work each week in the lord's fields. Alaine had heard complaints from his uncle about how tenants shirked their duties. 'Twas the first time he'd heard the argument firsthand from the other side.

The smithy leaned toward a farmer. "'Struth, John, if you would take a whetstone to that plow of yours, the planting would not be so hard on your ox team, and you would be spared sixpence fine every year."

"I sharpen the blade every winter!"

"Then mayhap you do it wrong."

"And I suppose you could do better?"

The other men at the table groaned. The smithy tossed his hands in the air, giving up the argument. Alaine smiled at the farmer's suddenly chagrined expression. All knew the smithy could do better.

Watt gave John a friendly slap on the back. "Methinks the ale has affected your wits."

"Aye, well, Nelda always did make a heady brew."

Alaine strummed the lute.

"A cup of ale, a maiden's kiss, 'twill weaken the mind, but leads to bliss!"

To the sound of the men's appreciative laughter, Alaine glanced toward the kitchen, where a particular maiden had hastened off to after he sang the ballad.

She'd said not a word, simply left the taproom, leaving Alaine to wonder if something in the song offended her, but couldn't for the life of him figure out what. Fascinating creatures, women. Just when a man thought he knew what would please them all, one proved him short of the mark. Of course, Grace wasn't like most women he knew. Her hands bore the redness of labor. She dressed in the drab, rough-weave wool of peasantry, not the colorful, smooth silk of nobility.

What might please a woman who toiled daily to survive? He'd already chopped wood and mended a latch for her. What else could he do? Bah, he was a minstrel, not a woodcutter or carpenter or innkeeper. He'd have a smile out of Grace tonight with one of his songs or he had no right to call himself a minstrel.

"What say you, smithy? Will I ride on the morrow or walk?"

"Walk. You could probably take the mare with you, but on a lead. Best not put added weight on her leg for several days."

"'Twould be better if I left her in Watt's care, then."

"Aye, especially if Watt's knees foretell the snow rightly."

"My knees never lie," Watt stated. "At least we will not send you on your way with an empty belly, Alaine. I told Grace to sacrifice an old hen, make pies of it."

The smith wagged a finger at Watt. "Blessed you are

with such a daughter. If my Rob possessed a dram of sense..."

Watt held up a staying hand. "Quietly, if you will. I do not think Grace has forgiven your son yet."

"Nor have I. Lucky am I she does not hold the son's idiocy against the father." The smith heaved his bulk from the bench. "Time to get the rest o' my chores done so my good wife allows me out tonight to hear your lute again, minstrel. 'Tis rare we have such fine entertainment of a winter's night."

The other men rose and echoed the smith's sentiments. Alaine assured them he'd play again after supper, restraining his curiosity over Grace and the smith's son, wondering if Grace had suffered a hurt of the heart. How recent? How deep?

Watt no more than closed the door behind his friends when Nelda ran into the room, screeching.

"Rats!" Nelda hiked up her skirts and climbed atop a trestle table. "Oh, Watt, there be rats in the kitchen!"

Thwap! Thwap!

"Nelda, come down!" Watt ordered, his attention divided between his terrified wife and sounds of the chase coming from the kitchen.

Alaine laid his lute on the table. "Care for your wife, I will see to Grace."

Grace stood near the worktable, armed with a broom. A mouse darted from beneath a stool, hoping to escape into the taproom.

Thwap!

With the mouse trapped under the broom, Grace looked so proud of herself Alaine had to smile.

"You have done this before." His comment startled her, surprise wiping away her pride. He wished he'd kept quiet.

"Far too many times for my peace of mind." She eased the pressure on the broom. The mouse lay still. "Trouble is, I no more than get rid of one and another finds his way in.''

Alaine picked the rodent up by the tail. "Do you know where they come in?"

"Aye. They burrow their way into the storeroom. They think the grain sacks their private larder."

"Let me get rid of this fellow and we will have a look at his doorway."

Alaine hustled out the back door and tossed the mouse into the shrubbery at the back of the yard. A scoop of snow and quick wipe against his tunic served as a wash for the nonce. When he again entered the kitchen, Grace was plucking chicken feathers.

"My thanks," she said. "I do not mind swatting mice so much as I dislike disposing of them."

"Shall we plug their doorway so you need not swat?"

She glanced at the storeroom. "Later, perhaps. I need to ready this chicken first or we will have a very late supper."

He shrugged a shoulder. "Then show me where it is and I can plug while you pluck."

Her mouth pursed, she pulled out a feather with more force than necessary. "You are a guest, Alaine, have earned your meal by chopping the wood. You need do no more."

True enough. So why did plugging a mouse hole seem a vital task for him to perform?

"Consider the service done in payment for Yseult's stay in the stable tonight."

Grace's shoulders sagged. She glanced at the arch between the kitchen and the taproom. "Father is displeased with me for the bargain we made. He'd be truly disheartened if you should get so much as a sliver in your hand. I will not ask it of you."

Stubborn woman. He crossed the room and laid his hands on her shoulders. A delightful warmth shot through his veins. He struggled to not respond to her shudder, to the sensual glow that brightened her sapphire eyes.

"You do not ask—I offer. My hands will suffer no harm."

She closed her eyes, took a long breath, then wetted her lower lip. What meager possession he retained of his senses prevented him from pulling her against him, kissing a mouth that begged a man's kiss. She opened eyes still bright with the awareness of what little space separated their bodies, of his hands on her shoulders.

"If you insist, then I will show you."

She slipped away. He took a moment before following her into the storeroom, a moment needed to regain his composure.

Grace pointed toward the back wall behind a barrel that, given the odor, held salted fish. "Back there. You can see the hole readily enough. Here, let me get my pallet out of your way."

She grabbed hold of the straw-stuffed sack of heavy linen that served as her bed and pulled it across the room.

Alaine stared at it, realizing that in this room, on that pallet, Grace stretched out to sleep at the end of her workday. In this tiny room, with the salted fish, a grain sack and various kegs and crates, Grace unbraided her golden hair and stripped down to her chemise to take her rest.

A beautiful lady deserved a maid to attend her, scented oils for her bath and lotions for her hands, should sleep on a down-filled mattress. Grace had none of these, nor could he give them to her. But he'd ensure no more mice disturbed her slumber if he had to build a whole damn wall to do it. And while he was about the work, he'd try to banish the vision of himself stretched out on that pallet beside Grace.

With the evening came the snow her father's knees had foretold. Grace only knew the state of the weather because each person who entered the inn shook snowflakes off an outer garment before settling onto a bench.

She didn't have time to see how much snow had fallen. She barely had time to keep all of the ale cups full.

The inn hadn't seen such a crowd in many a month. Most of the village's men had wandered in to listen to Alaine's music.

The object of their curiosity perched on a tabletop, singing a song about a dairymaid's amorous adventures in a meadow. As minstrels were wont to do, he'd placed a cup on the floor at his feet to collect tributes. She couldn't begrudge him the coppers tossed into his cup, not when the money box behind the counter now contained enough coins to actually jingle.

Certes, how could she begrudge anything of the man who worked for over an hour to prevent the mice from nibbling on her last sack of grain? The same man who'd eaten two meat pies, proclaimed the simple meal tastier than that he'd been served in an earl's castle. She suspected he overstated, but the compliment stayed with her even now, several hours later.

'Twould be handy to have a man about the place who threw himself into chores with such zeal. 'Twould be nice if the same man could lure patrons into the inn as did the minstrel. And if he could look at her as if she were ripe fruit, ready for devouring, make her tremble with desire...ah, such a fantasy.

The tanner waved his ale cup in the air. Grace grabbed the pitcher off the counter and headed across the room.

The dairymaid cavorted with her knight in a bower of crushed grass and heather, the man vowing to hold the maid precious in his heart. The song ended when the knight abandoned the maid in the grass and rode off, giving no thought to marriage. The men hooted and hollered at the knight's conquest and escape. Grace wondered how much they'd appreciate the knight's lack of honor if the maid in the song were one of their daughters.

She filled the tanner's mug. "There you are, Hugh. A tasty batch, is it not?"

"Aye, and 'tis even better when served by the most beautiful maiden in the village."

She'd heard the phrase uttered before, by nearly every man in the village who hoped for a free mug of ale. They should know better by now.

"Then mayhap I should charge more for an ale when poured by my dainty hand."

The tanner winked at her. "Ah, Grace. Someday some fortunate man will meet your price and pay it gladly. You mark my word."

Grace opened her mouth to ask what he meant, but everyone's attention turned once more on Alaine. From the lilt of the lute and the expression on his face, all knew he began another ballad. No one understood the words; no one cared.

Grace quietly made her way back to the counter and leaned against it, putting the pitcher down without a sound.

She rested her chin on her upraised fist and wished she understood the words of Alaine's song. Then again, 'twas probably best she didn't. 'Twould hurt to hear over and over about a gallant knight and his lovely lady, and of the kisses they stole in the moonlight—only to have the knight desert the lady.

Some man will meet your price.

Had she set her price too high? A man to share the work, to bear the burden of caring for her parents. An honest, decent man to laugh and cry with during the day and converse and make love with at night. Surely 'twas not too much to ask.

As often happened during the ballads, Alaine's gaze wandered her way. She no longer allowed herself to feel flattered or flustered by the attention. She was the only woman in the room besides her aged mother. Naturally, a minstrel would sing a love song to a woman. He meant nothing by it.

Grace heard the inn's door open. Two males, one a man of middling age, the other a lad, stepped inside. Their heavy woolen cloaks and fur hats were burdened with snow. She hustled over to greet the newcomers and ushered them to a table near the hearth.

They eased off their outer garments, revealing long tunics of tightly woven wool in a hue of forest-green. Nobles, Grace realized. For good service and a comfortable pallet, which Grace strove to give every patron, some nobles paid very well.

Softly she asked, "Ale? Or mayhap warm cider?"

The older man looked at her as if she'd offered him nectar from an ancient god's golden flagon. "Cider. And food. The four men of our escort are seeing to our horses. They, too, need feeding." He glanced at the crowd, pausing a longer moment on Alaine. "Have you enough pallets for all of us?"

"Pallets aplenty," she assured him. "I will fetch your cider then see to the rest."

On her way into the kitchen, she stopped to send her father out to the stable to ensure the escorts settled. Within minutes she'd readied enough cider to warm all of the newcomers through. For the nobles she warmed meat pies; to the escort she'd serve soup from the iron kettle hanging in the hearth.

By the time she carried the food and drink out to the nobles, Alaine stood near the nobles' table. The lad's eyes drooped so heavily Grace wondered if he'd stay awake long enough to eat.

The older man laughed lightly at whatever comment Alaine made, then reached for his cider. "My esteemed minstrel, I, too, have eaten at the Earl of Shrewsbury's table. No finer victuals to be found anywhere."

Alaine pointed at the pie. "That pie will change your mind. Grace, you had best heat his lordship another one straight away. He will not be able to resist."

Grace blushed at the praise, wholly unlike her. "If his lordship wishes."

"Likely I will," the man said on a sigh. "We did not stop for nooning for fear of being caught amidst the worst of the storm. Glad I am we go south, not north."

"Deep, is it?" Alaine asked.

"In places. Not impassable, but makes for hard travel."

The villagers, now aware of how bad the weather turned, finished whatever ale remained in their cups and then headed for their homes. Before going up the stairway, the noble gave her two pieces of silver.

"For your good care of us, mistress, and the incomparable meat pie," he said, then herded his son up the stairs.

Soon the inn was quiet, everyone gone to pallets—except Alaine. He strummed the lute and hummed while she wiped down the tables, too exhilarated from tonight's good fortune for sleep. The vision of roasted goose for Christmas had returned, and now she had the funds.

She poured the last of a pitcher of ale into a mug and set it down beside Alaine. He'd entertained the crowd all evening, certainly earning a free ale.

She glanced into the cup at his feet. Several copper coins winked back at her.

"You did all right for yourself."

"Enough to pay you in advance for Yseult's oats until after Twelfth Night, I should think."

A full fortnight away. After the Christmas season.

Grace eased down onto a bench. "Probably, but take the coins with you. Given the weather, you may need to stop at an inn tomorrow night."

"True." He took a sip of ale. "I cannot say I look forward to two days' walk in the snow. But the morn is still many hours away. What say you to another song?"

"Please, not another dairymaid or shepherdess."

"As my lady wishes," he said, then strummed the lute.

Grace crossed her arms on the table, recognizing the tune. 'Twas one of the love ballads he'd directed her way all evening. Only this time no one raised a mug to distract her. No one entered the taproom to disrupt the magical spell he wove.

His gaze never strayed from her face, as if every word he sang were written for her ears alone. The inflection of his voice, the magnetism of his very presence drew her deeper into the sweet fantasy of being the lovely lady the gallant knight desired, made her vulnerable to the desire in Alaine's eyes. 'Twas both thrilling and terrifying to know her pallet lay in a small but private room only a few steps away, far from prying eyes and ears. If she took Alaine to her pallet, gave him what he wanted, no one but the two of them need ever know.

Dangerous thoughts she had no business thinking, couldn't afford to act upon.

Alaine sang the last verse, knowing he'd somehow lost Grace. The dreamy glaze in her eyes cleared. Her spine straightened.

He inwardly chided his presumption. True, that canzo had touched the hearts of many a noble maid and sometimes led to a night of passion. Grace didn't understand the words, though she'd certainly understood his intent and refused to succumb.

The innkeeper's daughter was made of sterner stuff than he'd reckoned with in a long time. And oddly enough, he wanted Grace more than any woman in memory.

Her beauty rivaled that of any woman he'd ever met. She'd gone about ensuring that a room full of people were content, with the gracious warmth sometimes lacking in women of his rank. Grace quietly went about her business without seeking praise, blushing when he complimented her on her cooking.

For all the copper in his cup, he'd failed dismally to-night. He hadn't made Grace smile.

He strummed the last cord. Grace rose from the bench, walked over to the counter and reached for something behind it.

"A lovely song," she said, coming toward him. "I would be remiss if I did not give you your due." She tossed a silver coin into his cup. "I wish you better fortune at Darby Castle than you have had during your stay here."

Last chance.

"The night is not yet over. We could—"

"Nay, minstrel, we will not."

Chapter Four

Grace ate her cheese and bread, determined not to join in the argument. 'Struth, she didn't know whose side to take.

Alaine prepared to leave for Darby Castle. Her parents insisted he must wait another day and let other travelers trample the snow on the road first.

"Watt, I appreciate your concern, but I am already a day late."

Her father huffed. "Get yourself deep into a drift and you may not get to Darby Castle at all. You heard his lordship same as I. Snow up to his horse's knees in places. Not a good day for a long walk."

The noble and his son had already left the inn, headed south. Their comments on the road behind them only served to heighten her father's worry. Never had Grace seen him argue so pointedly with a patron's decision to continue a journey, no matter how ill-advised.

"Only in places," Alaine countered.

"Enough places where you might lose the road altogether. Then where will you be?" Father tossed his good hand in the air. "Lost, wet and frozen, that is where. Why take a foolish risk when waiting one more day will make the journey safer?"

Father's argument made sense. The road might prove treacherous. However, after what had almost happened between them last night, Grace wanted Alaine gone.

She still couldn't fathom why she had given him the silver. A penny in his cup would have made the same statement, that all she owed him for his song was payment of the same kind the others gave in tribute. She'd spent a restless night thinking about the silver. Thinking about Alaine.

Once, alone and burning in the dark, she considered going upstairs to fetch him, tell him she had changed her mind. She'd won the battle against temptation when remembering the men of the noble's escort also slept in the common room. In the dark she might very well wake the wrong man!

Best Alaine leave and remove the wanton temptation of his magnificent body and voice. Best he go before he could do her another kindness. Before she must again witness his alluring smile. Before her curiosity and restless body prodded her to lose her common sense.

Alaine swirled the cider in his cup, staring at the amber liquid that nearly matched his eyes. "I suppose a delay of one more day might be wise."

'Twould be agony.

Delighted, Mother applauded the decision. "You will play again tonight, will you not?"

Alaine flashed her a smile. "I might be persuaded."

Mother rested a hand on his forearm. "Might I also persuade you to sing one of the ballads in English, the one that begins *la dossa votz?*"

The song he sang late last night, for Grace alone, the melody and inflection pure seduction.

"Mother, you should not ask so much—"

"Madam asks nothing untoward," Alaine said, interrupting Grace's protest. "If I can find the right words to fit the melody, 'twould be a pleasure to honor her request.''

Mother giggled. "How gallant of you, good sir."

Alaine dipped his head and waved his arm in as courtly a bow as she'd ever seen executed while sitting.

The two were actually flirting with each other. Well, if they wanted to trade silly pleasantries for the rest of the day, 'twas fine with her. She picked up her empty cup and tin plate, but hadn't risen from the bench before her father leaned forward.

"Grace, what is the name of the tanner's girl?"

The young lady who'd audibly sighed over Alaine's bare-chested wielding of the ax yesterday. "Marie. Why?"

"I intend to hire her for tonight, if her folks allow."

Grace inwardly winced, both at her father's choice of hired help and the hit to her pride. Father had never before suggested she fell short when serving patrons. Nor did she want to spend any more of the profits than necessary. She'd already erred badly in giving Alaine the silver. And to have to listen to Marie sighing over Alaine...

"We managed last night, the three of us. Why hire Marie?"

"Because tonight the men will bring their families."

Grace couldn't imagine it. "The women never come into the taproom, much less the children."

"They will tonight. Best be prepared."

Alaine worked on the translation he had promised Nelda, but another verse intruded, the words chasing around in his head.

Usually a melody came to mind first, then the words to fit the rhythm and mood. This time the sentiments, a mixture of angst and joy, begged expression. Knowing what he wanted to say and the best way to say it, however, proved difficult.

He knew damn well to whom he owed the inspiration—

Grace, whom he hadn't seen for most of the morning. He supposed she avoided coming into the taproom because he'd taken her father's sensible advice and stayed. She would rather he packed up his lute and left.

He certainly hadn't argued very long or hard this morning, could have been well on his way hours ago. But then he'd not have the chance to bring the smile to Grace's face he'd vowed to have of her last night.

'Twas the other thing he'd craved last night that scared her today, he was sure. His passion. His desire to touch and taste the woman with the sapphire eyes who bedeviled him yet this morn.

So where was the vixen who inspired love songs and tortured his body? Alaine went in search of a fresh dose of inspiration.

He found Grace in the stable, leaning on a pitchfork outside of Yseult's stall. She gave him a tight-lipped smile, then turned her attention back to the stall. From within, the smith's voice soothed the mare, complimenting her fine manners.

"How does she?" Alaine asked.

The smith rose and dusted his hands against each other. "The swelling eases. A few days' rest is all she needs. A prime companion you have here. Must cost you a lot to keep her."

"Aye, but she is worth the expense, and more. I have gone without mine own supper a time or two so Yseult might have hers."

The smith laughed. "Ah, what we men do to keep the females content. Woman or mare, if treated badly, they become contrary creatures."

Grace patted Yseult's withers. "'Struth, if a female is contrary, 'tis usually some man's fault, is it not?"

Yseult tossed her head and snorted in complete agreement.

The smith lost his smile. "My apologies, Grace. I did not mean to remind you of past hurts."

Grace looked surprised by the remark. "Truly, I spoke only in general. I do believe you more upset over the matter than I."

The smith's fingers curled into his palms. "Mayhap I am. I had not thought my son so foolish."

"Have you had word from Rob?"

"Nay, not in all these months. Upsets his mother."

"So I imagine. Give your wife my greetings."

With that, Grace left the stable.

She may have fooled the smith, but not Alaine. She hurt over whatever the smith's son had done.

'Twas none of his affair. He didn't need to know what the lout of a man had done to Grace. He should let the matter be.

"What happened between Grace and your son?"

The smith gave a long sigh. "They were betrothed for a time. I thought Rob finally coming into his proper manhood when he asked Grace to marry him. Then he came home one day as angry as a bee denied nectar, said he would not marry Grace if paid a fortune. Refused to say why. Two days later both he and the miller's daughter turned up missing."

Alaine fought his unwarranted anger without success. "Rob broke the betrothal and then ran off with another woman."

"Truth to tell, I think Grace tossed Rob out and he took consolation with Bess." The smith shrugged his shoulders. "No one knows for sure what happened because neither will tell."

Alaine spent his anger by attacking the woodpile. By the time he put the ax down, he'd chopped a month's worth of wood. Still, he doubted that if Rob should appear in the yard he'd be able to restrain his hands from wrapping around the lout's neck.

He gathered up an armful of wood to toss into the taproom's hearth. That done, he followed the sound of a knife hitting the worktable in the kitchen. Mayhap Grace's mother could shed further light on her daughter's failed betrothal. Nelda was nowhere to be found; Grace chopped turnips and wild onions, likely readying them for the always simmering soup pot in the hearth.

Come to think on it, he hadn't seen her parents all morning, either. The entire family seemed to have disappeared when he began to work on his song.

He snitched a slice of turnip and drew a reproving glare, Grace's sapphire eyes snapping with annoyance. A man could drown in those eyes, sometimes calm, sometimes stormy, too often weary. "Nearly done?"

"Nearly." She glanced at the storeroom. "I should probably toss in some carrots, too."

"I will get them," he offered, and went into storeroom. Grace had placed her pallet back to where it belonged, the thick mat large enough for two people. 'Twas far too easy to envision Grace sprawled on the pallet, her unbound golden hair—

Carrots. He'd come into the storeroom for carrots.

He found a few of them readily enough, then looked around for more. Surely there must be more in one of the other crates. He searched, only to peer into one empty crate after the other, which he'd half noticed yesterday and not given much thought to.

He did now, counted the meager food stores on one hand. A half a sack of grain, a partial barrel of salted fish, a quarter round of cheese, a crate of apples, a few more turnips.

Jesu, with several months of winter left, there wasn't enough food laid by to see the mice through until spring, much less three grown people!

It hit him then that the Brewers might have truly sacrificed a hen for last night's meat pies. So why had Grace given him a silver piece last night, coin she could ill afford to part with if needed to purchase food for winter?

He returned to the kitchen and handed her the carrots. "Sparse pickings in there. Hardly enough to feed the mice."

"Thanks to you the mice will feast no more."

"Not near enough food for three grown people to last out the winter."

She began slicing. "We need only enough to last us for a few days past Christmas. With the money you helped bring in last eve, I can buy more grain and cheese. We will not starve."

"And after?"

Grace glanced at the back door, then spoke just above a whisper. "We will no longer be here. By the grace of God we shall have a buyer for the inn and enough money to purchase a retirement for my parents from Glaxton Abbey."

Sell the inn? Alaine couldn't imagine Watt and Nelda Brewer anywhere but here in the Wayfarer Inn, offering up hospitality to villagers and travelers alike.

"A hard decision for your father to make, I imagine."

She took a long breath. "I have not yet discussed it with my parents, so would appreciate your silence. They deserve one last Christmas in their home."

They deserved more, and he could well imagine Watt refusing to bow to what was apparently Grace's decision— one Alaine found distasteful.

"Why sell?"

She paused in her chopping. "Because there is too much work for one person. My parents help out where they can, bless them, but are hampered by age and frailties. If Father could still do some of the heavy work, we might last awhile longer."

"You could hire someone to help out."

"If I had the money, I would, but I do not. The villagers

are willing to help when they can, but they have their own families and work to see to. 'Tis not fair to burden them any longer. I truly have no other choice.''

There were always choices. Alaine just didn't know what Grace's choices might be. Zounds, retirements at abbeys didn't come cheaply. Would the inn's sale cover the expense? He didn't know but could only assume Grace did.

''And what of you?'' he asked, needing to know.

She shrugged a shoulder and took knife to carrots again. ''I will decide after I see to my parents. Ouch!''

Grace stuck the tip of her forefinger in her mouth. A smear of blood marred the knife. He felt the sting as if it were his own finger sliced open.

Alaine held out his hand. ''Let me see.''

''Tis nothing, merely a little cut.'' She turned her hand to show him. ''Already the bleeding stops.''

So he saw, but he grasped her hand anyway to have a closer look. No dainty miss, Grace Brewer. Her hand was chafed, had likely seen its share of cuts and slivers. A strong, long-fingered hand too accustomed to hard work. The calluses wanted for soothing, the dryness for lotion. 'Twas the most beautiful hand on God's earth.

He kissed her palm.

Her fingers curled. She shivered, wiping his mind clean of everything but the woman who stood close enough to pull into his arms. She didn't resist his tug and melded against him perfectly, igniting a yearning so deep he had to kiss her or go mad.

The light touch of lips wasn't enough. Her lush mouth moved under his, kissing him back, inviting more with a sweet innocence he found utterly enticing. Untouched and untried was the innkeeper's daughter...and a fast learner. Her arms encircled his neck. She pressed so tight against him she must feel his full, hard arousal and pounding heartbeat.

Alaine couldn't remember wanting any other woman as much as he wanted Grace. Slow and lingering or hard and fast, he didn't care. In the storeroom on her pallet or right here on the kitchen worktable, either were fine with him.

Did Grace care? Alaine didn't think so, not if he judged the depth of her desire correctly, a match to his own.

Now, if he could only ensure her parents wouldn't walk in the kitchen door, or a patron wouldn't enter the taproom and call out to demand an ale.

Reluctantly he broke the kiss, but held her within the circle of his embrace, knowing he must let go soon. With Grace's cheek resting on his chest, he found the inspiration he'd been seeking for the next verse of his song. There could truly be no other. The declaration of love.

How odd that he had sung love songs to most of the highest ranking women in two kingdoms, and only now truly understood how it might actually feel to be in love. The pounding heartbeat, the yearning to hold and be held, to protect. The wish to give one's beloved pleasure in every way.

Tonight, without fail, he would make Grace smile.

Grace couldn't remember the last time she'd worked so hard while having so much fun.

Father had been right about the size of tonight's crowd. Men, women and children alike leaned against the taproom's counter, filled the benches and sat on the floor.

Father had hired Marie, who seemed to be having a good time pouring ale for the patrons. If only the girl wouldn't swoon whenever Alaine sang a ballad. Indeed, most of the women—even the long-married ones—went all dreamy eyed, especially the Widow Tucker. Grace wished the woman wouldn't look at Alaine as if he were honey for her bread.

As for the men, they behaved themselves admirably, drinking but not getting drunk while under the scrutiny of their families. Even the butcher, who normally must be reminded of his manners, seemed content to sip his ale and listen to the music. He'd also vowed to save her his plumpest goose in return for a dance.

Goose for Christmas. Coins aplenty for food. No more mice in the storeroom and enough chopped wood to last for weeks. All because Alaine's horse had suffered an injury, bringing the minstrel to the Wayfarer Inn's door.

And into her kitchen, and into her arms.

The kiss hadn't been a complete surprise. Sweet heaven, how she'd reveled in Alaine's tender hunger. She'd known his kiss would be pleasing, but hadn't expected her knees to weaken or her senses to take flight. If he hadn't possessed the will to pull away, to return to the taproom table where he'd been hard at work before and since, she might well have pulled him to the kitchen floor and insisted on more.

He'd give her more than kisses. Alaine would lie with her if she expressed willingness.

Her body was so willing she thought she might explode. 'Twas the niggling voice of caution that she battled.

Alaine now sang the ballad her mother wished to hear.

"I have heard the sweet voice of the wild nightingale," the song began, then went on to tell of a woman with a fickle heart and the man who suffered her misbehavior. Grace thought the ending unsatisfactory, for the woman hadn't changed her fickle ways or the man's suffering eased.

After the crowd's appreciation waned, from the back of the room a woman called out, "Another dance, kind minstrel."

Alaine laughed lightly. "I do believe I have played every dance you already know. Might I interest you in learning a new one, hardly known outside of France? 'Tis a graceful, courtly dance, the steps easily learned."

Agreement resounded through the taproom.

Alaine put his lute aside and held out his hand. "Grace, would you partner me?"

Her heart thudded against her ribs. She shouldn't. Someone might notice her attraction to Alaine, but she wasn't about to let any other woman seize the opportunity.

Alaine walked her through the steps, sometimes holding hands, others not. Bodies pressed close, then parted. Quick steps and slow, a slide and a bow. Through it all, his gaze locked with hers until she forgot other people occupied the same room.

He began to sing, putting steps and music together.

Grace fair floated across the floor, sliding into Alaine's arms and out, barely aware of the other couples sampling the steps. Would that the dance could go on forever, that she might spend the rest of her life in such carefree yet thrilling style. Dancing with Alaine.

Loving Alaine.

She nearly tripped over her own feet. Her common sense screamed a denial even as her heart whispered acceptance.

For the rest of the evening Grace grappled with her wayward heart and wanton thoughts. Was it possible to fall in love so quickly, with a man she knew near to nothing about? Or was she simply as entranced as almost every other woman in the room?

Normally she wasn't swayed by a man's desire. Alaine wanted her, she knew that, but he'd also taken the time to do small kindnesses without being asked. She could talk to him easily, a rarity not to be considered lightly.

Would it be wrong to give herself to Alaine out of love when so many women married and gave themselves to their husbands out of duty? Was it shameful to share one night of bliss with the only man she might ever love and truly want to be with?

By the time the children's eyes drooped and their parents reluctantly took them home, she'd put her doubts to rest.

For one night she would play the lovely lady to Alaine's gallant knight. Falling in love with a wandering minstrel, in the unseemly haste of only a day, might be the biggest mistake of her life. Not seizing the chance to know his passion, to find out if he felt more for her than lust would be the greater regret.

After the last patron ambled off toward home, and her parents climbed the stairs to their room, Grace threw the bolt on the door and put her plan into action before she lost her nerve.

'Struth, she'd spent so many years rebuffing men's advances she'd never given a thought about how to seduce one.

Grace slowly walked toward where Alaine sat on the table that had served as his stage, amazed her outstretched hand didn't tremble or her palm sweat. 'Twas tonight or never.

"Alaine, would you partner me?"

He stood and took hold of her hand, a good beginning to Grace's way of thinking.

"Liked the new dance?" he asked.

"I did, but I do not mean for us to dance. There is…another thing for which I need a partner, if you will have me."

"Another—" His eyes went dark with understanding. "'Tis an offer no man in his right mind could resist. I will, however, if you feel the least doubt. I would not have you suffer regrets come the morn."

Fair warning of his intent to leave her on the morn, with no obligations or regrets. No future existed for an innkeeper's daughter and a wandering minstrel, just a night of loving.

"No regrets, Alaine," she whispered, then leaned forward for the kiss to seal her fate.

Chapter Five

He granted her wish with a tender kiss, imbued with the promise of further delight to come. 'Twas more thrilling than she anticipated and yet less than thoroughly satisfying.

Grace sensed Alaine held his passion in tight rein. Without a word he swept her up and carried her into the dark storeroom.

"Have you a candle?" he asked just above a whisper.

"Aye, somewhere." Her legs unsteady, she fetched a short candle. "Will this do?"

"For the nonce."

He left the storeroom. Grace took a long breath, knowing Alaine would come back shortly.

And then what? Sweet mercy, she ached within her woman's places. Aches Alaine would ease, she was sure.

What was taking him so long? She resisted the urge to go out and light the candle herself.

She should do *something* to prepare for his return. The ladies in Alaine's songs sometimes "made ready" for their lovers, but the songs never said how. Nor had a one of the ladies awaited a lover in so bleak a bower as a storeroom, with only a straw pallet on which to take their pleasure.

Grace took refuge in the ritual of unbraiding her hair, the strands separating to the rake of her fingers.

She heard his footsteps and, when he walked in the door, was glad he held a lighted candle. The flame glimmered in eyes lit with approval and hunger.

Never had she felt more female.

Whatever last doubts she'd harbored over the wisdom of allowing Alaine into the privacy of her room and onto her pallet vanished with the snick of the latch.

He placed the candle on an ale keg. Grace lifted her arms, an invitation he quickly accepted by hefting her up and burying his face in her bosom. She thrilled to the strength that held her in so intimate an embrace, to the warmth of his breath in the valley between her breasts. The tips hardened and tingled, begging for more than the nuzzle of his nose.

"I shall take the greatest care with you, Grace, I swear."

"As a gallant knight cares for his lovely lady."

"Just so."

"Then I shall be content."

"Oh, more than content."

The statement intrigued her. "More than?"

The sensuous slide down his long, lean body drove her nearly witless, especially when the vee between her legs encountered the hard bulge in his breeches. With her feet on the floor, she reached for the ties of her gown.

"Not yet," he said, clasping her hands at the back of her neck. "'Tis one of the pleasures I intend to partake of slowly, peeling your garments off. 'Twill ensure I see and taste every inch of you."

Grace struggled for patience, her imagination taking flight over where he wanted to look, what part of her he wished to taste. He dipped his head for another kiss.

She clutched fistfuls of his tunic, glorying in the sensation of floating, leaving behind her cares and worries. For the next little while her world consisted of only her and Alaine in a softly lit storeroom that seemed more and more a scented bower with each passing moment.

Her innocence enticed him.

Grace might lack skill, but her enthusiasm flourished. She responded with abandon to deeper kisses. Her slight start of surprise at the touch of tongue to tongue sent a jolt of need to his already aching loins.

He fumbled with the ties at the nape of her neck; she deftly unbuckled his leather belt and let it drop to the floor.

Alaine gathered fistfuls of her gown, easing the skirt upward. Grace did the same to his tunic, slowly raising the hem until able to sneak her hands beneath. Her fingertips skimmed the bare skin along the tops of his breeches until she halted at the lacing.

His control coming undone, Alaine sucked in his breath, willing Grace to tug on the string and free him. Her hesitancy reminded him that she'd likely never undressed a man. Would the sight of him please Grace or frighten her?

'Struth, he'd die a slow, painful death if fright overcame her and she asked him to halt. But halt he would, if she asked.

Reluctantly he broke the kiss. He saw no reserve in her expression, only an unasked question.

"Your gown first," he said.

She raised her arms, giving a permission he immediately took, until Grace stood before him in only her shift—a sheer white veil that hid nothing.

The dark circles at the tips of her breasts drew his hands like iron to lodestone. Within moments both her shift and his tunic lay on the floor, next to the pallet where he and Grace pressed flesh to naked flesh.

Grace didn't think there was any finer place to be than molded against Alaine, his hands stroking her side, his lips tasting the hollow of her throat.

Grace now knew the full meaning of wanton.

She tried to lie still, allow Alaine to do as he pleased

without interference. 'Twas near impossible. Her hands simply wouldn't be still, not when his broad shoulders begged a caress.

Soft skin covered unyielding muscle. This man she lay with played a lute and sang as sweetly as a lark, yet his body spoke of physical labor. A puzzle, was Alaine, and she had only tonight to sort out and fit together the pieces.

Then he rolled her over and lowered his mouth to her breast. His rough tongue licked a sensitive nub and sent her reeling. His hand slid downward, over her hip, then inward, over her thigh, until his palm rested between her legs, over the ache she most wanted eased.

"There, Alaine. Oh, please."

"Here?" His palm pressed against her need.

Grace's sharp intake of breath shot straight to Alaine's heart. Would that he could pierce her without causing pain and drawing blood. Impossible. Unavoidable. Best to do the deed swiftly and thoroughly.

He slid his finger into her wet, tight place. Her body rose up to meet him. He stroked her velvet sheath, heightening her arousal, readying her for his entry.

First he had to get his breeches down. He rolled, reached for his lacing and ended up pinned to the pallet.

Grace wasted no time on pleasantries. She did to him as he'd done to her—spread light kisses over his chest, having her own sweet way with his body.

She slid downward. He held his breath. Then the minx slipped her tongue into his navel and he damn near lost his wits.

"Have mercy, Grace."

Her head came up. She smiled wickedly.

"Do you hurt, too, Alaine?"

"The most delicious hurt you can imagine."

She placed her palm on the bulge in his breeches. No amount of fabric could shield the heat, certainly not the layer of wool between her hand and his male parts. Then she untied the lacing and freed him to the open air and her gaze.

She stared at his staff with widened eyes, driving him wild. Tentatively, with the tip of her forefinger, she touched the head. "You are bigger than I expected."

Through the sizzle of heat and boost to his pride, he heard her hint of worry, and wondered who she compared him to.

He raised up on his elbows. "Expected?"

A rosy hue bloomed on her cheeks. "Sometimes, when the men drink too much ale, they…talk."

Knowing how men bragged when in their cups, Alaine could imagine what Grace might have overheard, likely in bawdy terms.

"Did their talk frighten you?"

"Nay, merely made me curious."

"And is your curiosity satisfied?"

"Not entirely."

She tugged on his breeches. He lifted his hips, then lay still as she removed his garment and boots. Shamelessly she ran her hands up his legs, along his inner thighs, but stopped short of putting her hands where he most wanted them.

"I will not object if you satisfy your curiosity entirely."

She grasped him gently, her cool fingers enclosing him. He lay back and fought for control.

"'Tis as velvet over steel," she whispered, then grew bolder, becoming more skilled with every movement of her increasingly busy hand. He let her fondle him as long as he dared, then pulled her up atop him.

No other woman had ever fitted against him this perfectly. Her soft curves melded along him in singular unity as if designed for him alone. Even as he took pleasure in the joy of skin against skin, in the kisses and caresses that led them ever closer to the physical coupling, Alaine couldn't ignore the stirring deep within his soul.

This woman, Grace, touched him in places no other woman had begun to reach.

Over the years he'd bedded other women, high- and lowborn alike, and generally enjoyed the experience. He'd given and taken pleasure with no other goal in mind but to assuage his lusty urgings.

Tonight, with Grace, he craved more.

He had no right, yet he yearned to possess her so completely she'd never want to couple with any another man. He had no right to her heart, yet he yearned for her love.

'Twas unfair to Grace to wish her eternally bound to a minstrel who roamed the kingdom, to a man she might see but a few times a year. 'Twas against both human nature and common sense for Grace to remain unwed—and to keep herself celibate, except for during his visits.

She'd not be satisfied with such a life.

While his wishes battled with what couldn't be, Alaine rolled Grace to her back and worshiped her beautiful body and bold spirit with the ritual older than time, fresher than spring.

Grace wondered at the sudden urgency of Alaine's loving, but couldn't give complaint. Never had her spirit soared so high. Each brush of his skin against hers focused her needs more acutely. Even as she writhed beneath Alaine's caresses, Grace yearned for the relief she sensed just out of her reach.

The candle sputtered. Grace feared losing the light, wanting to witness every moment until the end, in whatever form that might take.

"Alaine. The candle."

"Have you another?"

"Not in here."

He nudged her legs apart and rose up on his knees. A fingertip to her wet woman's place raised her hips off the pallet.

"This may hurt a bit, but not for long."

Beyond caring, she could only whisper, "Then hurry."

He placed his hands on her hips, lifted her to meet him, then slid inside. His entry caused a sharp pang, quickly over with, replaced by the wonder of his full possession.

Just as she became accustomed to the joining, he braced his hands on the pallet and leaned forward, causing an entirely new sensation Grace considered divine.

Alaine maintained complete control until Grace moved. She rose to meet his rhythm, taking him in deeper with each stroke. She fitted around him like a scabbard especially made for a sword—tightly yet gently, fully, with no room to spare. On the verge of release, from somewhere deep within, he drew willpower he didn't know he possessed, then thanked the Fates when the woman he wanted to pleasure burst apart in glorious fashion.

She went over the edge with her head tilted back, her expression a mixture of pain and bliss. The tremors of her inner tumult caressed him in intimate waves, lapping at the edges of his control until he plunged to the depths and succumbed.

When had a woman ever responded to him so readily with such hunger? Never. Had he ever been more willing to delay his own pleasure for a woman's sake? Not in memory.

In the aftermath of the grandest lovemaking he'd ever known, Alaine realized he must move soon.

Then a sweet smile captured Grace's lips and he didn't think he could bear to budge for the rest of the night.

She stroked the side of his face. "Now I understand why the ladies in your songs take such risks to be with their lovers."

Lovers. Aye, he and Grace were lovers, yet the word rang shallow, wholly inadequate for what they'd shared. Nor did he wish to be compared to the knights who loved their ladies and then left them for months on end, sometimes never to return. But wasn't that what he would do come morn? Leave the Wayfarer Inn and Grace until after Twelfth Night.

And after, what then? Where would she go and what would she do after she sold the inn?

Alaine rolled onto the pallet, bringing the object of his concern with him, unwilling to put any space between them just yet. He held her close and listened to her breathe, unable to imagine Grace in any place other than Wayfarer Inn.

"Grace, what would it take for you to keep the inn?"

She sighed softly. "A miracle."

He'd never performed a great feat, much less a miracle. "I should like to help, if I can."

Her head shifted on his shoulder. She kissed his cheek. "You have. I now have enough coin to purchase a goose for Christmas and hire a village boy to chop the rest of the wood. We will be warm and decently fed until I can find a buyer, even if after Twelfth Night. You are very good for business, Sir Minstrel, and I thank you."

Good enough to thank him by giving herself to him? He couldn't bear the thought that she'd made love with him out of a twisted sense of returning payment.

Nay, not Grace. She'd be more forthright, give him coin. What had happened between them was the result of undeniable physical attraction. She'd desired the coupling as much as he.

"Have you enough to purchase the retirement for your parents?"

"Nay. For that I need to sell the inn. Must we talk about this now?"

Alaine wanted to, but acknowledged that tonight should be spent loving, not talking. Time enough in the morning to find out how much money Grace needed to fix up the inn so she could stay in business. He'd return the silver she'd given him, knowing it not enough to make a big difference but enough to give her a few more days in her home, where she belonged, where he'd know where she was, where he knew her to be safe.

Her hand skimmed his belly. His loins stirred. The need to possess her again overcame him.

This time he didn't need light. He knew her body intimately, had learned where she liked most to be touched and kissed to bring her to bliss. He could see her in the dark as well as if a candle burned bright. Never would the vision of her pleasured smile leave him, burned as it was into his memory forever.

Chapter Six

Grace woke alone, the room dark but for a wisp of daylight seeping in from under the door. She closed her eyes and lay motionless, still replete and full of wonder.

Alaine made love as grandly as he sang. While her flesh yet hummed from the stroke of his fingers, she recalled the sweet love words he'd whispered in the dark. She knew her lips didn't taste like honeysuckle. Nor was her skin as smooth as rose petals or her hair as sleek as the finest silk. She didn't possess a fragile or dainty bone in her whole body, yet Alaine had likened her to a vessel fashioned of porcelain, to be cherished and handled with delicacy.

If only her lover weren't leaving this morn.

Grace swallowed hard to hold back useless tears. She'd known all along her minstrel must leave for Darby Castle to entertain for the Christmas season.

My minstrel. An unwarranted claim of possession. Alaine belonged to no one, owed no loyalty to anyone but himself—and his music, his greatest love, his very soul.

No regrets, she'd promised him, and truly couldn't say she sorrowed over the decision to lay with Alaine, though she'd rather not have to tell him fare-thee-well this morn.

Grace flung back the coverlet—and groaned.

Sweet mercy, her body ached from the vigorous activity

in which they'd engaged, especially those muscles deep within her that had yearned for Alaine's invasion and now protested because he had. A smear of blood stained her inner thighs and the bed linens, evidence of her loss of virginity, proof that she'd yielded to Alaine. Without question, she'd do so again, if he was of a mind, when he returned after Twelfth Night.

'Twas the surety of his return that kept her tears at bay while she dressed. Alaine intended to come back to fetch his horse when finished entertaining at Darby Castle.

'Twas a minstrel's life Alaine led, going from place to place to play his lute and sing his songs. He was good at and enjoyed how he made his way in the world.

Still, mightn't the time come when he wished to settle in one place? Make a home and take a wife. Sire children.

Grace sighed and chided her imagination for embarking on such a foolish flight. She had nothing to offer him as enticement. No dowry, certainly. Soon she'd not even have the inn, which might interest a man used to long hours of sometimes arduous work. She couldn't imagine a man of Alaine's ilk trading a carefree life for one of chopping wood and mending mouse holes.

Too much to hope for.

Or was it? He hadn't minded chopping wood overmuch. He surely possessed a body designed for laborious tasks.

Grappling with the vision of a life spent watching Alaine chop wood, Grace opened the door and stepped into the kitchen.

"Good morn, Grace!" Her mother stood near the worktable on which was spread a variety of food. "I was about to wake you. We have more visitors!"

"So early?"

"'Tis nearly midmorning. You slept overlong."

Midmorning? She'd never slept so late! Grace knew why. Did her mother? Hopefully not!

She glanced at the door, her heart falling.

"Has Alaine left?"

"Not as yet. He converses with the newly come travelers while I fix him a food packet."

Grace tossed on her cloak. "From where are the travelers?"

"London, I believe. Alaine knows them."

Then the travelers were likely headed north, in the same direction as Alaine. How nice 'twould be if he could make his journey in familiar company. Safer, too.

"How odd that he should meet up with acquaintances."

"Oh, more than acquaintances, I would say. Noble, too. Have a good look at his lordship's conveyance. A right fancy wagon if you ask me."

Her curiosity high, Grace went out the kitchen door.

This noble traveled in style, with a large contingent of horse-borne guards and several oxen-drawn wagons. 'Twas easy to pick out the lord. Richly garbed, gold winking from several fingers, he stood near a high-wheeled wagon. Atop the wagon bed loomed a red velvet canopy from which hung matching heavy drapes. Whoever rode inside would stay warm and dry. A right fancy wagon, indeed!

Grace glanced about for Alaine and saw him coming out of the stable—with Yseult on a lead, making his way toward the noble's fancy wagon.

If Alaine took his mare with him, then he had no compelling reason to return.

Alaine tied Yseult to the back of the wagon. "My thanks, Henry. You are sure she will not slow your progress overmuch?"

The noble gave Alaine a friendly cuff on the shoulder. "No more than this damn snow. Truly, 'tis the least I can do to see you *and* your horse home safely."

Alaine had a home? He'd not mentioned one. And wasn't he on his way to Darby Castle?

"Aye, my uncle spares no expense during the season,

and Yseult will be glad of the pampering from the stable lads. My thanks for your kind offer.''

'''Twas kind of your uncle to invite us to celebrate the season at Darby. 'Struth, 'twill be a grand Christmas.''

Grace groped for answers, and could come up with only one stunning conclusion. Alaine journeyed to Darby Castle, and from the sound of it, his uncle was the castle's lord.

Noble blood flowed through Alaine's veins.

The velvet curtain parted to a female hand. ''Father, are we nearly ready?''

''Aye, dearest, nearly.''

The curtain parted farther, revealing a lovely young woman. She smiled at Alaine.

''Do remember to bring your lute, Alaine.''

He gave her a gracious bow. ''Lady Constance. Since you are so good as to share your wagon with me, I shall certainly strive to be good company.''

''And my ladies and I shall strive to be your most ardent admirers, will we not, ladies?''

From within the wagon came female laughter, and a chorus of agreement.

Nearly overwhelmed, Grace wanted to run back into the storeroom, throw herself on her pallet and pull the coverlet over her head. She couldn't move.

For the first time she saw Alaine as he truly was—a noble playing at being a minstrel—instead of the wandering entertainer she'd wanted him to be.

She should have guessed Alaine's rank the moment she'd set eyes on Yseult, a much too expensive and quality horse for anyone but of knightly or noble class.

He's not coming back.

Grace tried to breathe, to cope with the onslaught. With her world tilted badly askew, she barely heard Alaine call her name.

She stared at the man she'd thought the most marvelous

being in the world. Whom she had led to her pallet and then dreamed of a life with.

Nobles dallied with innkeeper's daughters. They married women of their own rank. Ladies with dowries, soft hands and sweet-smelling bowers.

Mercy, how foolish she'd been.

The urge to scream at Alaine for misleading her nearly won out. Except he hadn't made her any promises, indeed, hadn't been the one who initiated their love play last night. He even, quite honorably, suggested she might have regrets.

All illusions shattered, Grace gathered up the shards of her pride and answered Alaine's summons. With each step toward him, she gained further control over the tears she refused to shed. Alaine mustn't see how badly she hurt.

Grace dipped into a curtsy before Henry, a gesture every noble expected from a peasant.

"Henry, this is Grace Brewer, the innkeeper's daughter," Alaine said. "She assists her parents in the running of the Wayfarer Inn."

Henry gave her the barest nod of acknowledgment.

Forcefully reminded of her position, Grace sought refuge in her role as caretaker of the Wayfarer Inn.

"Greetings, my lord," she mumbled, then turned to Alaine with what she hoped a stoic expression. "My mother prepares your food packet and will bring it out anon. Is there aught else you require of us before you depart?"

Alaine's eyes narrowed. She chose not to wonder what he was thinking, for it no longer mattered. Within minutes he'd be gone and life would go on as if he'd never been here.

"Nay. I believe I have everything I need."

"Then I shall bid you all good journey."

More than ready to escape, Grace took her leave. She

got no farther than three steps when Alaine appeared in her path. Though tempted to walk around him, she halted.

"A rather terse farewell," he commented, bewildered.

What did he expect? The embrace and parting kiss of a lover? One night of bliss didn't make them lovers, only a man and woman who'd shared a pallet. He was about to walk out of her life without remorse. She owed him nothing in return.

"I beg pardon if I offended, my lord. I did ask if there was aught else you required."

His hand rose as if to touch her. She stepped back, knowing she couldn't bear it. His fingers clenched before his hand fell back to his side. If it was sorrow that flashed in his eyes, it was quickly gone.

"You gave no offense. Indeed, my stay here has been amiable. I would recommend the inn to any traveler requiring a good meal and soft pallet."

She wanted to scratch his eyes out.

"Your kindness is appreciated. Do mention the inn to all and sundry, minstrels in particular, who will be welcomed most warmly. I have learned they are very good for business."

Christmas day dawned cloudy and gray, but nothing could stop the revelers in the great hall from feasting, drinking and generally having a grand time. Seated in a high-backed chair on the dais, Alaine sipped at an after-supper goblet of fine wine, watching a group of small boys try to imitate—without much success—the feats of the acrobats who had performed last eve.

Holly and colorful silk banners decorated the hall. An enormous Yule log crackled in the hearth.

Guests had robed themselves in their finest garments, most in jewel-hued velvet. Fingers glittered gold and silver in the firelight.

Uncle Matthew had begrudgingly admitted that Alaine

might have made a good choice in trading sword for lute, a gift Alaine always hoped for but never dared expect. A bit later he'd pick up the lute, lead the guests through the traditional carols and, perhaps, sing them the song he'd finally finished this morn.

A perfect Christmas, or it would be if he could shake his bad humor.

Good for business.

Grace had as much as admitted she'd slept with him as payment for his entertainment, and wouldn't mind the company of another minstrel she could welcome most warmly.

He'd expected an affectionate parting and received a brusque send-off. Even after two days of pondering, he wasn't sure how the woman who'd been so warm and giving could turn so cold and contrary.

Regrets? Possibly. Or mayhap he'd said or done something to offend her—though he had no notion what that might be.

Just as he'd always remember the pleasured smile on Grace's face, 'twould now be marred by the bluntness of her rejection.

And why was he wallowing in melancholy over a rebuff by a woman he'd now never see again? What sense was there in going back to the Wayfarer Inn to see a woman who welcomed him only for his value to her in coin?

Why, in a grand hall filled with cheerful people, did he feel so damn alone?

"Alaine? Where are you?" From beside him, Aunt Faye leaned over to put a hand on his forearm. "You sit here beside me yet seem so far away."

He managed a smile for the woman who'd been like a mother to him and done her utmost to make his homecoming joyful.

"Not so far that I do not hear you."

"'Tis not like you to be so quiet or still. You have not

been gone so long that I do not know you as well as I did from the day you came to us. Give over, Alaine.''

Well he remembered the day he'd arrived at Darby, grieving for his parents, who'd succumbed to severe fever, unsure of his welcome. Matthew and Faye, his only living relations, had given him a true home without reservation. As a child, he'd wept on Faye's shoulder. As a man, he'd not burden her with a tale of woe on a day meant for joy.

''Mayhap I mellow in my advancing age.''

''And mayhap you think my wits grow dull in mine.''

''Never.'' He kissed her cheek. ''I merely need a distraction from my own thoughts, is all.''

''Hmm. Well, be closedmouthed if you wish, but I will have the truth from you yet, mark my words. In the meantime, tell me, do you intend to sing us your new song this night?''

He'd told no one of the song. ''What makes you believe I have prepared a new song?''

Faye flashed a wicked smile. ''When I passed your door last night, I heard you playing. Since I did not recognize the tune, I assumed you prepared a new song. Am I right?''

Alaine inwardly sighed. ''Right, as always.''

She tilted her head. ''Is it the song that troubles you? Does it not flow as you wish it to?''

'Twas his finest work yet.

''I believe the song good, but you must judge for yourself.''

''I can barely wait to hear.''

She turned back to her meal. Alaine glanced around the hall, noting the whereabouts of several men he wished to speak to about buying the Wayfarer Inn, a few of whom he'd already approached. All of them had the means.

Grace had dismissed his wish to help her, but then, she hadn't been truly aware of his ability to help. Nobles were always looking for ways to increase their fortunes. He needed to convince only one of these men to purchase the inn and let Grace and her parents remain as caretakers.

How were the Brewers celebrating Christmas? Had Grace bought the goose for their meal? Had she noticed that he'd placed the silver coin—as well as all the coppers the villagers had placed in his cup—in her money box?

Uncle Matthew rose from his chair, a signal to all that the feast was done and the evening's revelry should begin. Alaine reached to the floor for his lute and a silver bucket.

Carols soon echoed from the holly-decorated rafters. Wine and ale flowed freely. Alaine lost count of the number of toasts offered to Matthew and Faye's good health. Gold and silver coins overflowed the bucket at his feet.

Toward the end of the evening, when Faye's stares became more expectant, Alaine strummed a loud, discordant flourish that never failed to silence a room.

Into the ensuing hush he plucked bright tones and began the as yet untitled song of the lovely lady and the knight who loved her. He'd chosen the style of an *alba*—a song of impending dawn—in five verses, each a mingling of praise for the beloved and curses against the coming of morn when lovers must part.

He sang first in the expected French, letting the music and the words course through him, then began again in English.

Alaine envisioned Grace, her loving hands roaming his flesh, the smile of pleasure curving her lips. He missed the sound of her voice, the spark of mischief glittering in her eyes, the scent of woman that belonged to Grace alone.

> "Of that sweet wind that comes from far away
> Have I drunk deep of my beloved's breath
> Yea, that of my Love so dear and gay
> Ah God! that dawn should come so soon!"

Would that the end had not come so soon. Would that he could return to the inn and he and Grace could begin again.

Would that he knew what had gone amiss.

The last tones reverberated through the hall. Alaine put his lute aside, his heart heavy and emotions drained. The sound of a woman's teary sniff turned his head. Indeed, several of the women's eyes were red rimmed.

The hall erupted in a cacophony of shouts, banging cups and stomping feet. Alaine stood to accept the accolade, his pride boosted by the volume and length of their appreciation. Yet, 'twas a hollow accomplishment, for the woman he wanted to play the song for, who'd inspired him, would never hear it.

Faye approached him, wiping away a tear. "Now I know why you are so morose. You must love and miss her very much."

She might have punched him in the gut, her words hit so hard. Miss Grace? Aye, more than he could say.

Love?

Was it love that befuddled one's mind when beholding a woman of such rare beauty that only he seemed to see it? Did love make a heart yearn for a touch, a kind word, a smile? Had love goaded him to hurry home—not so much to see his family but to find a buyer for the inn?

He'd been singing of love for years, and only now truly knew the emotion firsthand.

"I suppose I do," he told his aunt, and a strange, not unpleasant, quiet settled in his soul.

"Then why did you not bring her home with you?"

Would Grace have come if he'd asked? Likely not. She saw her duty as clear—care for her parents. She'd not have left Watt and Nelda alone at Christmas. 'Struth, she mightn't have accepted an invitation anyway, given her mood the morn he left.

"I do not believe my love returned."

"Fool woman."

Her ire on his behalf made him smile. "Grace is no fool."

"A lovely name, Grace." Faye tilted her head. "Alaine, have you told her of your love?"

A lump formed in his throat, unsure if he could ever tell Grace for fear she'd either not believe him or, worse, not care. He shook his head.

"Fool man."

His aunt flounced off in a huff, leaving him standing alone with his lute and bucket of coins. Not a fortune, but a hell of a lot of money.

Enough to buy an inn?

He bent down to finger the coins. What if he bought the Wayfarer Inn? Grace and her parents could hire the help they needed to have the place fixed up. Buy whitewash, nails and latches. Planks for the fences. Patching for mouse holes.

And Grace? If he eased her burden to so great a degree, might she smile at him once more, mayhap grow to love him, even marry him?

Dare he ask for so much in this season of miracles?

More snow had fallen. However, several horses in his uncle's stable were more than capable of enduring a harsh trip to the inn. His aunt and uncle wouldn't be happy about his leaving before the Twelfth Night celebration, but his aunt might understand, and perhaps he could bring Grace back with him.

Alaine hurriedly scooped up the coins, then went to find his uncle, planning to leave on the first morn he thought it safe for both man and beast.

Chapter Seven

Grace placed the largest of the three meat pies on her father's trencher. The last scraps of the Christmas goose, drowning in thick, spicy gravy, wrapped in flaky yet sturdy crust, was a shameless attempt to improve his humor.

She'd already endured his silence—after his short, pointed tirade—all morning, ever since she dared utter the word *retirement*. If he didn't start talking to her during nooning, the remainder of the day would be very long, indeed.

While Mother hadn't been talkative, she hadn't lapsed into furious silence. Grace knew that if she won her father over then her mother would follow his lead.

Intent on returning to normalcy, she sat down to her own meal. The pie tasted like dust, went down her throat in a lump and hit her stomach like a rock. She ate half before she pushed it aside.

"You cannot ignore me forever, Father. Pretending a problem does not exist will not make it go away. I know you do not care for my solution, but neither have you suggested another."

"The inn is our home. I will not leave," he muttered, then took another bite of pie.

She'd heard the exact sentiment this morn, just before

he'd stomped out the door. He may not have softened his position, but at least he wasn't shouting.

"I know the thought of leaving distresses you."

"Then we will not leave."

"We cannot afford to stay."

Mother crossed herself. "The Lord will provide. He sent Alaine to us, did he not?"

A blessing and a curse. One could argue that a darker power had arranged for his horse to stumble and twist her leg. Without Alaine's visit, Grace couldn't have afforded the Christmas goose. Because of Alaine's visit, her parents considered the money box a treasure chest.

They'd been innkeepers most of their lives. Surely they knew the extra money only a reprieve, not their salvation—just as she now knew her time with Alaine only a bright moment of joy, not a prelude to future happiness.

She'd come to peace over their difference in rank, and realized his music was his first and all-encompassing love. She had yet to forgive herself for her brusque manner the morning they'd parted. He'd done nothing to deserve her anger and waspish tongue. Alaine must think her a harridan, but there was nothing she could do about it now, no way to ask his forgiveness.

"Alaine's visit filled the money box, but the funds will dwindle over winter. I doubt the Lord has arranged for another minstrel to come our way anytime soon." She leaned forward. "That is why I want to make arrangements for you with the abbot now, while we still have the extra funds."

Father dusted crust crumbs from his hands. "Better to spend the money on whitewash and nails."

"And who will spread the whitewash and pound the nails?"

"I will help you, so will your mother."

Grace bit her bottom lip to keep from blurting out that

neither one of them had the strength or energy for heavy or grueling work.

"So we spread whitewash and put in a few nails. What good would it do? Business has not been good for the past two years, ever since…your wounding. I see no reason to think 'twill be better next year." She sighed. "I accept that the dire state of the inn and lack of patrons is my fault—"

"Not so!" His ferocity set her back. He glanced at the arm wounded when protecting Grace from an attacker. "'Tis that blasted noble's fault, damn his hide. He was not satisfied with my blood. He threatened to ruin us, to spread the tale to all and sundry of how we ill-treated guests."

Grace gasped. "A lie!"

"True, but he thought himself ill-treated because I would not allow him his way with you. He considered a wench to warm his pallet as part of the service due him, and believed I should order you to bend to his wishes. When I did not, he decided to teach us a lesson on how to serve our betters."

Grace felt the blood drain from her face. "Why did you not tell me this?"

"You had already left the taproom in tears. I saw no reason to upset you further. We were prepared for a lull in business, Grace. Perhaps not this long or this harsh, but 'twas expected."

"And you expected your arm to fully recover, did you not?"

"I did," he admitted. "But when I finally accepted the loss, you had already taken over so many of the chores that I thought 'twould not matter, that we could still wait out the lull. I believe we still can."

"I believe he is right, dear," Mother injected. "And now we have an ally in Alaine."

Confused, Grace asked, "What can Alaine do now that he is gone?"

"He can help us rebuild our reputation. He enjoyed his stay here, he told me so. If he recommends us to his friends, especially his minstrel friends, we could be prosperous again come spring."

'Twas too much to hope that a good word from Alaine would lead patrons to the inn's door. She also doubted her parents knew she'd given him a less than warm fare-thee-well.

Truly, he'd made her no promises, done all one could expect a man to do to ensure she'd have no regrets. And she hadn't, not until realizing Alaine's noble birth, a circumstance neither of them could change, placed him far out of her reach.

What was done was done. He'd gone back to the world in which he belonged, one of privilege and comfort and music. She expected nothing of him, and neither should her parents.

"'Tis a fragile string on which to tie our future. We could starve before Alaine thinks to mention the inn to any of his friends, longer still before they pass our way in their travels."

"So we give up?" Father asked. "Do we let the bastard who set out to ruin us win? Nay, Grace. We have not held out this long to give up now."

His pride had suffered so severely she hated to deal it another blow, but if 'twas what it took to make him see the reality of their situation, then strike she would.

"Who is truly the winner if the inn falls down atop our heads, or we end up in early graves? Mother will fall first, then you, if I do not precede you by working to exhaustion. Is that winning, Father?"

His eyes narrowed. "You so blithely consign us to graves if we stay. 'Struth, Grace, you make it sound as if finding a buyer will be so easy. Just where, in the dead of winter, with the inn in disrepair, do you intend to find someone willing to purchase and fix everything that needs repair?''

A very valid question, one to which she'd given much thought.

''I will go to the abbot. If he does not wish to purchase the inn, then he may know of someone who does. I may even be able to convince him to barter the inn's ownership for your retirement.''

Father opened his mouth, closed it again.

''What of you, Grace?'' Mother asked. ''You have said nothing of your plans.''

'''Tis my hope the new owner will let me stay on, serve ale in trade for bed and bread. If not, I shall have to look for work elsewhere. Heaven knows, I have the experience to manage an inn, not just serve ale.''

Her parents exchanged a look she knew well—one of concern over their child's well-being.

''You must not worry over me,'' she said firmly. ''I am young and healthy and capable. I can care for myself. What I can no longer do is provide for the two people I love most, in the manner they deserve. If I know you two are sheltered and fed, within calling distance of the monks' aid if it is needed, 'twill give me peace of mind.''

Father shook his head.

Grace pressed onward. ''Would it not be nice to rest for a change? Enjoy your remaining days without the hardship of rising early and working till the sun sets?''

'''Tis what I have done all of my life, Grace. Without something to do, what sense rising?''

Grace thought hard and fast. ''Then work in the abbey, with the monks who oversee the abbey's hospitality. Surely they would welcome the aid of a man who knows how to treat guests. And Mother might lend a hand in the brewery, or the kitchen. You need not be idle, simply work at a more leisurely pace.''

Both were silent for a long time. Mother finally asked

in a small voice, "If the abbot sees fit to purchase the inn, might he let us all stay as caretakers?"

Grace had no notion. 'Twas not the way things were usually done. The hope on her mother's face was painful to behold.

"I can but ask. Father, what say you? The weather has turned mild again. I could go to Glaxton Abbey and be back within the space of a day."

He glanced from her to her mother and back again. His chest rose and fell twice before he answered. "Ask."

Seeing no one in the yard, Alaine dismounted in front of the Wayfarer Inn, dropped the reins of the battle-trained horse to the ground and sped into the taproom.

Watt and Nelda sat at the trestle table nearest the hearth, so forlorn neither uttered a greeting, merely stared at him. On the verge of tears, Nelda's bottom lip trembled. Something horrible had happened. His heart thudded against his chest.

"Where is Grace?"

Watt cleared his throat. "She left several hours ago for Glaxton Abbey, to see the abbot."

His knees nearly gave way with relief that Grace was alive and well. Then he realized why she'd gone to the abbey, to purchase the retirement. She couldn't have sold the inn so quickly! But apparently she had, somehow, if she was off to purchase the retirement. Hellfire and damnation, he'd arrived too late with a sack of money in his pack and a much rehearsed marriage proposal on his lips.

Grace didn't need his money, his help—him. She'd done well enough all on her own.

Alaine eased onto the bench beside Nelda. She gave him a wan smile.

"What brings you back so soon?" Watt asked.

Love of Grace. Misguided belief in miracles.

"I had hoped to purchase the inn."

Watt's eyes narrowed. "Grace told you of her plans?"

Alaine understood her father's anger. "Only in passing, and only because I pressed her. To whom did she sell?"

"She has not—yet. She goes to bargain with the abbot."

His stomach flipped. Hope welled up as he bolted from the bench. Chances were she'd already arrived at the abbey. Chances were she'd talked the abbot into the purchase. Did he have a chance in hell of catching Grace before it was too late?

"Watt, come get my lute."

Alaine was out the door and had his belongings unstrapped from the horse's back before Watt shuffled out the door. He handed the lute over, then pulled down the heavy pack containing a few pieces of dry clothing sprinkled generously with coins.

"Alaine, what are you about?"

Alaine led the way into the inn. "Off to catch Grace before she sells the inn." He dumped the pack into the corner. "Wish me good fortune and pray Grace is a bad bargainer."

"What would a minstrel want with an inn?"

"I want Grace. The inn just happens to come with her."

Nelda finally smiled. "Good fortune, Alaine."

Watt frowned. "Grace always makes a good bargain."

"Then hope I catch her before she has the chance." Alaine hurried toward the door, then stopped. "I assume the abbot will somehow know she has permission to negotiate on your behalf."

"She carries a parchment. Grace wrote it out, and I put my mark to it."

Damn.

The road to Glaxton Abbey proved little better than a well-worn path to the east. For the entire two leagues, Alaine pushed the horse as fast as he dared over the snow-slicked ground. A set of footprints marched along the path, leading him steadily eastward.

Grace's footprints.

He noted where she rested, saw where she must have slipped and fallen, and prayed as hard as he'd ever prayed that she wasn't hurt, but that her journey proved so taxing she walked slowly.

What if she arrived in good time? Abbots were busy people, especially during Christmas. Perhaps the abbot wouldn't grant Grace an audience right away, would make her wait until his schedule allowed—perhaps tomorrow.

Alaine doubted his luck would run so much in his favor.

The horse withstood the rigors of the ride. Within sight of the abbey, Alaine urged the beast to a gallop across the wide expanse of cleared land surrounding the imposing stone buildings.

The gate stood open. He passed through and brought the horse to a halt just within, then bore down on the first monk he spotted.

"I seek a young woman who came here this morning to see the abbot. Where might I find her?"

"Likely the abbot's office." He pointed. "Through that door, up the stairway. You will find the abbot's secretary at the top."

"My thanks, good monk."

"May the joy of this most holy season be with you, my son."

Joy of the season. Alaine held the good wish close as he again ground-reined the horse and sped up the stairway.

He'd visited enough abbeys in his travels that the wealth of the Church no longer awed him. He ignored the gold-gilt frames surrounding paintings of saints and deceased bishops. The bright tapestries held no interest. Only the round-faced, tonsured monk sitting behind a desk of dark, richly carved wood could help him find his own treasure.

"I seek Grace Brewer. Is she here?"

The monk rose from his chair and waved a hand toward

the huge, ornate doors to his right. "She is speaking with the abbot. If I might inquire—halt! You may not—"

Alaine stepped through the doorway and quickly closed the door behind him.

Grace stood before the most ostentatious desk Alaine had ever seen, her hand outstretched, holding a piece of parchment.

"Grace. Wait. You need not sell the inn."

She spun around. Her eyes went wide. "Alaine?"

He crossed the room quickly. "One and the same."

The abbot, garbed in the full regalia of a man in high position in the Church, rose from his thronelike chair. "Who are you, young man?" he huffed. "How dare you enter my chamber both uninvited and unannounced?"

Alaine did him the courtesy of a courtly bow. "Alaine of Darby, Your Grace. Forgive the intrusion, but I must speak with Mistress Brewer forthwith." He snatched the parchment and grabbed hold of Grace's hand. "The Wayfarer Inn is no longer for sale. Come, I will take you home."

He tugged. She resisted. He should have known this wouldn't be so easy.

"What do you mean the inn is no longer for sale?"

He couldn't envision making explanations and begging Grace's beautiful hand in marriage in the presence of an abbot. 'Twould be hard enough in private. So he took the easy way out.

"Your father has changed his mind." A small lie, and Watt would certainly do so later. After all, there was enough money in his pack to buy the inn four times over, or so Uncle Matthew had assured him.

Her brow furrowed in confusion. "But—"

"Give the abbot his due, my dear, then we shall be on our way and the abbot can return to his prayers."

The abbot came around his desk, his mouth pursed. "Unhand the girl."

Alaine never hesitated. "I think not."

"Alaine of Darby, you say?" he asked, the question a threat.

"Sir Alaine of Darby, nephew of Lord Matthew, dear friend of Lord John of Gaunt."

The mention of John deflated the abbot, as Alaine knew it would. He'd have to apologize to John for invoking his name, but guessed his friend wouldn't mind when given the reason. This time, when Alaine tugged Grace's hand, she dipped a small curtsy and followed him out the door.

Too confused for rational thought, Grace grabbed hold of one of the many questions racing through her head.

"Who is John of Gaunt?"

"The king's exchequer."

"The king's—" Grace halted at the top of the stairway, pulling Alaine up short. "You are a friend of the king's exchequer?"

"Actually, I am the king's favorite fencing partner and the queen's favorite minstrel. May we go now?"

"Nay. Hold a moment." Grace willed her composure into obedience as best she could, having been dragged from the abbot's chamber by a minstrel who refused to let go of her hand.

Well, she was holding on rather tightly, too, had no intention of letting go unless she must.

What was Alaine doing here? He'd planned to stay at Darby Castle until after Twelfth Night. He must have gone to the inn and talked to her parents, who'd told him where to look for her or, more likely, sent him after her. The utter grief on their faces upon her departure this morning still haunted her.

"Father changed his mind?"

He smiled, like a little boy caught in mischief. "Come, I will explain everything on the way home."

At the bottom of the stairway stood a large, mean-looking black stallion. Alaine dropped Grace's hand to pick up the reins. Once mounted, he reached for her hand again.

"Think you can swing up behind me?"

Grace looked at the great height and shook her head.

Alaine chuckled. "Then give me both hands, use my foot for a boost."

'Twas an awkward mounting, but she soon sat crossways on his lap, his arms around her for support. A cozy seat, or would be if she weren't up so high. She turned her face into his shoulder until her stomach settled. The horse's gait was smooth, and Alaine's body warm. Lulled into contentment, she wished the inn more than two leagues away.

She hated to disturb the quiet peace of riding through the countryside snuggled up to Alaine, but those questions returned to nag at her.

"You said you would explain."

She felt him sigh.

"I suppose I should first tell you that your father has not truly changed his mind, not yet. He will, however, when I tell him about the buyer I found for the inn."

Grace stiffened. "You lied to the abbot? What buyer?"

He took a long time to answer. "Me."

She sat up straighter, the better to look at his set jaw, to vent her disbelief and growing ire.

"Alaine, you chopped wood to earn your supper that first night. Now you ask me to believe you have enough coin to buy the inn?"

"I do. 'Tis at the inn, in my pack."

Alaine braced for the tirade he felt and saw coming. Then a single tear trickled down her cheek.

"We have no need of charity, Sir Alaine. Set me down and I will go back and see if the abbot is yet agreeable."

Sir Alaine? He halted the horse. "I do not purchase the inn out of charity. I do so because...because..."

Jesu, he'd never stumbled over words before. 'Twas how he made his livelihood. He'd so carefully planned exactly what he would say to her, and now that single tear tied his tongue in knots.

No words seemed the right ones, not even the song he'd written for her.

"Because I want you, Grace. The inn and taking care of your parents just happen to come with you."

She pursed her lips. "Me?"

"If you will have me. Marry me and we shall raise a whole new brood of innkeepers."

Her anger eased, but not her reservations, apparently.

"Knights do not marry innkeepers' daughters."

"Aye, well, someone once told me I could not become a minstrel, either, and I did so anyway."

"Oh, Alaine." She wrapped her arms around his neck.

He liked the feeling, but not the tone of her voice. Very aware she hadn't given him an answer, he hugged her hard, nuzzled into her neck, seeking her scent to give him courage.

"I love you, Grace, cannot imagine my life without you. The money is yours to do with as you please. Fix up the Wayfarer. Buy another inn in some other town. Toss the money into a river, for all I care. Just let me share your life, let me wake beside you every morning."

She backed away, eyes wet, her smile heartbreakingly sad.

"I love you, too, Alaine. I would marry you in an instant if I knew you wouldn't grow to hate me for it."

He opened his mouth to object; she placed a finger on his lips.

"Alaine, what of your music? It is your soul. You would die inside if you must give up being a renowned minstrel for chopping wood and mending mouse holes."

Granted, he'd miss the traveling, the excitement, even

the money. But the music? How did he make her understand?

He kissed the finger at his lips, removed her hand.

"The music never leaves me. I can make people happy or bring them to tears. It used to be enough, but not anymore, not since you entered my heart and became a part of the music."

She didn't look convinced. "Could you truly be happy singing only in the taproom of an inn?"

"Should I feel a pressing need to entertain a larger crowd, we can go up to Darby Castle and I can sing my fill. My uncle would be delighted. In fact, if I do not take you there within days my aunt may never speak to me again."

"Surely not."

"On my honor." He brushed a long strand of her golden hair back from cheeks beginning to dry, a mouth touched with a true smile. "I swear, my love, if I had to choose one over the other…well, I could be happy just singing you love songs every night. You inspired one, you know."

"Did I? Sing it for me."

"Tonight, just before dawn."

She sighed and curled up into him again. 'Twas nice, but she hadn't yet given him an answer.

"Grace, you do mean to marry me."

She smiled up at him, her eyes shining with love, giving him the answer he craved without words, setting them both on a path to forever and ever.

"I should be a fool not to marry you," she said wryly. "Have you not heard how very good minstrels are for business?"

This time the words held no sting, only humor. Minx.

Alaine set the stallion to a comfortable pace, the words to a new song coming together. One about a minstrel, an innkeeper's daughter and miracles.

*   *   *   *   *

TORI PHILLIPS

After receiving her degree in theater arts from the University of San Diego, Tori Phillips worked at MGM Studios, acted in summer stock and appeared in Paramount Pictures' *The Great Gatsby*. For the past twenty years she has been a docent and actress at the Folger Shakespeare Library in Washington, D.C., where she researches material for her historical novels. Tori has written short stories for *Teen* magazine and *Sassy* magazine, freelance newspaper features, poetry, and has published four plays for Dramatic Publishing Company. She has won a number of writing awards, including the prestigious Maggie Award for Excellence in Historical Romance, and her work has been nominated by *Romantic Times Magazine* for a Reviewer's Choice Award. *Publishers Weekly* praises Tori, saying that "she's literate, witty and tells a good story." Tori lives in northern Virginia with her husband, Marty. When she is not working at her computer, she relaxes by reading and ice skating—though not at the same time. Tori loves to hear from readers. Please write her at P.O. Box 10703, Burke, VA 22009-0703.

Please address questions and book requests to:
Harlequin Reader Service
U.S.: 3010 Walden Ave., P.O. Box 1325, Buffalo, NY 14269
Canadian: P.O. Box 609, Fort Erie, Ont. L2A 5X3

TWELFTH KNIGHT
Tori Phillips

To three very special little friends of mine:
Maddie, Ryan and Kelly.

Chapter One

"Some excellent jests, fire-new from the mint."
—*Twelfth Night*

Snape Castle, Northumberland, England
November 1553

"I am out of patience with your peevish humor," thundered Sir Guy Cavendish to his only unmarried daughter, Alyssa. "'Tis no matter if you want it or not. I vow that you shall be wed before February."

Alyssa stared at her father with disbelief. Normally the most patient of men, Guy had allowed the infamous Cavendish temper to rise to surface. She took a deep breath. "I refuse to marry anyone you have to *buy* for me, Papa. I am not a goose in the marketplace."

Guy stuck out his chin. "If you were as gentle as your sisters, I would not have to offer a princely fortune to entice suitors for you."

"*Mais oui,*" Lady Celeste added from her chair by the hearthside. "True beauty begins within your heart and so radiates outward. That is how you will win a man's love." She flashed a smile at her tall husband.

Alyssa rolled her eyes to the ceiling of the counting room. How could her intelligent parents be so obtuse? "I refuse to play the fool to catch myself a bigger fool. And I am *not* like Gillian," she added vehemently.

Why couldn't her parents understand how much Alyssa hated being a twin? She loathed being regarded as one half of a whole; the mirror image of sweet, impossibly perfect Gillian, whose sugary smiles and mealymouthed platitudes reaped universal approval. Yearning for recognition of her own unique attributes, Alyssa pursued an independent course that had often led to misunderstandings and punishment. Adversity had only strengthened her resolve to be herself.

Sighing, Celeste returned to her embroidery. "*Ma foi!* You speak the truth. Gillian has a happy marriage and a babe on the way. Don't *you* desire this same happiness for yourself, *cherie?*"

Alyssa looked away. Of course she did! But not with a husband who had to be purchased. "I won't be shackled to a knave."

Guy narrowed his eyes. "What was so wrong with Sir Nathaniel Falwood that you felt it necessary to dispatch him with his lute hanging around his neck like a ruff collar? He comes from a good family."

Alyssa snorted. "Oh, he had a nice face—and a scheming mind. While he praised my beauty out of one side of his mouth, he asked you countless questions about my dowry with the other. He found your wealth considerably more interesting than my company."

Guy ran his fingers through his silvered hair. "You never gave Lord Falwood half a chance to prove himself."

Alyssa tossed her head. "I knew the measure of that hedgepig before he opened his mouth. You should be glad that I saved your estate from his grasping fingers."

Guy squared his shoulders. "Enough of this prattling, missy! I grow weary of arguing with you. You are already two-and-twenty with nary a marriage prospect within a hundred miles. A few more years of this stubbornness, and you will become too sour for even my gold to sweeten. My mind is made up. Come this Christmas season, I will host as many young men of the court as I can lure with the fortune you spurn. By the thirteenth day of Christmas, you will be betrothed to one of them!''

Alyssa opened her mouth to protest, caught her mother's warning look and remained silent. Spinning on her heel, she fled from the chamber. She did not pause until she had reached the sanctuary of her bedchamber. Scooping up her beloved cat that dozed among her pillows, she held it against her cheek. "How can my parents do this horrible thing to me, Mika? This year, I wish that Advent would last forever.''

Queen Mary's court at Greenwich near London
November 1553

Hearing his name called, Sir Robert Maxwell looked up from the thorny chess problem on the board before him. He smiled when he saw his boyhood friend stride down the gallery toward him.

"How now, Nate? Back so soon? Methought you had gone a-wooing.''

Sir Nathaniel Falwood sank into the opposite chair. "Peace, Max! I am lucky to have escaped with my life.''

Max chuckled. "So you had second thoughts about wedding?''

Nate touched a fresh scar on his cheekbone. "Aye, when I met the hellcat. 'Tis no great wonder her father offers such a rich dowry.''

Max twirled the ivory queen piece. "Indeed?'' he murmured.

Nate grimaced. "I hear that my Lord Cavendish has just raised his stakes—twelve thousand pounds in ready cash plus the title to a plot of land that brings in two thousand pounds during a good year.''

Max whistled through his teeth. Though he was a rich man, the Cavendish dowry took away his breath. ''Is the lady a hag?''

Nate shook his head. ''Nay, that is the devilish part. The wench is a beauty with hair the color of midnight and bright blue eyes. Her figure is tall and slim and her breasts are full ripened, as far as I could see, but mind you, she did not allow me a close inspection.''

''A modest woman?''

''A shrew straight from hell and therein lies the problem.''

Max replaced the queen piece on the board. ''*Not* a modest maiden? No giggles, no sudden blushes? No voice that stammers or is tongue-tied?''

Nate barked a wry laugh. ''Hardly! Gentle manners are unknown to Alyssa Cavendish and her words are laced with vinegar and wormwood. She would enchant a unicorn if she smiled, but I never saw her do so, except—'' He stopped suddenly.

''Except when?'' Max prodded. This reluctant bride sounded very intriguing. ''Tell me what made the lady smile.''

''When she crowned me with my lute and said I was out of tune,'' he snapped. ''And she is no lady by any definition of the word.''

Lounging back in his chair, Max pondered Nate's description of the Cavendish girl. His extensive experience with women had taught him to look for underlying reasons when frowns and tantrums blotted out smiles and sweet disposition. Perhaps unhappiness was the key to Lady Alyssa's churlish behavior. His interest warmed. ''I turned thirty years on my last birthday,'' he mused. '''Tis time I settled down. Tell me more of this minx.''

Nate gaped at him. ''Surely you jest! I would not wish

Alyssa Cavendish on my worst enemy, let alone my best friend. There are enough posies here in Greenwich to tempt you.''

Max waved away the idea. ''Young girls are too bland for my taste. I seek a woman with some fire in her blood.''

Nate shook his head. ''You are already rich enough. I cannot think why you wish to consider a match made in hell.''

''She's that bad, eh?'' Max grinned.

''You have lost your wits. I tell you plainly, Alyssa is a shrew.''

Max's grin widened. The idea of taming this spitfire to his will would be a welcome diversion from his tedious life. ''I wager you a thousand gold crowns that I can win the heart of this paragon of misdirected virtue.''

Nate slapped his knee. ''Sweet revenge! I would be glad to relieve you of your money, if you insist on this tomfoolery.''

''You think I cannot do it?''

''Exactly!''

Max held out his hand. ''Then we have a wager. Agreed?''

Nate shook it firmly. '''Twould be worth twice that amount to see you married to that baggage.''

A ghost of a smile hovered on Max's lips. ''Did I say anything about *marriage,* Nate? My wager is only to win the chit's affection.''

''God's death! I should have remembered what a rogue you are.''

Max's brain was already spinning with plans for this new adventure. He knew of Sir Guy's open invitation to the court's bachelors to join the Cavendish family at Snape Castle for the Christmas festivities. Max would be there, but not in the obvious guise of a suitor. He would gain entry to Alyssa's heart through the back door. He had to work quickly to gather everything he would need. Christmas was a scant five weeks away.

Snape Castle, December 23

Molly, Alyssa's maid, peered around her mistress's door. "Are ye deaf, m'lady?" she asked. Having dressed Alyssa since she was in leading strings, Molly was the only person in the house who dared to speak to Alyssa with such impertinence. "Can ye not hear the trumpets?"

Alyssa dismissed the cacophony blaring below her window. "Another suitor, I warrant? Does this make three or four?" In self-defense, Alyssa planned to spend as much time in her chamber as possible to avoid the bandycocks that now strutted around Snape's great hall.

Molly crossed to the window, rubbed the mist from one of the panes, then looked out. "Nay, m'lady. 'Tis the Lord of Misrule who has come."

Alyssa pretended to yawn. "Ah, well, let us pray that Peter Sheepshanks has learned a few new jests and songs for this season. I swear he has not changed one jot of his repertoire for the past five years. Even his best gibes last Christmastide were wearisome."

Molly chuckled. "Ye are in for a surprise, m'lady. 'Tis not old Peter at all, but a new man straight from the court, they say." She pressed her nose against the glass. "By my larkin, he *is* a handsome devil!"

Alyssa looked up from her embroidery frame. "Indeed?"

"Come see for yerself." Molly rubbed the pane again with her sleeve.

Alyssa jabbed her needle into the cloth, then sauntered over to the window. Any new entertainer would be better than rusty Sheepshanks. She rubbed a diamond pane and peered out. The courtyard below seethed with more activity than at Gillian's wedding over a year ago. A train of mules filled the enclosed area. Several young men, dressed in colorful tights and tunics, unloaded a large number of heavy-looking boxes and lumpy canvas bags.

Two mounted pages, also dressed in colorful motley, continued to blow on their beflagged trumpets. The boys' puffed cheeks were red with the cold air and their exertions. In the center of the chaos was a broad-shouldered man astride a prancing milk-white charger.

The handblown glass distorted the player's features. Alyssa opened the window for a better look. Molly stood on tiptoe behind her.

"See?" crowed the maid in Alyssa's ear. "He is a fine piece of work."

"Hush up, Molly," snapped Alyssa. "You have the voice of a bullfrog."

The new Lord of Misrule must have heard the maid. Glancing up at the window, he caught Alyssa in his gaze. For a long breathless heartbeat, the man stared boldly at her; mischief glinted in his dark eyes. Then his handsome face creased into a wicked grin. Sweeping off his peacock-plumed hat, he bowed from his saddle. The highlights in his dark brown hair gleamed in the sun's wintry light. Then, in a single graceful motion, he alighted from his horse and turned his back to her while he directed his minions where to put his excessive baggage.

"Fills out his tights nicely, don't he?" Molly observed.

Alyssa did not reprimand Molly for her wanton comment. The man's green-and-white-striped hose stretched around his muscular thighs and snugly curved over his tight backside. Alyssa could barely breathe. Her heart jolted into her throat and lodged there. Blood pounded in her temples. She gripped the stone windowsill for support.

"Oh, there will be some high jinks in the kitchens this coming fortnight," Molly predicted with relish. "I'll not be surprised if that handsome scoundrel seduces at least three of the scullery maids."

Something in the pit of Alyssa's stomach skittered as she watched the man lead his burdened minions to one of the storehouses. Walking with a jaunty spring in his step, there was no mistaking the Lord of Misrule's air of command. Shocked by her unexpected reaction to this overblown jester, she slammed the window, rattling the glass panes.

"Cease your prattle, Molly." Alyssa returned to her sewing. When she picked up her needle, her hands shook.

Molly laughed. "Mark my words, m'lady," she tossed over her shoulder as she left. "Our new Lord of Misrule will capture many a heart."

"Misrule, indeed," Alyssa snorted, then added "Hell's bells!" under her breath when she pricked her finger.

Though the flamboyant stranger did not appear at supper in the hall that evening, his arrival was on everyone's lips. Alyssa was grateful that she was spared the ordeal of conversing with the three suitors who dined in a gaggle at the other end of the table. What a ragged trio of cony-catchers!

Sir Jeremy Mackarel spoke with a stammer and walked with a limp. Sir Lionel Scudamore, who slurped and burped his way through the meal, was no better than a common ruffian disguised as a gentleman, while Sir Lucian Dugdale swore like a drover and laughed like a jackass. Out of the corner of her eye, Alyssa studied them in order to devise her best strategy for sending them scuttling back to court before New Year's Day. At first, she barely paid attention to the talk of the new entertainer.

"Sheepshanks sent a fine letter of recommendation," Guy informed the company. "I had no idea that old Peter could wield a quill."

Alyssa sopped a chunk of bread in the dregs of her soup. She highly doubted that dull-witted Peter had written anything more complicated than an *X* beside his name. She suspected that the gaudy stranger in his scandalously tight hosiery had penned the glowing letter himself.

Lady Celeste grinned. "Oh, la-la! He made me laugh before he had even doffed his cloak. That one has a merry heart."

Alyssa stared down at her cabbage soup. *Everything makes Mamma laugh—except me, of course.*

"And his name," added Gillian, now returned to Snape with her Scottish husband to await the birth of their first child. "Sir Hoodwink!"

An interesting choice of an alias, Alyssa mused. Papa would be wise to lock up his silver and gold plate before that highwayman popped them into one of his sacks. Speculating on the contents of the entertainer's intriguing baggage occupied Alyssa for the remainder of the simple meal. Since earliest childhood, she could never wait until the gift exchange on New Year's Day. Annually, she discovered her mother's latest hiding place and peeked at her presents as well as everyone else's. Let silly Gillian be surprised; Alyssa gloried in her foreknowledge.

The lure of Sir Hoodwink's crates and bags was too tempting to resist. Alyssa would do a little private investigating later, while everyone else was asleep in their beds. After all, she reasoned, it was in Papa's best interest to know if this stranger had secretly smuggled firearms for his hirelings to overwhelm the castle during the holidays.

The bright moon in the clear, cold sky shed enough light for Alyssa to find her way to the storehouse. To her relief, the horde was unguarded. No doubt Hoodwink's men were drinking and flirting in the castle's warm kitchens. Alyssa chided herself for neglecting to bring some implement with which to pry off the lids of the wooden crates. The canvas bags presented no challenge to untie. The first one held a number of little gowns decorated with garlands of silk ivy vines and holly leaves. The workmanship was exquisite, but who could possibly wear them?

"Finding everything to your satisfaction, mistress?" asked a deep voice just behind her.

Alyssa involuntarily jumped. Angry at being caught, she whirled round to defend herself. The Lord of Misrule's dark eyes regarded her with amusement as he stepped in front of the door to freedom. A slow, lazy smile spread across his too-handsome face.

"Do my fripperies please you?" he drawled.

Alyssa squared her shoulders, despite the fact that her knees shook. "Pretty things, but far too small for me to wear."

"They were not made for *you*," he purred in the back of his throat.

His mocking tone stung Alyssa. She realized that she was fast losing control of this admittedly ticklish situation. "Indeed? Then do you hope to train the castle's mice to perform a galliard for our amusement?"

He chuckled. "Pray tell me, lass, are your mice so clever?"

He stepped a little closer to her. She caught a faint whiff of an exotic musk mixed with an essence of lemon. Though Alyssa had inherited a tall stature from her father, she found that this Hoodwink rogue overshadowed her. His shoulders strained the seams of his garish doublet. She swallowed hard but refused to back away.

Alyssa gritted her teeth. Obviously, the man didn't know who she was. "Curb your insolence, knave. I am a lady of this manor."

His smile grew wider. "You lie," he replied in a velvet tone.

Hot rage filled her. "How dare you!" She slapped his grinning face.

Swift as a snake, he caught her wrist before she could deliver a second blow. "I swear I will cuff you if you strike again," he murmured in her ear in a honeyed voice.

"I am no gentleman and your behavior proves what I just said. You are no lady."

Alyssa pulled her hand from his grasp. No servant dared to speak to her with such boldness. "And you are a knave disguised in rich apparel."

Instead of contradicting her, Hoodwink laughed as he leaned casually against the door frame. "Is that the worst you can call me, Lady Alyssa? I have heard that your waspish tongue is infamous in Northumberland."

She glared at him. "If I am a wasp, best beware of my sting."

He shrugged. "Then I will treat you as I would any wasp—pluck out the stinger before it can do me harm."

Alyssa had the sensation that she was sliding down a slippery slope. "So you intend to cut out my tongue?"

"Nay, my lady, I would remove the stinger from where it lodges—in the wasp's *tail*." He allowed his implication to hang in the air between them before adding, "Do you still swear that you have a stinger?"

Alyssa's cheeks burned with humiliation and she blessed the darkness of the storeroom that hid her blush. "*Where* did you learn this crumb of intelligence?" she shot back.

"From my mother's wit."

"Indeed?" Alyssa felt on firmer ground now. "My condolences to your witty mother for having such a witless son."

"Are you always so peevish, Mistress Disdain, or is your temper merely the result of a scanty supper?"

She skirted around him. "'Tis my fashion when I see a crab."

He eyed her like a cat at a mouse hole. "Is there a crab nearby?"

"If I had a looking glass with me I would show you one."

He pretended to be shocked. "What? Do you mean my face?"

She applauded him. "Again I am stunned by your brilliance."

He took hold of both her hands. His touch was gentle—and warm. Not until that moment did Alyssa realize how chilly she was.

"The hour is late. Though this discourse is pleasant, I confess I need my sleep," he murmured, caressing her fingers. "So I must evict you from my bedchamber, unless of course, you plan to seduce me. Do you?"

Alyssa snatched her hands away from him. Her heart thumped against the confines of her bodice. "You are a swine!"

He bowed her out the door with a melting smile. "And a pleasant repose to you as well."

Alyssa stalked away with murder in her heart—and the most disconcerting flutters in her stomach.

From the deep shadows of the storeroom, Max watched the young woman pick her way over the slippery cobblestones. He admired her straight back, squared shoulders, the tilt of her proud head and the enticing sway of her skirts as she moved. His blood warmed. *Her hands trembled when I held them.* He recalled the flicker of unguarded emotion in the depths of her ice-blue eyes—a yearning or fear? Whichever was the case, Lady Alyssa's behavior was something more than mere perversity—and it intrigued him.

His manservant, Tom Jenkins, joined him. "Is *she* the one you came to wed?" The youth whistled under his breath. "Better you than me, my lord. I would rather be horsewhipped every morning in the town square."

Max clapped the lad on the shoulder. "Aye, that is my Lady Disdain. And my wager with Sir Nathaniel is that I would win her *heart* to me. Marriage was not part of our bargain."

Tom chuckled. "Ah, now I perceive the nut and core of it. You will teach that shrew a sharp lesson that she will never forget."

Max closed the door, then turned to his servant. "How so, Tom?"

"You will baste this goose in the same sauce that she cooks the ganders who court her. Let her see how she likes the taste of rejection."

Max stroked his chin. "You think that I plan to make this woman the target of others' ridicule?"

"Aye," Tom agreed, heedless of his master's serious tone.

Max retrieved the little gown that Alyssa had dropped on the floor. He carefully folded it, then replaced it in its bag. "Mayhap my plans may change a bit during this fortnight," he remarked.

Christmas Eve day dawned clear and cold. Max breathed a quick prayer of thanksgiving for the good weather. Working his way around the crowded stable yard, he tested the horses' girths to make sure that none of the Cavendish family would be spilled into the snow. When the household gathered outside, eager to gather the traditional greenery for the hall's decorations, Max noted that Alyssa was not among the laughing company.

He cast a quick glance at the window where he had seen her yesterday. Though the sun's rays reflected against the glass, he thought he detected some movement behind the panes. Lady Alyssa might spurn this holiday pleasure, but he would command her presence when it came time to hang the garlands of holly and pine. Custom demanded that the entire household must obey the Lord of Misrule for the next fourteen days.

Several hours later, after the family and their guests had dined on their midday meal, Max prepared to pounce upon the elusive Alyssa. While the Cavendishes cheered the arrival of the massive Yule log with songs and applause, Max intercepted Alyssa just as she reached the stairway to the upper gallery.

"Oh, ho, mistress mine, we meet again!"

Alyssa gave him a haughty look. "Step aside! You are in my way."

He merely grinned. "How clever you are to have noticed that!"

"Remove yourself," she commanded, and her cheeks turned pink.

Max pretended to ponder her request, while he watched her out of the corner of his eye. Her heightened color accentuated her beauty. He must not push her too far now if he had hopes to win her affection later. "There is a word that I fear has gone missing, my lady." He rubbed his brow. "'Twas hanging between us only a moment ago. Ah! I have it! I did not hear you say 'please.'"

Alyssa's face changed to a reddish hue. "I will not banter with a servant." She lifted her hand to slap him.

Max wagged his finger at her. "Softly, gentle mistress," he said in the most seductive tone he could muster under the circumstances. "My warning of last evening still stands."

Her beautiful blue eyes grew very large. "You would *dare* to lay a hand on me with my father watching?"

Max chuckled. "Aye, methinks I would."

Squaring her shoulders, she challenged him with a fiery look. "Very well, strike me, if you are foolish enough." She swung at him.

Anticipating her, Max ducked and lifted Alyssa over his shoulder.

Her squawk of outrage caused everyone to look in their direction. She pounded his back with her fists. "Put me down," she railed from her upside-down position. "I vow you will regret this madcap action."

"You forget that I am the Lord of *Misrule*," Max whispered. "During this fortnight, I can say or do whatever I please. Be of good cheer, my lady, or 'twill be *you* that will look more foolish than I." In a louder voice, he addressed the stunned revelers. "See what prize I have caught by the stair! A sweet lark come to make our festivities merrier!"

"Have your brains dribbled out of your ears?" Alyssa hissed at him as he carried her to the center of the large chamber.

"Not yet," he murmured. "Now, smile and pretend that all is well."

"In a pig's eye," she muttered.

As Max had hoped, his announcement was greeted by laughter and applause from the others, led by Sir Guy himself. Max wished that Alyssa could realize how much more pleasure she would have if she joined in the merrymaking instead of making herself unhappy out of spite—or fear. Once again, he had caught a flash of that most basic emotion in her eyes when he had scooped her into his arms. He set her on her feet, then dusted her with his silken handkerchief while she fumed in silence.

"Oh, la-la, Sir Hoodwink," said Lady Celeste. "Our Alyssa has not helped to decorate the house for several years now. 'Tis good to see her in our company." She smiled at her angry daughter.

"This churl flouts me!" Alyssa sputtered. "Send the fool away!"

Max leaned down and whispered to Alyssa so that only she could hear him. "I ask you to be the judge, my lady. Who is the greater fool—he that keeps the Christmas spirit in his heart and on his lips, or she that closes her heart to the joy and good cheer around her?"

A sheen of tears filmed over her eyes. Alyssa turned her head aside. "Very well, master of fools. I will remain, but I swear, I will do nothing."

One of the ladies by the hearth giggled. "You had best

believe my sister, Sir Hoodwink. She is as stubborn as a mule when she wants to be.''

Max searched for the speaker and nearly gasped aloud when he spied her sitting by the fire. With the exception of her obvious pregnancy, the young woman was the exact image of the spitfire before him. Though Max had known many women, never before had he chanced to meet identical twins. He glanced at Alyssa. She continued to stare at the opposite wall, but he noticed that her lower lip quivered a little.

So that is the way the wind blows. He wondered what it would be like to live with a mirror image of himself day after day. He decided that he would hate the experience. He wished he had known of Lady Gillian before he had embarked upon this particular course with Alyssa. Now he was in too deep to withdraw without losing whatever ground he had gained. He would have to play this part to the end, but gently.

''Will you join us in the decoration, Lady Alyssa?'' he whispered.

''Indeed not!'' she replied in a clear voice that everyone heard. ''Continue. I will stand here and contemplate my foolishness.''

Gillian giggled again. Many in the hall joined her. ''See, Sir Hoodwink? She nourishes her stubbornness so that we will all look at her.''

Max saw Alyssa quiver. How long had this cruel baiting between the sisters been going on, he wondered. Why hadn't someone stopped it before the canker had festered into such a painful sore?

Alyssa vowed not to move until the last holly twig was tied into place. Staring at a bare stone wall, she listened to the laughter around her. Every so often, the Lord of Misrule uttered a new jest. Some of his gibes were extremely clever; they nearly ensnared her with their wit. She had to bite the inside of her cheek to keep from laughing.

A wave of self-pity welled up behind her eyelids. She wished she had not been forced into this uncomfortable position or made to look the lackwit that Hoodwink had said she was! Why did she feel compelled to stand like a garden statue while everyone else was having fun? It was so unfair!

Yet she knew that the minute she relaxed, she would attract the most unpleasant attention. Her family, the servants and, most of all, those wretched suitors would tease her for her weakness. That would hurt her more than the stiffness in her knees or the pain between her shoulder blades. She gritted her teeth. Alyssa Cavendish would never yield to a jumped-up jackanapes like Sir Hoodwink. She would die on the spot first.

The winter's short sunlight had dipped below the great window in the hall by the time the company finished turning the chamber into a fragrant green bower. When the last serving maid disappeared toward the kitchens, Alyssa sighed, rubbing the back of her aching neck. Once again she turned toward the stairs to her bedchamber.

She halted when she saw the Lord of Misrule watching her. "Haven't you had enough amusement for one day?" she snarled.

He moved closer to her. "I was about to ask you the same question, my lady," he murmured. He slipped his hand under the veil that covered her hair and gently massaged the tight muscles at the nape of her neck.

Though shocked by his bold move, Alyssa did not pull away. His touch was sure and skillful. He made her want to purr like her cat, Mika. She knew she should upbraid him for this unseemly behavior—and she would—but not this exquisite minute. A small sigh escaped her lips.

"Better?" he whispered, his thumb circling behind her ear.

"Aye," she replied in a voice that was barely audible.

"You know, Lady Alyssa, we would have been glad of your help."

"Ha!" Alyssa should stop him this minute, but his fingers continued their delicious—that is, their *distracting*—dance along her shoulders above the neckline of her gown. Something fluttered in her breast. She had the most overpowering urge to lean back against him.

"You are smiling," he murmured, and his breath fanned her cheek.

Alyssa gave herself a little shake. "Am not!" She glared at him.

Using the tip of his finger like a painter's brush, he traced her lips.

"A smile or two is not too expensive," he observed. "And 'twill buy you more good opinions than a wealth of witty retorts."

Alyssa blinked. His words made good sense, but she would rather cut out her tongue than admit that she might have acted in a rash manner this afternoon. Not trusting herself to make a retort, she dashed for the stairs.

His chuckle followed her. "We will spar again soon, my lady!"

Once in the safety of her chamber, Alyssa tried to banish the infuriating man from her mind, but Sir Hoodwink refused to disappear like a bad memory. Lying on her bed with Mika in her arms, she mused on the rogue's too-handsome face, his too-seductive voice and his too-sensual touch. No man had ever affected her like this. Alyssa found herself at a loss. Sir Hoodwink—or whatever his name was—disturbed her in every way. She hated him for making her the butt of the family's amusement, yet at the same time, she couldn't wait to see him again. "I look forward to our next sparring match with pleasure," she told her cat.

After supper, the Lord of Misrule ordered the entire household to don their heavy cloaks and furs. His nimble pages appeared, almost by magic, bearing blazing torches and baskets filled with more holly sprigs. Led by Sir Hoodwink, the Cavendish family, including pregnant Gillian attended by her redheaded husband, trooped outside to the barns and stables where they gave the traditional Christmas Eve blessing to their curious livestock. Over every horse stall, cattle crib and chicken coop the Cavendishes hung their holly for protection against evil spirits and for good luck during the coming year in memory of the Christ child who had been born in a stable and warmed by the humble animals there.

Alyssa had always liked this part of their family tradition. It signaled the beginning of a fortnight filled with feasting and gifts. Of course, she pretended that she found the whole exercise boring so that everyone would entreat her to smile and to enjoy herself. But this year, Gillian had captured the family's interest simply because she was heavy with child. If Gillian was so afraid of slipping on the icy paths between the barn and paddock, she should have remained in the hall next to the fire. Piqued that her twin was once again reaping all the attention, Alyssa ignored the others. Taking a small bit of holly, she entered the dark stable, calling softly to her favorite gelding.

"Hush there, Dilando," she crooned. "'Tis only me. Good evening, love," she whispered as her horse nuzzled her, looking for a treat. "'Tis time again to bless you." She slipped a small piece of carrot to her pet. Then she looked up at the crosspiece above Dilando's stall.

In past years, her father had hung up her holly for her, but this year he stayed close to Gillian. No matter, Alyssa thought. She was perfectly capable of doing it herself. All she needed was something to stand on. There must be a cask, or perhaps a small ladder, nearby, if only she could see where she was going. Still whispering endearments to her horse and the other half-wakeful beasts nearby, Alyssa searched in the dark.

"Hell's bells," she muttered when she stubbed her toe on a rake.

"I doubt that the devil will be ringing any bells this Christmas Eve," drawled a honey-sweet voice from the darkness.

Alyssa froze, tingling half with fright and half with pleasure. "Sir Hoodwink! Methought you were shoveling a path for my sister."

He came up behind her. "Lady Gillian has more than enough help as it is. Methinks *you* are the lady in distress."

Blood pounded in Alyssa's temples as she inhaled his heady, exotic scent. "I am never in distress," she assured him, trembling as she spoke.

"Of course not," he agreed. Then, without warning, he placed his hands around her waist and lifted her off the ground. "Hang high your holly over this most fortunate horse, my lady. I shall not drop you."

Alyssa could barely breathe. No man had ever attempted such liberties with her. "I do not expect you to drop me, Hoodwink," she replied as she looped the holly over the top of the crosspiece. "There, 'tis done. Now you may put me down."

Without a word, he lowered her—slowly so that she slid down the length of his body. Alyssa felt the hard muscles of his chest, the straightness of his legs and the…the firmness between them.

She wet her dry lips. "You may release me," she whispered.

"Indeed, mistress?" he replied, his fingers stroking her back.

Even though she was tightly corseted and wearing a thick cloak, the skin under her clothing burned where he touched her. *Will he attempt to kiss me?* she wondered, half-hoping that he would try. His manner was certainly brazen—and made this adventure in the stable very exciting.

Alyssa pulled herself together. What if her parents found them in this near-embrace? "Unhand me, Master Misrule. You forget yourself."

He chuckled. "Not yet, my lady. But the fortnight has barely begun." With that thinly veiled insinuation, he dropped his hands. "After you." He bowed to her with a flourish.

When Alyssa stepped into the cold stable yard, she discovered that the rest of her family had already returned to the castle. Obviously, no one had given a thought to her whereabouts. She could have fallen and broken her leg without anyone knowing—or caring. Her warm feelings of the past five minutes evaporated. Without a backward glance at the only person who had sought her out, Alyssa stamped her way through the dirty snow to the castle's side door.

As usual, the celebration of Christmas Day began with the family's attendance at three Masses: midnight, dawn and midmorning. Then the first of the season's great feasts began. After Snape's elderly priest had blessed the food, the Lord of Misrule held up his hands for silence.

"'Tis time to light the Yule log," he announced. The assembled family and guests applauded, Alyssa among them.

Usually Papa lit the great log that would burn throughout the next two weeks. Alyssa glanced at her father with familiar anticipation. But instead of rising, Sir Guy settled back in his great chair with a mysterious smile on his lips. Alyssa stared at Hoodwink. The chatter in the hall grew quieter. Who would the Lord of Misrule choose for the honor?

With a swagger, the entertainer crossed the open space to the high table. He paused in front of Alyssa—and winked at her in the most shocking yet titillating way.

"With your kind permission, my lord, I choose Lady

Alyssa to light the Yule log as she is the only maiden among the Cavendish family. Her purity will sanctify our fire.'' Sir Hoodwink offered his hand to her.

Alyssa's cheeks grew warm under his smiling gaze. Holding her breath, she waited for him to add some spiteful barb to his pretty speech.

Instead, he asked, ''Will you serve as our torchbearer, my lady?''

Gillian, sitting on her left, gave her sister a little nudge. ''Don't gawk at him, Lissa. Get up before he changes his mind.''

One of the lackeys held her chair as she struggled to free the skirts of her mulberry damask gown from the carved legs of the high table. Meanwhile, her father led the company in applause. Her ears tingled. Applause for her? Hoodwink gave her icy fingers a little squeeze.

''Chin up, my lady,'' he whispered as he paraded her down the center aisle between the lower tables toward the massive fireplace at the end of the chamber. ''Let everyone admire your beautiful blue eyes.''

What mischief hid behind his smile? ''Will the log explode in my face?'' she asked.

He cast her a doleful expression. ''Tush, Lady Alyssa. Would I do anything so unmannerly to such a sweet lady?''

They arrived next to the hearth. Before them, the huge oaken log lay in splendor, surrounded by a pile of dry kindling. A crown of green holly leaves and red berries wreathed the top. The Lord of Misrule lit a waxen spill and held out the flame to her. ''Do you dare to take the risk?''

Of course she would! Alyssa had never refused a dare. She grasped the lighted spill. ''Let us see how sweet I am.'' Taking a deep breath, she plunged the taper into the tinder. Instead of an answering blast of gunpowder, the fire licked the bundles of twigs around the log.

Louder cheers erupted around the hall. Alyssa slowly turned to face her family, their guests and the servants. Everyone was clapping their hands, stamping their feet—and actually *smiling* at her. The shock of their universal approval caught her off guard. Her lips trembled as she smiled in return.

Sir Hoodwink took the spill from her shaking fingers and tossed it among the blazing faggots. "There now. That didn't hurt much, did it?"

Alyssa was too overcome with her emotions to think of a suitably tart reply. Instead, she savored the company's warmth as Hoodwink led her back to her seat. Her good mood lasted throughout the twelve courses of the dinner until several giggling chambermaids carried a mistletoe kissing ball into the hall. Alyssa closed her eyes while the rest of her family and guests greeted this wretched holiday tradition with glee.

She hated the kissing ball. Who wanted to be bussed by some wet-lipped, drunken lout? she had told herself over the past five years when no one had attempted to lure her under the green sphere. She had no desire to stoop so low for such a disgusting trifle. Kissing balls were for wantons or idiots.

Alyssa remained in her chair while the rest of the family—even Gillian, looking like a round pudding—clustered under the archway where the chamberlain tied up the mistletoe with red ribbon. The green mass glistened with dozens of pale white berries. At a signal from the Lord of Misrule, the musicians in the gallery struck up a merry reel. Nimble dancers filled the floor. When Lord Dugdale made a halfhearted attempt to invite Alyssa to join him, she waved away the shambling coxcomb, ignoring the look of relief on his drink-reddened face.

The dance's tempo grew faster. Every now and then a man would swing his partner under the ball and kiss her while the none-too-surprised woman squealed her pleasure.

Alyssa curled her lips with distaste, though her foot kept time with the infectious music. She was not aware of Sir Hoodwink's presence until he whispered into her ear.

"You do not dance, mistress?"

Alyssa jumped at the sound of his voice but quickly regained her composure. "I dance right well, if I have a mind to it."

He chuckled. "And what is the state of your mind at this moment?"

She wet her lips. "I find...that is—"

He did not allow her to finish. "Your toes have already made your decision, my lady." He took her hand. "Up now and let us foot it."

She tried to jerk away but his grip was too strong. "Churl!"

He had the nerve to laugh. "Show me how well you can dance, mistress mine. Or are you afraid that I will trod on your hem?"

"I would not put any wickedness past you," she snapped.

He pulled her out of her chair. "Dance with the devil, then, if you dare to dance with me. Will you risk it?"

The suggestive tone in his voice affected her in the most unexpected way. "I will lead you a merry round, Misrule. Your feet will cry for mercy before I have finished with you!" She dragged him to the cleared floor.

His eyes flashed. "I accept your challenge with great pleasure."

The reel segued to an equally abandoned branle, followed by a quick-paced galliard. Alyssa actually enjoyed herself. Hoodwink was a superb dancer. Though she executed a number of complicated figures, he kept up with her, measure for measure. People stood aside, applauding them as they twirled around the floor. A breathless hour later, Alyssa's energy began to flag toward the end of a mourisque. As if he read her mind, Hoodwink circled her off to the side where she could rest and catch her breath.

Alyssa blotted the perspiration on her forehead with her handkerchief. "You dance well, Master Misrule," she conceded.

A corner of his mouth twitched. "A compliment from Lady Alyssa?" he asked with mock surprise. "I am honored."

She fanned her face. "Well, don't be. 'Twas a slip of the tongue."

"Where else does your tongue slip?" he whispered.

She stepped back, her defenses instantly alert. "How now?"

He took another step closer to her. "Tell me, my lady." His dark eyes sparkled in the firelight from a nearby torchère.

She sidled away from him. The warm nearness of his body made her senses spin. "You...you are—"

He slipped his arm around her waist and drew her to him. The very air around them seemed to crackle like the lightning of a summer's sudden tempest. Before she had time to think, his lips covered hers. His kiss, far from being hard or cruel, shattered her reserve with its gentle power. Ecstasy spiraled through her. His persuasive touch demanded a response that she was helpless to resist. Rising on tiptoe, Alyssa returned his kiss with a hunger that took her by surprise.

Rumbling low in the back of his throat, the aptly named Lord of Misrule deepened his sweet assault. His tongue lightly traced the fullness of her lips, sending shivers of desire racing through her. Alyssa moaned under his caress. Lacing her fingers around his neck, she pressed against him. Suddenly he broke away from her, leaving her mouth burning with the fire of his touch. Dazed and confused by this introduction to a passion she never knew she possessed, Alyssa looked up at him for guidance. His eyes smoldered deep in their sockets before he lowered his lids.

Without a word, he reached over her head and plucked two of the waxy mistletoe berries from the kissing ball. "These are your tokens by custom, my lady," he said with a strange hoarseness in his voice. He took her hand and placed the tiny fruit in her palm.

Every nerve in Alyssa's body burned. "You have miscounted, you rapscallion. Only one kiss passed between us."

He drew in a deep breath before he answered. "Nay, bewitching mistress. I kissed you, then you kissed me back. That makes two."

Her tongue touched her love-swollen lips. Her mind spun beyond her common sense. "I kis…kissed *you?*" she stammered.

His hooded gaze bored into her. "Aye, you did," he whispered. He stepped backward, then dipped a graceful bow to her. "And now I must attend to my duties, mistress mine. I bid you a sweet good-night."

Alyssa blinked. "You are a thrice-wicked man," she murmured. She could still taste the honey of his kiss.

He flashed her a grin. "And dream of me, Alyssa," he added.

"Churl!" she whispered after him. Then she dashed up the stairs.

For the second night in a row, sleep eluded her. When it finally came, she dreamed of the Lord of Misrule and his bold, delicious kisses.

Chapter Two

Though December 26 dawned cloudy and cold, the weather held long enough for the traditional Saint Stephen's Day horse races. By the time the company returned to the castle for dinner, scattered snow flurries swirled around them. The bracing wind had given everyone a sharp appetite for the feast. Platters heaped with joints of roast beef, legs of mutton and whole suckling pigs followed one after another. A heap of fresh-shucked oysters glistened in a huge tureen. Chickens basted in honey made the rounds of the tables, high and low. Sir Hoodwink, showing no fatigue from his exertions during the morning's races, kept the company amused with many clever songs fresh from Queen Mary Tudor's court. Even Alyssa's suitors looked happy.

Just before the sweet course was served, a fanfare of trumpets brought the hilarity of the great hall to a standstill. An unfamiliar young pageboy marched down the central aisle with great solemnity. Alyssa leaned forward in her seat. The child was dressed in a white satin tabard. The letter *A* with a crown over its apex, made of a ruby-red ribbon, decorated the front. The Lord of Misrule stopped the page.

"What ho!" he cried out. "Who are you? Where do you come from?"

The little boy bowed to the Lord of Misrule, then he bowed to Sir Guy and Lady Celeste seated at the center of the head table.

The child announced, "I am the servant of my master, the Twelfth Knight, and I come from the land of…" He paused for a brief moment while he tried to remember the rest of his speech. "From the Land of L'Amour," he finished with a triumphant grin on his face.

"Bravo!" Celeste applauded the child.

Alyssa's attention was drawn to the intriguing package the page held between his small hands. She itched to know what was inside the large box covered in red satin and tied up with a ribbon made of gold tissue.

Hoodwink patted the boy on his shoulder. "On behalf of my Lord and Lady Cavendish, you are welcome to Snape Castle. Whom do you seek?"

"Who will be so lucky?" Gillian whispered beside Alyssa.

Alyssa hoped it wasn't going to be another present for her sister's babe. Not even born yet, and already the child had a trunkful of darling things. Alyssa pinched herself under the table. She should be ashamed to be envious of an innocent still in the womb.

The page looked around the hall with wide hazel eyes. "I bring a gift for the most worthy lady in the land," he recited.

Alyssa's shoulders slumped. Obviously the beautiful box was for Mamma. No doubt Papa had arranged this surprise for his beloved Celeste. How lucky her mother was to have found such a loving husband! Alyssa sipped her wine and tried to banish the yearning in her heart for a marriage like that of her parents—or Gillian.

The Lord of Misrule turned to face the entire hall. "And who, pray tell, is this most fortunate woman?"

The page puffed out his chest. "The Lady Alyssa Cavendish!" he shouted. He looked at the high table. Astonishment filled his expression when he saw the two identical women sitting side by side. He tugged on Hoodwink's gaudy doublet. "Please, sir, which one is she?"

With a dramatic flourish, Sir Hoodwink pointed to Alyssa.

Trembling with excitement and aware that all eyes were upon her, Alyssa scrambled to her feet. "Here I am!" she called to the page.

"Why you?" Gillian muttered behind her napkin.

Her twin's open disappointment cheered Alyssa. "Why not?" She grinned as the boy advanced toward her. "'Tis high time, too!"

"Mayhap 'tis nothing but snails and toads," Gillian sulked.

With a smile for the page, Alyssa all but snatched the lavish box out of his hands. She glanced down the table at her trio of suitors and was delighted to see that they were as surprised as everyone else in the huge chamber. Alyssa basked for a moment as the center of attention. Then she untied the ribbon and lifted the lid.

Nothing slimy jumped out at her. Instead, resting on a bed of white satin, was an exquisite tree, about ten inches high, made entirely of boiled sugar. Three golden pears of marzipan hung from its branches. Perched at the top of the tree was a feathered partridge fashioned from a candied fig. Alyssa's mouth watered at the sight. She held up the box so that everyone could see—and envy—the gift she had received from an unknown admirer.

"Please thank your master. I will enjoy this to the last crumb."

Grinning, the page bowed, then skipped back down the aisle. A babble of voices broke out in the hall as the guests and retainers discussed the unusual present. Alyssa returned to her seat.

"Those pears look most toothsome," Gillian hinted.

Alyssa plucked one from its branch and bit into it. "Aye," she agreed.

Gillian narrowed her eyes. "Do you intend to eat the whole thing?"

Alyssa gave her twin a smug smile. "Aye, 'tis a gift for *me,* Gillie, not *us.* I intend to savor every morsel."

Gillian wrinkled her nose. Alyssa knew that her twin really wanted to stick out her tongue, but now that she was a married woman, Gillian was expected to be too mature for such childish behavior.

Alyssa ate a second pear. "'Tis heaven!" she told her pouting sister.

By the time she finished the third pear and the figgy partridge, Alyssa knew she had had enough sweets, but she didn't dare put the box away for a later time. Gillian would tease her unmercifully—or worse—filch a large piece of the tree for herself. Still smiling, Alyssa broke off one of the leafy boughs and sucked on it. The sugared treat made her teeth ache with its oversweetness. She cast a sidelong glance at her sister, hoping that Sir Hoodwink's ghost story had distracted Gillian's attention. No such luck. Her twin stared at the dismembered tree like a terrier at a rat hole.

"Methinks you will be sick if you eat it all," Gillian observed.

Alyssa swished a bit of wine around her mouth to rinse away some of the cloying sugar from her teeth. "Nonsense," she snapped.

She broke off another branch. There was still the whole trunk to eat and it looked very thick. She prayed that it was hollow. With a sinking sensation, Alyssa realized that she should have offered some of her treat to Gillian and their mother at the outset. Now her pride would not allow her to concede her miscalculation and give in to Gillian's entreaties.

Alyssa's stomach revolted against the sugar. It took all her fortitude to swallow the final bite of the trunk. She drank a little more wine to wash the whole mess down. She massaged her groaning stomach. A dreadful bubble rose to her throat. She gripped the arms of her chair until the skin over her knuckles turned white. Chill perspiration dotted her brow.

I must not be sick! Sitting perfectly still, she calculated the distance to the nearest garderobe at the far end of a long corridor off the hall. *Miles from here!* Alyssa whimpered behind her pressed lips. The sugared bubble rose higher. She was overcome with a great desire to gag. Hell's bells, she thought as she bolted from her chair. *Please let me make it to the privy!*

Clamping one hand over her mouth and lifting her heavy skirts with the other, Alyssa raced through the dancers, flashed past several startled servants and ran headlong down the endless corridor to the tiny alcove. She barely made it. After emptying her stomach of the tree, pears, partridge and her dinner, Alyssa stumbled outside the garderobe. Feeling weak and clammy, she sank down on a nearby bench. Though she was more miserable than she had thought possible, she refused to give in to tears. Closing her eyes, she rested her head against the cold stone wall. As soon as she regained her strength, she would crawl up the stairs to the comfort of her bed. Someone sat down beside her.

"Go away," Alyssa mumbled.

Max shook his head at the wretched figure beside him. He never expected that Alyssa would eat the entire subtlety at once, but he would not chide her for her gluttony now. She had paid the price with interest.

"Feeling better?" he asked in a low tone.

Alyssa's eyes snapped open. Recognizing him, she looked away. "'Twas very warm in the hall," she mumbled. "I…I was overcome."

Max set down the small tray he carried. He poured a steaming brew from a covered jug into a brown-glazed mug. "Drink this."

She shook her head. "Is it your jest to kill me?"

Max swirled the cup to mix the steeping herbs. "A stomachache is no laughing matter, my lady. Drink up. 'Twill help."

She glanced at him, then at the cup he offered. She bit her lower lip. Max wished he dared to gather her in his arms and soothe away her physical distress, as well as the deeper one in her soul.

"'Tis only a bit of chamomile and rosemary with a few mint leaves," he continued. "A gentle remedy for a gentle lady."

"Ha!" she snorted, but without her usual fire. "Do I look so pathetic that you must treat me like a limp lily?"

Max ignored the barbed question. Instead, he remarked, "'Tis a pity that you are missing all the merriment. One of your swains, Sir Jeremy, is playing Hoodman Blind and is making a goodly mess of it. He will nurse bruised shins in the morning."

A tiny smile touched Alyssa's lips. Then she sighed.

Max held up the mug. "Do you dare to take this risk?"

She arched one of her lovely dark brows. "That you have laced your potion with belladonna?"

He grinned. Even when down, she still had spirit. "Exactly so."

Without another word of protest or thanks, she took the cup and sipped its contents. "Will I grow green or sprout feathers by midnight?"

Max leaned back against the wall. "Time will tell," he replied.

In silence, Alyssa drank more of the concoction.

"I regret that I cannot kiss you at this moment," Max remarked.

Alyssa gave him an incredulous look. "Methinks you

would be mad if you wanted to. But, for the sake of argument, Hoodwink, why don't you take such a bold liberty? Nothing stopped you last evening."

Max smiled to himself. *So my kiss did not offend her. Good!* Aloud, he replied, "Alas, there is no mistletoe." He pointed above them.

Another little smile flitted across her lips. "For that omission, I am sure you give much thanks."

Taking her cold hand in his, he grew more serious. "I give thanks that you are feeling better enough to jest with me. You know, my lady, in the future, you may find that sharing your bounty with others will be more beneficial to your health."

She tensed but did not snatch her hand away from his. "Is that your physic? Are you a doctor as well as the Lord of Misrule?"

He grinned at her. "Aye, my specialty is broken hearts."

"Oh?" Alyssa looked away. "Then you had best look elsewhere for a patient. My heart is perfectly sound."

"Is it?" he whispered as he bent down and kissed the back of her hand. Her skin was as smooth as satin against his lips.

She gasped under her breath, trembled, then withdrew her hand. "I am suddenly very tired. No doubt your witches' brew has begun its work. I bid you good-night." She rose and turned toward the stair.

He stood behind her. Though he longed to sweep her into his arms, his prudence counseled him to leave well enough alone for this evening. "May your angel guide you to your rest."

She looked over her shoulder; a true smile lit up her face. "My thanks for the angel. Usually gentlemen tell me to go to the devil."

He laughed at her wit, then doffed his hat to her. "Ah, but as you already know, Alyssa, I am no gentleman."

She smiled at him in reply before she disappeared around the corner of the staircase. Max listened to her soft footfalls as she ascended to her chamber. Sweet Jesu! What a beautiful smile she had! And what a sad heart! He prayed that he could help her—not for the sake of his half-remembered wager—but for herself.

Blowing snow from the previous night's storm kept all but the hardiest revelers inside Snape Castle on December 27, the second day of Christmas. By the time dinner was announced in the early afternoon, the bored Cavendish family and their guests looked for the Lord of Misrule to surprise them with a new entertainment.

Between the meat and salad courses, while Sir Hood-wink conducted a raucous game of forfeits, unseen trumpets trilled a fanfare. Like a sprite from fairyland, the little page, holding a covered birdcage, appeared in the far doorway. The company grew quiet as the child made his way toward the head table. Hoodwink stopped him.

"You have come again, little messenger?" he asked the boy.

The lad blinked then replied, "Aye, sir. I am here, aren't I?"

Even Alyssa laughed at his adorable innocence.

"And you have brought another gift?"

The child nodded. "Aye, sir, but 'tis not for you."

Following more laughter, Hoodwink said, "Indeed? Then who does your master honor today?"

Drawing in a deep breath, the boy shouted, "The Lady Alyssa!"

Celeste leaned toward her grinning daughter. "Eh, *bien,* Alyssa! You have won someone's heart, methinks. But whose?"

Alyssa didn't care. She was much more interested in knowing what was inside the birdcage. Her mysterious suitor would soon show himself. In the meantime, she intended to enjoy his gifts—and all the attention that they garnered her. Rising from her chair, she beckoned to the page.

"Come hither, boy. Show me what the Twelfth Knight sends today."

The page placed the cage between the twins. Alyssa lifted the cover. Two pure white doves regarded her with black beady eyes. Alyssa felt a twinge of disappointment. She had so hoped for one of those brightly plumed parrots from the New World. She had heard that they could be taught to converse in English.

Celeste signaled to the nearest lackey. "Beautiful plump birds! Take them to the dovecote, James."

Alyssa's temper flared. These doves were *her* gift, not something for the kitchen. She grasped the cage's ring before James could whisk them away. "How could you think I would send these pets of Venus to be made into pies? The Twelfth Knight would be offended, methinks."

Alyssa's brother-in-law, Jamie Campbell chuckled. "Since when did you consider the feelings of your luckless suitor?"

Alyssa made a face at him. "I have my generous moments."

Gillian giggled. "Look, there is something else for you."

Alyssa returned her attention to the page. She almost gagged when she saw that he held another red satin box tied up with gold tissue. Reluctantly she accepted the gift. Her stomach lurched when she saw another sugar pear tree complete with a figgy partridge. She had no desire to even smell the sickening-sweet offering, much less taste it. Yet her pride balked at giving it away. The sugar tree was expressly sent for *her*. She would eat the sweets in the privacy of her chamber at a much later date—when her stomach could face it.

Then she caught sight of Sir Hoodwink. When their

gazes met, he lifted one brow in a silent challenge. He nodded to the box in her hand. She could almost hear him ask, "Do you dare to take the risk?"

Alyssa tossed her head back, shot a defiant look at the Lord of Misrule, then turned to Lady Celeste. "Mamma, would you care to taste this most exquisite subtlety?"

Gillian gasped under her breath. "Take care, Mamma. Perchance Lissa knows something unwholesome about these pears that we do not."

What a spiteful thing to say! Alyssa thought. She bit her tongue to keep from telling Gillian to fly to the devil. Instead, she turned up her smile. "Take some, Mamma. I swear the sweets are good—though very rich," she added.

Celeste's hand wavered over the sugar tree. Alyssa gnawed the inside of her cheek. She knew that her mother remembered the time that Alyssa had filled two dozen cherry tarts with ground pepper just because Lady Celeste had allowed Gillian to wear her pearl necklace to a family wedding instead of Alyssa. Her mother's hesitation humiliated Alyssa, an emotion that she had rarely felt. "Please, Mamma," she whispered.

Into the breach of strained silence stepped the Lord of Misrule. Without so much as a by-your-leave, he selected the plumpest marzipan pear and popped it into his mouth. He rolled his eyes with merry ecstasy. "A feast for the tongue, my lady," he informed Celeste. "Lady Alyssa is a most loving daughter to share this wealth with you."

"And…and for all my family," Alyssa quickly added, savoring Hoodwink's kind words. Even though she knew he was only playacting, at least it was for her benefit—something that didn't happen very often. She flashed him a smile of gratitude.

He rewarded her with one for her alone; it dazzled her with its brilliance and sent her pulse racing. Her breath stopped in the middle of her throat. Blood pounded in her ears. She swallowed.

Hoodwink took the box from her shaking hand. ''With your permission, Lady Alyssa, I shall distribute your gift.''

Sinking back into her chair, Alyssa could only nod in reply. While her parents, sister, in-laws, suitors and guests helped themselves to the partridge and pear tree, Alyssa's mind whirled with a gamut of perplexing thoughts. Who was this entertainer and why did he alone have such a devastating effect on her? Whenever he was nearby, her steady emotions rocked against each other inside her breast, leaving her giddy, breathless and in complete disarray. Hoodwink was a hireling for a fortnight, yet he confused her, enticed her, challenged her and engaged her as no man had ever done.

On the following day, the Feast of the Holy Innocents, the sun shone clear for the morning's sport. Max invited not only the castle's residents but also the villagers to the stable's paddock, where his minions had laid out a small but well-appointed racecourse. Colorful flags snapped from broomstick poles as the Cavendish family and retainers took their places on the spectators' benches. They broke into thunderous applause when Max announced that the Goose and Piglet Races were about to commence. He watched with more than a little relief when the excitable creatures actually performed well, chasing after one of the lads who lured them with food. Meanwhile, the guests watched and wagered on the eager piglets and befuddled geese.

Max glanced at Alyssa. Discarding her usual haughty look, she laughed with joyous abandon, especially when her chosen pig won several heats. Max's blood sang with her pleasure. The woman was a peerless beauty, full of fire and wit. All she needed was someone to call her bluff and prove to her that she was worthy of love. She needed someone like him. The more he knew Alyssa, the better he liked her. His wager with Nate receded even further in his memory.

Everyone was ravenous by the time the day's feast began. Snatching mouthfuls of food between jests and songs, Max waited for the appropriate moment to signal the trumpeters' fanfare. When the serving men prepared to enter the hall with the fowl course, Max held them back. He nodded to his little page. The horns filled the great hall with their brassy notes. The company immediately grew still. By now, everyone recognized the sound and they looked forward to the mysterious Twelfth Knight's latest offering. Max handed a covered dish to the little page.

"I will follow you," he whispered to the boy. Then he signaled to a second page, who carried another covered cage of doves as well as a satin box. The trio paraded down the aisle.

Alyssa half rose from her seat, her blue eyes shining with anticipation. The first page set the platter before her, then lifted the lid.

"For you, Lady Alyssa," announced the lad. Then, leaning across the table, he whispered. "'Tis capons, m'lady, with honey all over them."

Alyssa stared down at the three small chickens, roasted to golden perfection and glistening under their glaze. Max watched her closely as the second page presented the doves and sweets. It amused him to see her face slightly fall at the sight of the red satin box.

"All these gifts are for the Lady Alyssa," shouted the second page, also dressed in the white tabard with the crowned *A*. "From our master, the Twelfth Knight, who sends them to you with his compliments in praise of your beauty and sweet temper."

These last words elicited snickers from the tables behind Max. Alyssa had heard them as well. Red splotches stained her cheeks.

Jamie Campbell murmured to his wife, "Obviously this Twelfth Knight has never met your sister."

Max glared at the young man. Clearing his throat, Jamie looked down at his trencher. Max needed to do something immediately to save Alyssa from further insult. Striding to the center of the floor, Max rapped his ceremonial staff for silence. The sniggering ceased.

Max plastered a large smile on his face as he swept his gaze around the crowded hall. "The Twelfth Knight truly knows his lady's heart and the depths of her generosity." He shot Alyssa a warning glance and hoped that she would have the presence of mind to hold her tongue. Taking a deep breath, he continued. "My lady has kindly donated these most sumptuous fowl to the lowest table in the hall." He pointed to the table nearest the door where sat the elderly residents of the village's almshouse.

The old people looked stunned at their sudden good fortune. At the head table, Alyssa opened her mouth to protest. Max narrowed his eyes at her. *Do not undo the good I am doing on your behalf!* Max hustled the two pages to whisk away the capons. Then he led the company in applause for the lady's charity as the pages presented the succulent dish to the almsmen.

Alyssa glared at Max with a promise of warfare in her azure eyes. Then she opened the box of sweets. "Sir Hoodwink! Please give these delicacies to my brother-in-law." She wrinkled her nose at Jamie, who merely laughed. "'Twill no doubt sweeten his wit."

Her largesse took Max unaware for a brief moment before he led another round of cheers. As he received the box from her, he whispered, "You amaze me, my lady."

She returned his smile. "We will speak anon, Master Misrule. I have a bone to pick with you—a capon bone!"

And I will look forward to crossing my sword with you!

* n*x*m*nt. Then ifh*x her va

Later, during the dancing, Alyssa cornered Max near the kissing ball. "How dare you take such liberties with my gift!"

Max thought how ravishing she looked when her temper was up. "Tell me the truth, mistress mine, I command it. Didn't you feast upon the warm response to your surprising generosity? Were not the sounds of clapping and cheers better meat and drink to your soul?"

She dropped her gaze. "Aye, but—"

Max held up his hand for silence. "Then you have learned a very important lesson this day, Alyssa," he whispered. "The more that you give away, the more you will receive."

"Humph!" she muttered.

Max turned her so that she faced the hall filled with dancers. "Regard Sir Jeremy." He pointed to the tall young man who watched the merriment from the sidelines. "He would love to dance with you. After all, he is here because of you."

Alyssa barely glanced at her erstwhile suitor. "Him? He is awkward and bandy-legged. I'd sooner dance with a goose."

Max shook his head. Alyssa needed a few more lessons in graciousness. He slipped his arm around her waist. For a distracting moment, he wondered if she were as slim and willowy undressed as she was when encased in the constrictive armor of her corsets. The thought made him warm in his nether parts.

"Be wise before you speak, my lady. Sir Jeremy was born a cripple and has spent many painful years learning how to walk—and to dance. Surely his courage and perseverance should be rewarded with a kindness from the most beautiful woman in this castle?" He brushed a kiss on her earlobe. "Do you dare to take the risk?"

"I can do anything you suggest, my lord," she retorted.

He chuckled to himself. "Good, then you will not be afraid to dance with Sir Jeremy."

She said nothing for a moment. Then, lifting her head, she marched over to where Sir Jeremy stood. Max could not hear their words, but from the amazed expression on the young man's face, he knew that Alyssa had invited her suitor to be her partner. Max grinned as Alyssa led Lord Mackarel out to the floor.

Sir Guy joined Max. "Tell me, Sir Hoodwink, do you think that my daughter has drunk too much wine tonight?" The lord of the manor gave his entertainer a shrewd look. "I have not known her to do a kind deed for years now— unless 'twas for her own benefit. What say you?"

Max shifted his weight. It was too soon to reveal his true identity to Lord Cavendish. As the Lord of Misrule, he replied, "Wise folk do say that the Christmas season weaves a special magic on all of us, my lord."

Guy lifted one of his dark golden brows. "Do they, indeed?"

In silence, the two men watched Alyssa and Sir Jeremy dance. Every time Alyssa turned in their direction, she smiled at Max. After a few minutes, Guy remarked, "I am pleased to see my daughter so happy. Her laughter has become a rare thing since both her sisters were married."

Max cleared his throat. "Mayhap Sir Jeremy has touched her heart."

A slow smile crept across Guy's face. "Mmm, methinks I should look elsewhere to find the cause of her present joy. This fortnight will prove most interesting." He looked directly at Max. "Though I wish Alyssa wed, I will not allow her innocence to be squandered upon a mere fortune seeker. Above all else, I desire a good man for Alyssa, for she needs someone to help her lighten her heart."

"Amen to that, my lord." Max's respect for Lord Cavendish rose a notch. At least, her father recognized that Alyssa's melancholy was the root of her tempestuous ways. As for himself, Max knew that he must not overplay his hand just yet.

* * *

During the night, more snow blanketed the countryside around Snape. On the fourth morning of Christmas, the Lord of Misrule organized an impromptu snowball fight. Soon the castle's courtyard was filled with lusty shouts from the men and squealing giggles from the women. Tossing her fur-lined cloak over her shoulder, Alyssa joined in the fun. But soon the game grew rougher, at least in Alyssa's direction. Expressions darkened when people threw their missiles at her. Their balls were harder packed and some of the servants aimed at her head, instead of her body.

"Come help me, Molly!" she shouted to her maid as another icy ball struck her shoulder. She saw that it had contained a small stone. Fury welled up inside her. "Who threw that?" she shouted at the general mob. "Who dared to hurt me?"

Molly cocked her head. "Them who you have hurt in the past with your sharp words and your temper fits. Aye, 'tis only fair that they get their own back now."

Alyssa seethed, her anger mixed with humiliation. "If you are not going to defend me, then begone!" she yelled at Molly.

The maid merely laughed before she ambled away. Another snowball, also holding a stone, hit Alyssa in the back of her hood. Cursing under her breath, she packed her own ball with a good-sized rock in its core. Before she could hurl it at a clump of potboys, someone behind her grabbed her wrist.

"Good morrow, Lady Alyssa," Sir Hoodwink remarked pleasantly, his fingers locked around her. "A fine day for a fair game, is it not?"

Alyssa tried to shake him off, but he was too strong. "The game is not fair," she snapped. "Unhand me!"

Instead of turning her loose, he marched her out of the courtyard, ignoring her demands and insults. He did not stop until they were within the sheltered confines of her mother's icy rose garden.

"Go hang yourself!" Alyssa told him in a deceptively low voice, taut with anger at his boldness. "Didn't you see those kitchen scullions flouting me? They meant to hurt me!"

Hoodwink brushed the snow off her cloak. "Tush, my lady. 'Tis better to forgive than to seek revenge."

"Forgiveness is for the weak," she snapped. "I despise weakness!"

The man lifted her chin with his forefinger, forcing her to look into his eyes. "The Bible tells us that vengeance belongs only to God."

"Poppycock!" Her lip curled. "I care not a fig for holy writ!"

His eyes widened at her blasphemy. "Then I care not a fig for you," he replied, his voice dripping with contempt. He turned smartly on his heel and left her alone in the frozen garden.

Hoodwink's anger and his unexpected departure took Alyssa by surprise. Stunned, she watched his retreating back. A sudden pain of emptiness closed around her heart. She took a step after him, to apologize, but she stopped at the garden's gate. Why should she go tearing after a mere entertainer who sang for his supper? Choked by her pride and stung by the nagging realization that her rash tongue had brought this latest misfortune on herself, Alyssa stalked back to the castle.

The Lord of Misrule did not even glance at Alyssa during the interminable dinner. Stabbing at the portion of jugged hare on her trencher, she dined on her misery instead. Only the familiar trumpet fanfare roused her from her wallow in self-pity. This time the little page presented her with four wooden whistles, each one carved in the cunning likeness of a grinning blackbird. She thanked the child with stilted politeness. Though she had no idea what she would do with these toys, she would keep what was hers—no matter that the page stared at the whistles with longing in his hazel eyes.

When the second page placed the platter of three honey-glazed capons before her, Alyssa glanced at the Lord of Misrule. He pointedly turned his back on her. She steeled her resolve. Very well, she would show him who was the mistress and who was the minion. She put all three hens on her plate, one on top of the other. When the page delivered another cage with two more doves, she refused to send them to the dovecote, even though her chamber was already filled with the cooing, smelly birds. Finally the page proffered yet another red satin box.

"More pear trees!" Gillian chortled. "They are so delicious."

"Aye, they are," Alyssa agreed in a cold tone. She pulled the box closer to her. "And I will enjoy eating all of them." She regarded the gaping crowd in the hall with hot scorn in her eyes. "At least this mysterious Twelfth Knight has wit enough to appreciate me."

Celeste touched her daughter's sleeve. "*Mon Dieu,* Alyssa. Surely there are enough delicacies for you to share as you did yesterday."

Alyssa sliced through the golden skin of the topmost capon. "Why should I, Mamma? No one has been kind to me today, therefore I will not be kind to them." She stuffed a forkful of chicken into her mouth.

Sir Hoodwink continued to ignore her. Alyssa bit off a piece of the capon's leg meat. Why should she care what that man did? He was her inferior. Yet her heart craved for one sweet word from his lips or a fleeting smile in his eyes.

Alyssa tossed the bones of the first capon under the table where the castle's dogs vied for the scraps. Her stomach felt full and satisfied. She eyed the two remaining hens.

Again Celeste leaned over to her and spoke in a low

tone. "Methinks those tasty birds would be well received at the lower tables."

Alyssa knew that her mother was right, but her pride still rankled. She shook her head. She didn't want the second capon, much less the third, but she had declared her greedy intentions in such an obvious manner that she knew she couldn't retreat now. Instead, she dawdled over the fowl, cutting off a little piece here and there while toying with the rest. She prayed that the dinner would end soon.

When the board was finally cleared, Alyssa waved away the third capon that she had barely touched. Suddenly the Lord of Misrule appeared before her. Intercepting the serving man, he relieved him of her half-filled trencher. With a hard glitter in his eyes, he returned the plate to Alyssa.

"Finish what you have begun." It was a command, not an entreaty.

She shot him a look of pure loathing. "You have overstepped your authority, entertainer. I do not obey a lackey."

Putting his hands on the table, he leaned across to her. "Do you know the penalty for disobeying a command from the Lord of Misrule?" he asked in a dangerous undertone.

Alyssa tossed her head. "I tremble to hear it," she sneered.

Hoodwink gave her a vile grin. "You will be sent outside to the cold, snowy courtyard—where you will cool your temper in the stocks."

Alyssa gaped at him. Had this man completely lost his wits? She glanced down the table at her father. "Papa?"

Sir Guy did not contradict Hoodwink. Instead, he nodded. "An hour or two might suffice."

Her cheeks flamed with resentment and humiliation. The Lord of Misrule smiled his victory, then he whispered to her. "Rejoice and be glad, sullen mistress. You announced that you would eat all the capons, therefore I command that you will. You told your sister that you would have the pear tree only for yourself, and so you shall.'' He opened the confection box and pushed it toward her.

The sight of the sugary tree made her stomach turn over. Throwing down her napkin, she fled the hall and sought sanctuary in her father's counting room. Hot tears of rage and shame filled her eyes. She remained inside the dark, cold chamber for a long time, until she was sure everyone had forgotten her. Slipping out the door, she tiptoed toward the staircase.

Sir Hoodwink stepped from the dark shadows. Without a word, he slipped his arm around her waist. Taken by surprise at his gentleness, Alyssa did not protest. Closing her eyes, she gave herself over to his unexpected attention.

Silently Hoodwink untied the laces that kept her tight bodice in place. Alyssa held on to the wall for support. ''You are not behaving in a seemly manner, Misrule,'' she reminded him, though she was thankful to draw an unencumbered breath.

He pulled apart the stiff back panels. ''Neither are you,'' he observed, though his voice lacked the sharpness he had used at dinner. He unlaced her whalebone corset. ''I have always thought that women's fashions were barbarous.''

With a rush of relief, Alyssa turned to thank him, then she spied the red satin box in his hand. ''What?''

''Now you have plenty of room for this.'' He gave the box a little shake. The sugar tree rattled against the sides.

''Have you no mercy?'' she begged, pushing away the loathsome box.

''Do you?'' he countered.

She blinked at him. ''To whom should I show mercy?''

''To those who plague you.''

Alyssa started to say that people deserved her contempt for being so hateful to her, but Hoodwink lifted the box's lid. The rich almond smell made her want to retch. She held her hand over her stomach to quell its spasms.

"Please," she croaked. "Distribute that thing to who-ever wants it."

"The young turnspits in the kitchen have not had an opportunity to enjoy much of the merrymaking so far," Hoodwink remarked.

She twisted a ring on her finger. "What is that to me?"

He pointed to her hanging sleeves wherein she had stuffed the four blackbird whistles. "Methinks the boys would like those—if you do not require them for yourself, that is." He rattled the box of sweets again. "What do you think?"

Alyssa touched her bulging sleeve. She had to admit that Hoodwink's suggestion was both good and practical. She extracted the whistles from the deep folds and held them out to her tormentor. "Methinks you are despicable." She sighed. "Do I have your leave to leave you now?"

The Lord of Misrule put down the whistles and satin box on the nearby bench. Without a word, he enfolded Alyssa in his arms, pillowing her head on his shoulder. Gently he rocked her back and forth. Tired of fighting not only him but herself, she wound her arms around his waist and relaxed into his embrace. It felt so right.

They stood entwined in the darkened corridor for eternal moments, while the sounds of music and song wafted from the hall. Then Hoodwink began to sing under his breath, accompanying the minstrels in the high gallery. His bari-tone was surprisingly tender, as if he sang the old carol just for her.

For the first time in her life Alyssa felt at peace, pro-tected, even cherished in the arms of this most fascinating man. She drank in the comfort that he offered her. His large, warm hand splayed across her back, massaging the knotted muscles along her spine. A tremor passed through her. Snuggling closer to him, she felt his thigh tighten against her leg.

In the hall, the song ended. Hoodwink pulled himself away from her.

"I have forgotten myself, my lady," he mumbled between stiff lips. "I pray that you pardon me."

Alyssa put a hand over her breast. "There is nothing to forgive."

He snatched up the whistles and the satin box. "There is, though you do not realize it yet," he said under his breath as he strode away.

Alyssa wondered what she had done wrong. Had she said anything new to anger him? She pressed her hand against her fevered brow. She shivered. *Mayhap I am coming down with the ague.* Hoodwink must have noticed it. Still puzzling over the man's perplexing behavior, Alyssa climbed the stairs to her chamber, where Mika was pursuing his futile efforts to capture one of the caged doves. Sleep did not come easily.

Once Max was out of Alyssa's sight, he slowed to a walk. He slipped inside an inviting alcove, where he mopped his face with the back of his sleeve. Hot lust surged through his veins. He had held many a half-clad woman in his life, but he had never experienced the intense sensual power that Alyssa exerted over him. Leaning against the cold stone wall, he ran his tongue across his dry lips. Her fire had burned him clear through to his very soul.

Max knew that he had left Alyssa in a state of quandary, but how could he have told her that he had been within an inch of ravishing her? Without her protective barriers of sturdy corsets and multiple layers of outer clothing, he had felt the real Alyssa made of warm flesh and sinuous muscle that had quivered under his fingers when he touched her. The devil take it! He throbbed for her.

I must be more cautious in the future. Winning his wager with Nate was one thing, but desiring his intended victim had not been part of Max's plan. He realized that he wavered dangerously near the edge of an unexpected abyss. Would he fall?

Chapter Three

The following day during dinner, Max met Tom in the corridor between the buttery and the great hall. "Is everything in place for the parade of gifts?" Max asked.

Tom glanced over his shoulder at the three pages dressed in the Twelfth Knight's white tabards. "Aye, my lord, how goes your quest?"

Max gave him a wry smile. "Well, methinks. The lady grows more pliable daily. All it takes is a firm hand coupled with understanding."

Tom made a face. "And bribed with a king's ransom in presents." He held up a small velvet pouch and shook it. "What do you think your gentle lady will do with these once she sees them?"

"I hope that she will give them to her family as love tokens."

The valet snorted. "Nay, she'll keep them for herself. A few smiles and kisses from you will not banish her greed when she spies this gold. You will see anon."

Max cocked his head. "Time will tell." Signaling the trumpeters to sound the fanfare, the Lord of Misrule bounced back into the noisy hall. As he expected, the notes of the brass horns quickly brought the large chamber to a hush. At the head table, Alyssa sat up with an eager expression on her face. Max clenched his jaw. *Do not disappoint me, Alyssa!*

He held up his hands for attention. "Make way for the messengers from the Twelfth Knight."

With a solemn look marking his importance, the youngest page marched down the center aisle toward the head table. Alyssa rose to meet him. "What do you have for me today, little Cupid?" she asked with a huge smile.

The page leaned closer to her and said in a loud stage whisper, "You are supposed to wait until I announce it's for you," he admonished her.

The hall erupted with laughter including Alyssa. Max grinned with relief. Tom's youngest brother had beguiled the formidable lady.

The boy threw back his shoulders, lifted his voice and shouted, "For the peerless Lady Alyssa from her true love, the Twelfth Knight!" With a quick bow, he presented the velvet pouch to her, then withdrew.

Alyssa hefted the bag in the palm of her hand. "'Tis a rich gift by the jingle of it," she mused, enjoying her moment as the center of attention.

Gillian craned her neck. "Open it, Lissa! I long to see what's inside!"

Alyssa fumbled with the drawstrings then poured out the bag's contents into her hand. Her eyes grew larger. "Oh!"

Max wiped his damp palms on his red-and-gold tights.

"'Tis five golden rings!" Alyssa chortled. Before Gillian or their mother could reach for one, she slipped all five over the fingers of her right hand then held it aloft for all to see. "At last, something practical!"

Alyssa's haste took Max by surprise. She did not even look to him for his approval. Masking his annoyance at her greed, he motioned for the other two pages to come forward. "There is more, my lady," he called.

She grimaced when she saw that the pages carried more

whistles, capons, doves and another satin box. Reveling in her new treasures, she absently waved away the other gifts.

Things were not going as Max had planned. He cleared his throat. "'Tis a wondrous bounty from the Twelfth Knight. Don't you agree?"

Celeste prodded her daughter to look at the pages. Alyssa wrinkled her nose at the whistles. "Keep them," she told the boys. "I have no use for such trinkets when these lighten my heart."

Tom's middle brother couldn't suppress his glee. "You are most kind, my lady," he stammered. "And these hens?" He held up the platter.

Alyssa twirled the rings around her fingers. "Give them to…to whoever is still hungry."

While her charity gladdened Max, her reason behind it did not. He cleared his throat. "My lady, here are more doves!" Taking the cage from Tom's young cousin, he held it out to her.

Looking up from her new baubles, Alyssa rolled her eyes. "Not more feathers! Hell's bells! My chamber is filled with bird droppings and feathers. My cat is frustrated to distraction and the damnable cooing wakens me at an ungodly hour."

Alyssa's mother laughed. "Can it be that there are too many gifts? Methought you wanted to keep everything for yourself."

Max smiled at Lady Celeste. *Bravo!*

Instead of flaring up at this gentle chiding, Alyssa merely giggled and fanned her fingers in the air. "Take all the doves to the dovecote. Put them in pies! What do I care for doves when I treasure these more?"

Max twitched his lips. "As you command, my lady." How could he have misjudged her so badly? Obviously, she was not so pliable as he had imagined. "And the pear tree?" He held up the box.

Alyssa pulled her attention away from her rings. "Give

it to…'' She looked around the hall. Her gaze lighted upon
the three London fops. ''Give it to my suitors, Sir Hoodwink. Perchance the sugar of the tree will sweeten their
dispositions.'' Then she returned to her jewelry.

With a sigh of defeat, Max directed one of the pages to
deliver the boxed confection to the three men. Meanwhile,
Gillian leaned closer to Alyssa; the green look of envy
colored her expression.

''Pretty trifles,'' Gillian observed with a sneer that
didn't ring true.

Alyssa shot a triumphant grin at her sister. ''Aye, they
are. Tell me, Gillie, how many rings did your Jamie give
when he wooed you?''

Narrowing her eyes, Gillian barely masked her anger.
''Only one, but 'twas my betrothal ring and so meant much
more. The Twelfth Knight may shower you with gaudy
trifles, but who *is* he and what does he look like? Methinks
he must be poxy in the face and hobbled with age. My
Jamie is the handsomest man in the North save for Papa.
What's more, I married him for love, not for sugar trees
or golden rings.''

Alyssa merely laughed. ''Jealous, aren't you?''

With a tight smile, Max bowed to the head table and
returned to the coolness of the buttery passage. Tom ma-
terialized out of the darkness.

''What did I tell you, my lord?'' He chuckled.

Max stroked his chin while his mind concocted another
ploy. ''The night is still young.''

Tom shrugged. ''Those rings are glued to the lady's
fingers.''

Max glared at the youth. ''There is more than one way
to catch a trout. Since the hook will not do, I will try
tickling it.''

A noise woke Alyssa from her sleep. Outside, the night
wind whistled around the corners of Snape Castle. She

burrowed deeper into her feather bed. Something pattered against her window; not a steady sound but all in a jumble. Wide-awake and pricked by curiosity, Alyssa slipped out of her warm bed. She wrapped herself in a knitted shawl and thrust her cold feet inside sheepskin booties. Then she crept to the window and looked out just as a small shower of pebbles clattered against the glass.

She cracked open the window. "Ho, there! Who the devil are you?"

A beautiful Christmas carol, sung by a gifted voice, answered her question. Clutching the shawl more firmly around her, Alyssa sank down on the window seat and gave herself up to the music. No one had ever serenaded her. Though the wind blew in chill air, she did not close the window. Darkness blanketed the courtyard, but Alyssa was sure she recognized the voice of the singer.

When he concluded his song, she called down, "Well sung, Master Hoodwink! Your voice shames the nightingale."

He answered with a laugh. "Compliments instead of full chamberpots? I am honored, my lady."

Alyssa shivered, not with the cold, but with delight. "Sing more!"

There was a pause, and Alyssa wondered if she had once again ruffled his feathers. Then he replied, "The night air skewers me like a sharp knife. Throw down a token of your affection to warm me."

Alyssa cast a quick look around her small chamber, now emptied of the annoying doves. "I have a robe of rabbit fur," she offered.

He laughed again. "'Tis a noble thought, Alyssa, but hardly a love token. What of your new rings? Surely you have enough to spare."

Alyssa glanced down at her hands. Her rings shimmered in the faint light of her fireplace embers. She should have known that Hoodwink was nothing but a rogue and an opportunist! All he wanted was her wealth—just like every other man she had ever met.

"You aim too high for such a low person," she replied with ice in her voice and aching disappointment replacing the joy in her heart. "I do not have to buy favor with anyone, least of all a player like you."

"You do," the invisible singer responded with a light bitterness. "Ask your suitors why they came so far north to woo *you*. Surely they could have found someone more amenable closer to London."

Alyssa stiffened; the rebuke made her cheeks burn with humiliation. Without dignifying his gibe with a response, she shut her window with a bang that disturbed the dozing Mika in her lap.

"That man is the most churlish coxcomb who ever filled a pair of tights," she told Mika. Stroking the cat's black fur, she tried to banish the image of Hoodwink in his particolored hosiery. The truth of his words rankled her. "What have I done to deserve this woe?" she asked her purring companion. "At the end of this impossible fortnight, Papa expects me to choose one of those ill-begotten maggots to be my hus…husband. That jolthead in the yard spoke true, Mika. I am a fool for ignoring it. No one wants *me*, but only Papa's gold. No one but you." She wept openly, hugging the sleepy Mika to her breast before returning to her bed, tormented by the cold realization of her fate.

Fresh snow once more blanketed Snape on the last day of 1553, so the inventive Lord of Misrule introduced a morning filled with games of divination and fortune-telling. On several tables scattered about the hall were decks of Italian tarot cards. Another table held paper and quills for numerology and dream-telling. There was a larger table set with bowls of apples and small paring knives for counting pips and peeling the skin to see whose initial it would form. Most of the women, including Lady

Celeste, clustered around Gillian as they vied to predict the coming baby's sex and birthdate.

Alyssa played a game of solitaire by the fire. She had no interest in her future—she already knew it was going to be a long, unhappy marriage. She barely looked up when Hoodwink's minions carried in a large pie, the pastry still warm from the oven. Many colorful ribbons dangled from under the top crust.

"What ho!" cried the Lord of Misrule, parading the pie around the great chamber so that all could admire it. He stopped near Alyssa. "Here is a pie that hides your true fortunes, fresh baked this morning."

The company responded with laughter. Alyssa put down her cards—she was losing anyway. Would the knave make her the butt of merriment in payment for last night? She steeled herself for that eventuality. Let him try!

"Come!" Hoodwink invited. "Draw a ribbon and see what Dame Fortune has cooked up for you!"

Alyssa wrinkled her nose. *Why does that rapscallion have to look so handsome, even this early in the morning?* It would have been far easier to disdain him if he didn't have such a fine, manly figure; if his shoulders were not so wide; if his expression did not make one want to smile back at him. Despite her best intentions, a pulsing knot grew in her stomach.

The family and their guests drew out the ribbons. "Your fortune is in your face!" shouted one. "You will beguile a stranger in the coming year. Take care of your heart," another read.

Gillian greeted her fortune with a yelp of joy. "Talk of wonders! It says that my babe will one day be the light of the world! How did your pie know that 'tis I who is expecting a child?" She regarded the Lord of Misrule with a dazed look. "'Tis sorcery."

Hoodwink grinned. "Nay, 'tis only a game. Therefore,

be of good cheer.'' He offered the pie to Alyssa. One black silk ribbon remained.

Alyssa stared at the ominous-looking strand. She did not have to look around to know that all eyes were upon her. For once, being the center of attention was not pleasant. Silently she damned both Hoodwink and his pie to the lowest circle of hell.

''Do you dare to take the risk?'' the knave whispered to her.

She lifted one eyebrow. ''Of course! I expect the worst.'' Pursing her lips, she pulled out the last paper.

''Read it, Lissa!'' Gillian commanded in a loud voice. ''Mayhap it will tell how many men you will tar and feather in the coming year.''

With her sister's gibe stinging her ears, Alyssa unrolled the little scroll and read, ''Stop crying for the moon and look back to earth. Your true happiness stands close beside you.''

Startled by this unexpected message, she looked up—right into the lush depths of Hoodwink's dark brown eyes. ''Where *is* my happiness?'' she whispered to him, holding her fortune against her fast-beating heart.

''Closer than you can imagine—if you will but open your heart to it,'' he replied. Then he gave her a slow, secret smile that shook her equilibrium to its very core.

At dinner that day, Tom Jenkins sidled up to his master while the fowl course was being served. ''All is in readiness, my lord. The trumpeters await your signal.''

Max nodded.

With a smirk, Tom continued. ''Would you care to make a wager with me, my lord?'' He hefted a velvet bag. Inside five more golden rings clinked against each other. ''Will the lady part with any of these?''

Max shot him a wry look. ''You think that she is too fond of gold?''

"Why is one of Lady Alyssa's rings so important to you?" Tom asked. "You have a great fortune already."

"'Tis not for my purse, but for the lady's sake," Max replied as he watched Alyssa through the drapes. What a prize she would be for any man if she could only learn to love! "By sacrificing something she covets, she will reap a greater reward—or so I hope," he added to himself.

"Will you wager with me, my lord?" Tom prodded.

Max wasn't as sure of himself tonight as he had been last night, but his pride forced him to nod. "Agreed. Ten shillings on my lady's generosity."

Tom chuckled in the back of his throat. "I feel as if I have picked your pocket."

Max signaled the fanfare. Through the crack in the drapes, he saw Alyssa clap her hands with joyous expectation. Last night's five rings gleamed in the candlelight. Tom's middle brother stepped into the hall carrying a beribboned basket. Max followed behind him.

"My lords, my ladies," he called out though the chamber had already grown quiet. "'Tis the sixth day of Christmas and once again we are visited by the loyal servants of the Twelfth Knight. Page," he addressed Tom's sibling. "What do you carry and for whom is this gift?"

Out of the corner of his eye, Max saw Alyssa half rise from her chair. *Remember your fortune and look for your true happiness, lady mine.*

The boy lifted his voice. "I bring six gilded eggs laid by the finest geese in England to grace the table of the peerless Lady Alyssa." He tipped the basket slightly so that the company could see the goose eggs, hard-boiled and painted with miniature scenes of rural England framed in rich gilding. Alyssa led the applause. Each egg was truly a work of art. Max wondered what she would do with them.

"By my troth," she said when she lifted one out of its green satin nest. "'Tis the cleverest workmanship I have ever seen, isn't it, Mamma? The Twelfth Knight is obviously a man of most interesting tastes.''

"Yea, verily," Max muttered under his breath. He snapped his fingers for the second page to appear. On his silver platter he carried four more blackbird whistles, three luscious capons and the pouch containing the fateful rings. The littlest page followed behind with more doves in their cage and another red satin confection box.

As soon as Alyssa spied the pouch, she ignored the other gifts. "Stars!" she cried. "More gold!" She quickly shoved the rings onto the fingers of her naked left hand. "Now I am truly matched, am I not, Gillie?" she added with a look of triumph.

A cold lump formed in Max's gut. Tom would be richer by his master's silver before the New Year's bells had rung. Max stepped to the high table and pretended to admire the gifts he had gathered in London nearly a month ago.

"I see you have found happiness, my lady, but is it true?"

Alyssa showed him the ten rings adorning her long, slim fingers. "What do you think, Master Misrule?"

"I was wondering what you will do with the goose eggs, my lady," he said, hoping to divert her attention from her jewelry.

Alyssa looked at her mother who held one. "'Tis my pleasure to give them to my family," she replied in a grand tone. "Does it please you, Mamma?" she added in a more normal voice.

Celeste smiled warmly at her daughter. "They make a perfect New Year's remembrance and I am glad not only of this magnificent egg but more so because of the giver." She kissed Alyssa on the cheek.

Flustered yet encouraged by this show of unexpected affection, Alyssa quickly distributed the other eggs to her family and guests. Then she ordered the doves to the dovecote, the hens and the sugar tree to the village's mayor and his delighted family. With a mischievous grin on her face, she presented blackbird whistles to the castle's chamberlain, the captain of the guard and the head butler.

Holding up the fourth whistle, Alyssa announced, "'Tis the season for gift giving and yet none has gifted us more than our Lord of Misrule."

The hall cheered her remark. Max looked around him, somewhat taken aback by the warmth of the company. He bowed to the revelers.

Alyssa held up her hand for silence. "Therefore, Sir Hoodwink, I give you…" She paused, smiling at him.

Max held his breath. If it was a ring, then he had not only won back his money from Tom but, more importantly, he was well on his way to winning the lady's heart. If she gave him the whistle—well, it was a step in the right direction.

Alyssa handed him the fourth blackbird. "You have made us right merry, Master of Misrule. I pray this trinket will make *you* merry."

Max accepted the whistle with a deep bow. "You do me honor." Leaning across the table, he whispered, "Tell me, do you not feel weighed down by all your wealth?"

Alyssa shook her head. "One can never have too much gold."

Max bowed again. "King Midas said exactly the same thing." He left her staring openmouthed at him.

On the first day of the year 1554, the Cavendish family exchanged little presents with one another. Alyssa's gifts to her family seemed small in comparison to the bounty that she had received the past week from her mysterious admirer.

During breakfast, Alyssa fingered her golden rings under the table. Guilt welled up inside of her. *I ought to give one to Mamma, Papa—and even to Gillie.* But she had grown too fond of them. She wished that Sir Hoodwink had kept his remark about King Midas to himself. It had given her an uneasy night and a sour taste in her mouth this morning. Her rings felt as if they had grown heavier during the past twelve hours.

Alyssa's unease persisted through the midday's ritual blessing of the apple orchard and during the first part of the New Year's feast. The cooks had surpassed their usual excellent fare with the presentation of a succulent roast boar, ushered into the hall with the Boar's Head carol. When the trumpet's fanfare blew during the final sweets course, Alyssa's unease only grew, though not enough to dampen her curiosity.

"What novelty do you think your knight will send today?" Gillian asked her as the drapes parted. "More golden rings?"

Alyssa had no idea how to answer her sister's thinly veiled envy. Fortunately, the arrival of the first gift halted further conversation.

"Happy New Year's Day from my master, the Twelfth Knight," intoned the tallest of the three white-clad pages. "In honor of the seventh day of Christmas, he presents seven swans a-swimming."

The page placed an oblong mirror on the table before Alyssa. Seven tiny swans made of puff pastry, filled with thick cream and decorated with sugar icing eyes and beaks, swam across the glass. Having learned by uncomfortable experience not to covet the entire dish for herself, Alyssa took one, then graciously presented the remaining six to the other diners at the high table. The heaviness she had felt all day lifted a little, until the second page appeared with more decorated eggs, whistles, capons, doves, sweets—and another pouch containing five more golden rings. In short order, Alyssa dispatched the eggs to the chamberlain's table, the whistles and sweets to the children's table, the doves to the dovecote and the hens to her suitors. She could not resist the five rings as they were more richly fashioned than the previous ten. However, once they joined the others on her fingers, she found that she had trouble folding her hands together.

At the conclusion of the meal, but before the cloth was removed, the Lord of Misrule introduced a new custom called "Wassailing the Milly."

Alyssa glanced at Hoodwink. When he spied her look, he gave her a sly grin. *How now? Methinks he is up to something with this new trick.*

"Behold the Milly," Hoodwink cried as Tom entered the hall carrying a large, brightly painted box. On the lid was a pretty little figurine of the Madonna and her child. "Today the Church celebrates the Feast of Mary's Purification after the birth of Christ," Hoodwink continued. "'Tis a tradition in the southern and eastern parts of our land to give a gift from the heart to the Holy Mother and Child on this day." He pointed to the wide slot at the Madonna's feet. "The coins and jewelry that you give from your bounty will be donated to the poor for their needs this cold winter."

The men and women from the almshouse looked thunderstruck then clapped with joy. Alyssa slouched in her chair. "Peter Sheepshanks never did this tomfoolery when he was Misrule. Methinks Hoodwink intends to line his pockets."

"Not so," said Jamie as he pulled out his coin purse. "'Tis a custom I have observed for many years."

Gillian playfully nudged her husband's ribs. "Pay no attention to my sister. She is afraid that she will have to part with a farthing or two."

Gillian's rebuke made Alyssa's cheeks burn and she prayed that no one was looking at her. Just then, the minstrels struck up a lively carol as Tom approached the high table. Sir Guy dropped ten golden angels into the box. With a smile, Celeste unpinned her pearl and ruby brooch from her bodice and pushed the costly gem through the slot. The three suitors donated showers of silver coins.

Everyone seated at the lower tables had something to offer the Virgin on her feast day when the box was passed to them. Hoodwink cheered their generosity. It soon became apparent to Alyssa that she would be the last person to receive the box, and therefore whatever she decided to give would be the most conspicuous. She cursed the scheming Lord of Misrule for putting her in such an embarrassing situation.

Alyssa cast a furtive glance at the wealth that glittered on her fingers. Besides the fifteen golden rings, she also wore a slim silver one that Gillian had given her that morning as a New Year's token. Alyssa twirled the silver ring. Gillian should be honored if Alyssa gave her sister's gift to the Milly, being a gift of love. Glancing up, she saw that Hoodwink watched her closely as the alms box came nearer. Gillian removed a golden bangle from her wrist. Alyssa knew that Gillian particularly liked that bracelet. Next to his wife, Jamie held out his purse, ready to donate the whole thing to the Milly.

Alyssa tried to clasp her hands together under the table and discovered that the rings prevented her. Again she looked at the wily Lord of Misrule. When Gillian dropped her gift into the slot he shouted his approval and blew her a kiss. Something snapped inside Alyssa's breast. More than anything she wanted that knave of hearts to shout out his approval for her as well. She craved his special smile, his sweet kisses and the smoldering looks he gave to her alone. The golden hoops that encircled her fingers did not thrill her as much as the warmth of the Lord of Misrule.

Gritting her teeth, she stripped off all her booty of the past three nights, leaving only Gillian's circlet in place. When Tom stopped before her, his face perspiring freely from the weight of the box, Alyssa quickly dropped the handful of rings into the horde.

"Bless you, my lady," the young man whispered before he moved on. "Though you have now cost me ten shillings, I am glad of it."

Alyssa had no idea what the youth meant. He must have quaffed a few too many beers in the buttery. Sir Hoodwink flashed her a smile that sent her pulses racing in double time. Then he lowered his head and kissed her hand. Each bare finger received his tender, exquisite salutation. Alyssa feared she might swoon.

"Yours is the greatest gift of all in this company," he murmured between his kisses. "For you gave that which you most desired while others gave that which they did not."

Alyssa could not think what to say in reply. In fact, she found it very difficult to think clearly while he continued to worship her hand. Sir Guy broke the spell. Rising from his chair, the master of Snape Castle glared at the hireling who dared to make so free with his daughter.

"Master Hoodwink, attend me immediately after this repast," he commanded the Lord of Misrule.

Hoodwink released Alyssa's hand, but only after he had given her a reassuring squeeze. "Your servant, my lord," he replied to Sir Guy.

Alyssa swallowed hard. She wished that the Lord of Misrule had not been quite so obvious with his personal attentions to her. She knew how frightening Papa could be when he was angry. From the set expression on Guy's face, Alyssa knew that the volatile Cavendish temper was not far from the surface. *Thank heavens, Papa has no idea of the kisses that have already passed between us—or does he?*

After dinner, she tried to slip after them but her mother, guessing Alyssa's intention, kept her close by her side.

Max followed behind Lord Cavendish as the older man stalked down the gallery. Outrage radiated from the set of the lord's broad shoulders. The time had come for Max to declare himself and his intentions. He touched the paper inside the breast pocket of his doublet. He prayed that Nate's letter of introduction would mollify the formidable Cavendish. He rubbed the bridge of his nose. What exactly were his intentions and were they honorable? That was the sticking point. By now, he had dismissed his wager with Falwood.

Sir Guy pointed to his counting room. "Close the door behind you." He strode into the small chamber and threw himself into the only chair.

Max glanced back down the hallway to make sure that Alyssa had not shadowed them before he shut the door. Then he turned and bowed to the fuming lord. *One of us must remain calm at all times, if I am to escape with my skin intact.*

Sir Guy stared at him with unblinking blue eyes. "How dare you touch Lady Alyssa! Explain yourself but be brief. My fingers itch to flay your hide."

Not a promising start. Max drew in a deep breath. "Permit me to introduce myself anew, my lord. I am Sir Robert Maxwell of Mordrake Hall and more recently of Queen Mary's court at Greenwich."

Sir Guy's frown smoothed with surprise. "What say you?"

Max continued in a rush before the huge man caught his second wind. "I have here a letter of introduction from Sir Nathaniel Falwood, who lately paid court to Lady Alyssa—with poor results."

To Max's unutterable relief, a tiny smile fluttered across Lord Cavendish's lips. "Aye, 'tis one way to describe the unfortunate man's luck. I have reimbursed him for his lute. I understand he prized it greatly."

Max handed him Nate's letter. "Indeed, my lord. 'Twas from Venice."

Sir Guy broke open the wax seal. "Exactly what he told me." He lapsed into silence while he read the contents.

Max prayed that Nate's penmanship and spelling were better then his usual output. Max tried not to sway or fidget while his lordship deciphered the handwriting.

Finally Sir Guy looked up at Max. "Lord Falwood speaks highly of you and his recommendation is appended with the signatures and seals of several others with whom I am acquainted. Very well, Sir Robert, I accept your identity. Now tell me why the disguise?"

Max relaxed his stiff shoulders. "Would your lovely daughter have looked twice at me if I had come as one more suitor?"

Sir Guy grinned. "Unlikely. So you woo her in counterfeit?"

Max hedged his answer, since he wasn't quite sure of it himself. "I have come to win her affections. In truth, I am also the Twelfth Knight."

Sir Guy whistled. "You must be serious about my daughter."

The sticking point! Max winced inwardly. "Lady Alyssa's fire and spirit are equal to her beauty," he replied evasively.

Sir Guy steepled his fingers together. "You know the dowry?"

"Aye, my lord. 'Tis most generous, but I am rich enough without it." Max had no intention of deceiving Guy when it came to the family fortune. If he kept faith with his wager, he would leave Alyssa sadder, wiser and still unmarried. That possibility disturbed Max's flexible conscience more than being labeled a fortune hunter.

Sir Guy's eyebrows rose. "I've never heard *that* claim before."

Max smiled. "I have good air to breathe, my lord, and clean rain to wash me. I have the sun to warm my body and cheer my soul. I can afford food enough to satisfy me and a pallet to sleep upon at night. I have all that I need in this life save for one thing—sweet Alyssa's love." Max wondered if there was a special place set aside in hell for lying churls.

Sir Guy sat up straighter. "Do you jest with me, Maxwell? In all honesty, my daughter is no sweet kitten but a wildcat."

Max shook his head. "I saw the marks of your daughter's disdain on poor Nate's head and I have witnessed the tempest she is capable of brewing, yet still I crave your permission to woo her."

"I am not so sure that I want a lunatic for a son-in-law."

"There is method in my madness, Sir Guy. Trust me."

Lord Cavendish stood. "It appears I must. Therefore, you have my permission to pay court to Alyssa as either yourself, or the Twelfth Knight or Sir Hoodwink or whomever else you pretend to be for the next week. But mark me, sir, I will not have Alyssa hurt by you in the end."

Max did not answer him but merely bowed. For the first time since he had shaken hands with Nate Falwood, Max regretted the wager. The realization shocked him.

Chapter Four

That night and the following morning, Max kept his distance from Alyssa while he tried to sort out his jumbled emotions. The hurt in her eyes almost unmanned him.

Papa must have threatened the Lord of Misrule with dire bodily harm, Alyssa concluded when Sir Hoodwink turned away from her smile for the fourth time. Churl! Coward! She should have known better. After all, he was only a hired entertainer. She had allowed herself to be beguiled by his winsome smiles, his sweet singing and a few stolen kisses. Very well, she decided, she would cease to favor him with her better nature. If he wanted her friendship, he would have to wade through fire for it—or at least challenge her father's wrath. For her part, Alyssa would pay him no more attention than any other lackey.

But her memory savored the taste of his kisses and her body yearned to feel his arms around her once more. Alyssa found it difficult to pretend indifference when she saw him jest with her mother or sing a ballad to one of their guests. Restraining herself proved to be an uphill battle. By the midday dinner, she was close to exhaustion and tears.

Again the familiar fanfare of trumpets sounded. Hoodwink bounced through the drapes, grinning broadly at her.

It was the first time he had acknowledged her in nearly twenty-four hours. *If he thinks I am a slobbering puppy that will come at the snap of his fingers, Hoodwink is sadly mistaken.* She pretended to rub away an imaginary spot on her gown.

"Once more the Twelfth Knight's pages have arrived," the Lord of Misrule announced to the company. "They bear more fine gifts for the Lady Alyssa."

Gillian dug her elbow into her sister's ribs. "Look up, Lissa!"

Alyssa gave her twin a sidelong glance. "This daily parade grows tedious," she remarked, though she was dying to know what new present would be offered. Suddenly the tables near the archway erupted into laughter. Taking a quick peek through her lowered eyelashes, Alyssa saw eight of the most ungainly looking milkmaids accompanying a painted canvas cow whose rear half had trouble keeping up with his front half. As the "maids" came closer, she recognized them to be the kitchen potboys under their exaggerated face paint. She pressed her lips into a tight line to keep from laughing.

The "maids" and the gangly cow executed an hilarious dance that Alyssa realized must have required a great deal of practice for the boys. Glancing at Hoodwink, who stood on the sidelines, she guessed that he had been the master of this mummery. The Lord of Misrule was obviously in the pay of her mysterious Twelfth Knight. That explained Hoodwink's excessive baggage in the storehouse.

Alyssa ached to laugh as everyone else did, but she would not give Hoodwink the pleasure of her approval. Let him feel the sting of her indifference. When the dance concluded and the cow executed a sidesplitting bow before her, she yawned aloud. The potboys glanced one to another, first bewildered then crestfallen. Alyssa felt a little sorry for them. Far from displeasing her with their antics, they had been very entertaining, but she could not possibly admit it with Hoodwink hovering so near.

Guy frowned at his daughter, then tossed a pouch of coins to the tallest "maid." "Well done, sweet lass. You have won *my* applause even if *some* among us are too rude to agree."

The boy caught the reward, bowed to the master of Snape then signaled the others to follow him out. Hoodwink patted the leader on the shoulder as the boys filed past him. With a glare at Alyssa, he signaled for the Twelfth Knight's pages to appear. When she saw that they carried more of the same gifts she had already received, she pretended that one of her fingernails had split.

"From the Twelfth Knight, who sends the Lady Alyssa his most heartfelt love and esteem," announced Hoodwink as the platters of swans, honeyed capons, gilded eggs and the rest were placed before her.

Alyssa didn't even give the velvet bag of rings a second glance. Instead, she removed her napkin, rose and turned to Celeste. "I fear I have a most wicked headache, Mamma. This dumb show has only made it worse. I pray you excuse me." Not waiting for her mother's permission to leave the table, Alyssa gathered up her skirts and swept out of the hall. Though Hoodwink tried to catch her attention, she avoided him.

Once back in her room, she relaxed her guard. It was exhausting to play the injured party for hours at a stretch. She curled up with Mika on the window seat.

"Now we shall see," she told her cat. "I wonder how long 'twill take for Master Misrule to come a-creeping up the stairs to beg my forgiveness for his cold behavior. Let us say an hour, Mika, for he must first engage the rest of the family in some entertainment. Aye, an hour will suffice. Meanwhile I can rest and plan how I will greet him when he comes."

The clock in the tower chimed the hour, then another

half, but no one knocked on her door. Not even her doting mother had come to see if Alyssa felt better or to offer a posset for her headache. As the second hour crawled by, it was not her head that ached but her heart.

"Listen to the music, Mika," Alyssa pouted. She pressed her ear against her door. "Everyone is having a merry time down in the hall. Hell's bells! I can hear that knave's voice above the others. Everyone is enjoying themselves but me."

She flung herself down on her bed. Thinking that his mistress planned to retire for the night, Mika happily joined her. The fire in Alyssa's hearth burned lower; her candle sputtered in a pool of hot wax. Still no one came to check on her, not even Molly. It was as if Alyssa had disappeared. The long wait had given her time to think and she didn't like what she saw within herself.

"Do you suppose that I have insulted Hoodwink?" she asked the sleeping cat. "Did I push him too far? He is not used to my ways."

Tonight not even her mother had played their usual game. In the past, when Alyssa had stomped off in a sulk, Celeste followed her, attempting to soothe her daughter's thorny temper. After pampering and special attention, Alyssa would be sweet to please her parents, until something else pushed her back into Gillian's shadow. But tonight, no one had come after Alyssa. Had she played her harsh hand once too often? What if her parents were tired of her?

Alyssa dashed away a hot tear from her cheek. "I will make amends tomorrow, I swear." She would apologize to her parents and then seek out the Lord of Misrule and...and say something appropriate so that he would know that she had enjoyed the dancing cow.

Still fully dressed, Alyssa fell into a troubled sleep.

On the morning of the ninth day of Christmas, Alyssa was wide-awake before Molly appeared. Instead of berating her maid for not attending to her on the previous night, Alyssa asked her if she had enjoyed the evening's capers.

"Well enough, m'lady," Molly replied with a wariness in her voice as she laced her mistress into a fresh gown. "The Lord of Misrule is a merry rogue indeed. 'Tis a pity that ye were not there."

Has Molly always picked her words so carefully with me, or have I been the biggest fool in Snape and never noticed?

With her new resolution to make amends uppermost in her mind, Alyssa hurried to Mass. Afterward, she startled Guy and Celeste into speechlessness by hugging them both and apologizing for her ill temper. Before either parent could remark upon her changed behavior, Alyssa dashed down the stone walkway to the hall. She hoped to catch Hoodwink alone before he commenced the flurry of the day's entertainment. She was so immersed in planning what she would say to the Lord of Misrule that she almost ran headlong into her suitors, who had gathered together under the staircase.

Judging their manner to be furtive, Alyssa's natural defenses crowded out her more benign thoughts. *How now? What plot are these scantlings hatching now?* She slipped behind a tapestry and listened.

Sir Lucian opened the secret conference. "I do not know what course you two may take, but as for me, I have had my fill of the Shrew of Snape. There is not enough gold in Lord Cavendish's coffers to tempt me to a marriage bed with his daughter."

Sir Lionel nodded in agreement. "Aye, her ill temper of last night has soured me as well. I'll not wed the chit. By the rood, I pity her long-suffering parents. I hope there is some man in this wide world who will take her with all her faults if only to rid this house of her."

"'Tis a wonder her father has not yet drowned her," said Jeremy.

Anger and humiliation rippled down Alyssa's spine as she listened.

"Peevish beyond all reckoning."

"So selfish that she puts the greediest banker in London to shame."

"She has not one shred of loving grace within her. I cannot but wonder at this Twelfth Knight. The man must be mad to court her."

"In faith, she dotes on her ill temper and dines on her disdain."

"Yet I pity her," Sir Jeremy remarked. "For she will die an old, shriveled maid and never know the joys of sweet companionship."

"Save your pity for someone who deserves it," chided Lionel. "Let the devil take her for his dam. I'll have none of Alyssa Cavendish."

"Nor I!" said Lucian.

"Nor I!" said Jeremy.

Alyssa's first impulse was to march boldly among the knaves and pin back their ears with the vehemence of her tongue. But the voice of reason and prudence stopped her. Everything her suitors had said of her was the truth. The future that Jeremy had described chilled her.

"On the other hand, we cannot insult our host," Jeremy reminded the other two. "We must not depart together and appear to spurn his generous hospitality."

"Aye," the others agreed.

"Let us take our leave one at a time, each with some dire pretext or other, so that by Twelfth Night all of us will be miles away from Snape Castle. Thereby none of us will be forced to marry the witch," said Lionel.

"Well said. I can pack my saddlebags and be gone straightway after breakfast. The day is clear and the roads frozen. With luck, I can make York afore nightfall." Lucian glowed with more good humor than he had shown during his entire stay at Snape.

"And I will follow you on the morrow," added Lionel. "I shall say that my duty to Queen Mary compels me to return to court."

"That leaves me until Thursday," Jeremy said with a sigh. "I pray that the fair weather holds until then."

"Then we are agreed," Lucian concluded. "Let us disperse and be gone."

"Will you say a farewell to Lady Alyssa?" Jeremy asked.

Behind the tapestry, she strained to catch his answer.

He barked a laugh. "I'd rather be skinned alive. Let her father break the news to her after I have made my adieus. I never want to see the jade again." With that parting shot, he strode out of the alcove. The other two followed a few minutes later.

When Alyssa was sure they were gone, she stepped out from her hiding place. Tears blinded her eyes while her body ached as if she had been beaten. Never before had she heard herself described in such loathsome terms. She knew she was often abrupt with brainless half-wits, but never had she heard the term "Shrew of Snape" and how could they call her a jade—a woman of no reputation? Her virtue was spotless.

A man's arm, encased in a tight red satin sleeve, reached over her shoulder. A clean handkerchief dangled between his fingers. "Would you care to put this to use?" the Lord of Misrule drawled behind Alyssa.

Whirling around, she nearly toppled against him. How had the knave crept so close to her without her knowledge? "Do you often spy on ladies?"

He grinned. "Do you often eavesdrop on gentlemen?" he replied.

Alyssa clenched her hands behind her back. "I have no idea what you mean, sir," she said as coolly as she could.

He continued to wave the handkerchief in front of her. "Methinks that you do. Listening to private conversations is a nasty habit, Alyssa. Sometimes one hears things that they should not."

"You have no idea what evil filth dropped out of their mouths."

"I heard 'chit,' 'hellcat,' 'shrew,' and 'witch.' Did I miss any?"

She swallowed down a sob. "That litany is foul enough."

Hoodwink stroked her cheek and smoothed away the mark of a tear. "In truth, those lords were charitable in their speech."

Alyssa swelled with indignation. "You dare to call those hateful words charity? You are as vile as they."

He continued to stroke her cheek, brushing the tendrils of her hair back from her flushed face. "What they said was gentle in comparison to what is said about you beyond the safety of your home."

She gasped. "My name is bandied about the countryside?" She clutched the edge of the tapestry.

He stepped closer to her and slipped his arm around her waist. Genuine concern filled his face. "Into the very corridors of the court."

"In London?" she whispered. "'Tis hundreds of miles away. Do idle wag-tongues repeat those slanders about me even there?" Her legs could barely support her and she was glad of his strength.

"Aye," he whispered, dabbing her eyes with his handkerchief.

Who cared what a daughter of Sir Guy Cavendish said or did beyond the walls of Snape Castle? Hoodwink was paying her back for last night. And she had almost apologized to him! "I do not believe you," she said through gritted teeth.

He smoothed her hair over her shoulder. "I may be a

rogue but I am not a liar. Did you think that your harsh treatment of past suitors would escaped unnoticed? Why do you suppose your father has offered a sizable fortune to anyone brave enough to wed you? News of good deeds crawls along the byways while tales of wickedness fly like the wind and stick in the ear of everyone who hears them.''

She closed her burning eyes as if to blot out the dreadful truth. "I am not wicked," she croaked. "I only wanted people to admire me—not drag my name in the mud. If my father heard—"

"He already has," Hoodwink interrupted her. "How do you think he feels when he hears his own dear child so slandered in the marketplace? Yet he cannot challenge the entire countryside. 'Tis why he is desperate to find you a husband so that the tongues of gossip will be stilled."

Alyssa leaned against his shoulder. "The whole countryside," she repeated. When had things gone so awry? How had she been so blind? She had only wanted to be her own person. She pulled herself from Hoodwink's arms and blew her nose into his handkerchief.

"Our chimneys smoke much these days. Have you noticed the deluge of cinders in the air?" she gabbled. "They irritate my eyes something fierce. My warm thanks for the use of your cloth, Hoodwink. Now I pray that you excuse me." She tottered down the corridor on unsteady feet. Halting, she looked over her shoulder. "Oh, I almost forgot. I…I am most sorry for my…um…my poor manners last evening." The words were harder to say than she had expected.

He gaped at her. Then a sardonic expression replaced his surprise. "I trust you have recovered from your headache?"

"Aye, Master of Misrule," she answered. "And more than that, I have finally come to my senses." Then she left him before her tears returned.

* * *

"Methinks that Alyssa is ill," Celeste told her husband
as they made their way down the stairs for the day's feast.

Guy looked down at his petite wife on his arm. "How
now? Has her headache turned into a fever?"

"Nay, 'tis very strange. All morning and this early afternoon, she has been like an angel. When Sir Lucian made
his sudden farewells to me, she spoke sweetly to him,
wished him a sincere Godspeed and reminded him to stuff
lambs' wool into his boots for warmth on the journey.
Later, in the kitchens, I overheard her apologizing to Wat,
the turnspit, for acting so peevishly last night during the
boys' entertainment."

Guy lifted both his brows. "Alyssa made a trip into the
kitchens of her own volition?"

Celeste nodded. "And she even went so far as to help
with the setting of the table. And all the while, she...
smiles. Do you think her stomach ails her?"

Guy whistled, then patted his wife's hand. "'Tis more
like her heart."

Celeste gasped. Guy stopped her further questions with
a soft kiss.

"Banish your fears, my sweet. Methinks she is in love—
thank God!"

By dinnertime, Alyssa's sudden reversal of behavior had
been marked by everyone in the castle. Though he was
pleased, Max wondered if her sweet temper was merely
temporary or if a true change of heart had indeed occurred.
He regretted his bluntness with her that morning, but perhaps his dash of ice water over her fragile self-esteem had
worked. In the meantime, he intended to enjoy the new
Alyssa's company.

While the lamprey pie was being served, Jamie muttered
to Gillian, "Methinks this Twelfth Knight only pretends
to woo your sister. If he continues to mock her honor, I
have a mind to challenge him to a pass or two in the
tiltyard."

Gillian only laughed at her husband's chivalry. "Do not waste your time nor spill your blood for Alyssa's sake. She will reap what she deserves anon. You will see. Things always backfire in her face."

Max, who had overheard the exchange, glared at Alyssa's twin. Then he cast a quick glance at Alyssa and saw that she too had overheard her sister's cruel remark. He braced himself for a tempest.

Instead, Alyssa smiled at Jamie. "My thanks, brother-in-law, for your kind offer, but I am not the least offended—by anyone," she added with a smile at Gillian.

Max signaled for the fanfare to begin. As the trumpets' notes died away, the youngest of the Twelfth Knight's pages stepped into the hall.

"My lords and ladies, on this ninth day of Christmas, my master sends nine young ladies to dance for your pleasure. Please welcome the Holly and Ivy Fairies. If they misstep, please excuse them. They are very young," he added before he slipped back through the drapes.

The minstrels in the gallery picked up their cue and began the opening notes of the familiar carol, "The Holly and The Ivy." Max held his breath. Tom and his brother had rehearsed the little village girls daily during the past week. At their practice earlier this morning, the poppets had performed with winsome charm. However, since donning their little gowns, a rash of stage fright had gripped them. Crossing his fingers behind his back, Max hoped for the best as Tom pushed the first little dancer through the drapes.

The child was greeted with indulgent smiles and applause. Emboldened by her reception, she turned her back on her audience and hissed for the other eight to join her. One by one, the fairy sprites tripped into the hall. Though slightly out of time with the minstrels, the girls enchanted the entire company with their adorable looks and dainty roundelay. At the conclusion of their brief dance, they executed wobbling curtsies and were rewarded with a shower of copper and silver coins. At that point, the fairies lost their remaining decorum and crawled under benches and tables to retrieve their rewards. Max glanced at Alyssa.

Laughing, she clapped and tossed pennies for the little dancers. Never had Max seen such brightness in her beautiful eyes as now. When she caught him looking at her, she smiled and beckoned to him.

"I see that you are a miracle worker, Hoodwink," she whispered.

"How so, my lady?" he replied, basking in her delight.

"Your gowns look far better on the children than on our mice."

It took him a moment to recall the conversation of their first meeting in the storeroom. Then he turned his smile up a notch. "I am glad that you approve, my lady. Have I done well for the Twelfth Knight?" he added. He wondered if her quick wits had made the connection between himself and her elusive admirer.

She gave him an enigmatic smile. "I am sure the knight is pleased."

Just then the comical cow and his eight "maids" thundered into the hall, bringing another round of cheers from the company. The boys cut more outrageous capers than the day before and ended their performance by tossing handfuls of sweet comfits from their milk pails.

No sooner had the cow and his cohort withdrawn, than the page bearing the platter of pastry swans and basket of goose eggs appeared. Max watched to see what the new Alyssa would do with her gifts—particularly the rings. Like a queen dispensing largesse, she dispatched the swans and eggs to the lower tables. The whistles were given to the boys who had played the milkmaids. Once again the village's elderly folk were gifted with the capons, and the doves were sent straight to the dovecote. When she received the box of confectionery, Alyssa called for the eldest of the dancing maids and presented the sweets to her, reminding the child to share the rich confection with her friends.

Holding the velvet pouch in her hand, Alyssa turned to Lady Celeste. "For you, Mamma, and for Gillian," she said in a clear, silvery voice. "And I pray that they will give you joy for all the times I have given you sorrow."

Gillian could only gape at her twin, but Celeste stood and embraced her daughter. The two remaining suitors glanced at each other in disbelief. When the tables had been cleared away and the dancing begun, Max bowed to Alyssa.

"May I have the honor of partnering the most generous lady in the hall?" Though he spoke lightly, he meant every word.

With a smile, she nodded. During the grand pavane, as they moved down the length of the chamber, Max remarked, "You have given away all the Twelfth Knight's gifts. Do you therefore reject his suit?"

They turned at the bottom of the figure before Alyssa replied, "Nay, my Lord Misrule, I but followed your advice. You told me that if I gave away my bounty I would get more in return."

This answer was not what Max had expected. He circled around her, then asked, "Is that the *only* reason you have been so generous?"

She curtsied to him. "Nay, in truth, I find 'tis most pleasant to have people smile at me."

At the end of the dance, Max pulled her into a side corridor. Before she could ask him the meaning of his sudden action, he showed her by crushing her against him. He covered her mouth with his, giving vent to his fierce passion.

Alyssa had hoped he would kiss her again, but she wasn't prepared for his intensity nor her reaction. Her knees trembled and she clung to him lest she fall. Her senses, sharpened by the impact, sent her reeling. Her thoughts spun like rainbow whirligigs as he devoured her. When it seemed that there was no breath left in her body, he raised his head and stared deeply into her eyes before his lips seared a path down her neck and shoulders.

Alyssa wove her fingers into the thick hair at the back of his neck. She pulled herself closer, railing silently against the cumbersome layers of their clothing. Her fingers felt the muscular cords of his neck and she could only imagine what the rest of him was like under his shirt. For the first time in her life, she understood why lovers felt no shame to undress.

"Alyssa," he breathed in her ear, sending delicious shivers down her spine. "We had best return to the hall."

She held him tighter. "Why?" *Don't stop! Don't let go!*

"Methinks we are close to doing something rash," he said with an odd hoarseness in his voice. Between each word, he kissed her collarbone, her throat and along her jawline.

"I have always done rash things." She held him tighter.

"I know," he murmured just before his lips reclaimed hers.

Someone cleared his throat behind Alyssa, then Tom said, "My lord…er…Misrule, Sir Guy is looking for you. You had promised to perform some feats of magic."

"Spikes and nails!" Hoodwink whispered into Alyssa's hair. "'Tis a good thing he stopped me in time or I would have performed much more with you." After a quick kiss on the tip of her nose, he slid out of her arms and hurried back toward the boisterous revelers.

His servant, Tom, sketched a small bow to Alyssa. "Sweet dreams, my lady," he said with a knowing grin.

Alyssa pressed her burning forehead against the cool plastered wall. *How can I possibly fall asleep after that?*

During the night, the wind shifted, blowing from distant Russia. Snuggled deep in her feather bed, Alyssa listened to the windows rattle in their casements, but her thoughts were far from the weather. After long wakeful hours, she had come to two conclusions: first, she deeply loved Sir Hoodwink despite the fact that he was only a player. There had been something special about him from the moment he had ridden his fine horse into Snape's courtyard. Secondly, the Lord of Misrule was a confederate of the unknown Twelfth Knight. Tonight, the little dancers' gowns had confirmed her suspicions. If Hoodwink was in the pay of the Twelfth Knight, and the knight sent a marriage proposal to her father, things would become very sticky. Alyssa knew that when she chose the minion over his master, all hell would break loose.

On the other hand, what if Hoodwink *was* the Twelfth Knight?

In the small sleeping quarters off the storeroom, Max burrowed deeper into his blankets. Next to him, Tom slept, wrapped around a box that contained the survivors of three dozen frogs brought from London. Not for the first time since this mad enterprise had begun, Max longed for the comfort of his four-poster bed. Tonight, thoughts of Alyssa Cavendish sharing that bed tormented his imagination and kept him wide-awake. Max realized that he had finally fallen over the precipice. More than the mere attraction of Alyssa's physical charms, the woman herself had trapped him. In the depth of this cold winter night, Max admitted to himself that he was in love with the willful beauty, not for the sake of his inane wager with Nate, but for Alyssa. Winning her would not be difficult—not after the kiss they had shared tonight—but he must keep the secret of his wager from her. Alyssa would damn him to eternal flames if ever she learned of his original plan.

Lady Gillian Cavendish Campbell lay sleepless next to her snoring husband with her hands pressed over her huge belly. A sharp pain in her lower back had awakened her earlier. Now she waited for a second one. Several nights ago, she had experienced what her mother had called false labor pains. Gillian wondered if it was happening again. A second pain speared her lower back. Biting her lip, she endured its sharp pangs. Like the first, it receded, leaving the young woman feeling alone and afraid in the dark. Should she waken Jamie? Mamma and the village midwife had told Gillian that she would recognize true labor by the regularity of the pains. And they should be in her stomach, not her back. Gillian closed her eyes and recited comforting prayers for the Madonna's protection. She had not told anyone, not even her mother, how much she dreaded childbirth.

Someone shook Alyssa. Slowly she opened her eyes. Cold gray light filtered through the ice-coated windowpanes. She blinked. *When did I fall asleep?*

Gillian sank down on the bed. "Oh, Lissa, help me!"

The agony in her twin's voice banished Alyssa's drowsiness. "Gillie?"

Her sister's eyes looked enormous in her pale face, tears spilling from them. Gillian curled up on her side holding her stomach. Alyssa realized that her sister was in the throes of heavy labor.

"What the devil are you doing out of bed?" Her chiding covered her fear. "You should be in the birthing room. Where's Mamma?"

Gillian winced then went rigid. Alyssa knelt down beside her, grasped her hand and held Gillian until the pain had passed. When she had strength to speak, her twin replied, "They've all gone a-hawking."

Alyssa's temper flared. "And left you to fend for yourself?"

Gillian shook her head. "When Jamie rose at dawn, I

didn't say anything. Methought 'twas another false alarm. I didn't want everyone to think I was a goose.''

Alyssa pulled her fur-lined robe over her shift. Then she gently helped Gillian to sit up. "Do you think you can manage to walk a bit? We have got to get you into bed."

Gillian sucked in a deep breath. "If we hurry before the next pain."

"Are they coming fast?"

To Alyssa's horror, Gillian nodded. "Aye, soon after my water broke, about an hour ago. I do not know the time."

Alyssa rang the little bell that stood on her bedside table. "Molly! Dora! Where are the maids? I'll warrant that they did not go hawking."

Aided by her sister's hands, Gillian pulled herself to her feet. "No one came when I called. Methinks the house is empty."

"Hell's bells!" Icy terror gripped Alyssa's heart. What did she know about birthing? Less than Gillian. Yet it appeared that Gillie's fate and that of her babe were now literally in her hands.

Supporting her twin around her waist while Gillie held on to her shoulders, Alyssa guided her slowly down the corridor to the small inner chamber that their mother had prepared for Gillian in early November. Another pain engulfed her twin just as she lay down on the bed. Alyssa held her again until the contraction passed, then she got her under the covers. Thankfully firewood and tinder had already been laid in the cold hearth with a large stack of dry, split logs piled beside it. Alyssa's shaking fingers fumbled with the flint before she struck a spark. Within a few moments the flames leaped high, taking the chill off the room. Alyssa lowered the heavy drapes that hung over the door to keep out the draft. Several layers of thick rugs covered the stone floor.

Once the room was as warm as she could make it,

Alyssa located the two birthing ropes that Lady Celeste had left folded beside the bed. She tied them to the headboard's posts. "Here, Gillie." She laid the looped ends near her sister's head. "When the next pain comes pull on these."

Gillian nodded, her eyes half-closed. "The midwife said that I should have sips of red wine for strength," she murmured.

"Wine!" Alyssa rushed to the door. "I'll get a pitcherful, and, Gillie, don't you dare...uh...*do* anything until I return."

"Hurry," Gillian pleaded.

Never had Snape seemed so large to Alyssa as she ran through the castle's empty chambers searching for help. In the massive kitchen, she finally encountered two potboys who had been left to turn the meat spits and to mind the large black kettles that simmered with savory-smelling food. Though Alyssa had eaten only a light supper last night, she could not face even the thought of food now.

"Wat!" She grabbed the elder of the two. "Where *is* everyone? Why did no one answer my call? Where's Molly?"

Wat, ignorant of Alyssa's distress, shrugged. "Sir Hoodwink took all the fine folk a-hunting this morning. Since there was no one left here, everyone else went to the village for some holiday cheer with their families."

"And put us in charge," added young Todd.

Alyssa ran a hand through the disheveled tangle of her hair. "God save us! When will they return?"

Wat wrinkled his forehead. "I know not, my lady. 'Tis the dinner hour now. The snow must have driven folk to shelter."

"Snow?" Standing on tiptoes, Alyssa looked out the small window cut high in the wall. A blizzard raged outside. She swore under her breath.

Wat put down his basting spoon. "What's amiss, my lady?"

I have two children, and a woman in birth pangs. I cannot show any weakness now or Gillie will be lost. Swallowing her panic, Alyssa replied, "My sister's time has come. We need the midwife."

Todd untied his apron. "I'll go to the village, my lady. 'Tis less than a mile. I'll run all the way. I'll bring help."

Alyssa's throat closed up. Cold sweat formed on her brow. She hated the thought of sending this child—no more than nine—out into such vile weather, but she needed help desperately. "Very well, but wrap up warmly." Glancing around the kitchen, she spied someone's long woolen cape. She snatched it off the peg. "Wear this over your coat."

Todd looked reluctant. "'Tis the cook's, my lady. He'll beat me blue for even touching it."

Alyssa had no time to quibble. She had to get back to Gillian as soon as possible. She tied the cloak around the boy's shoulders. "Wear it, Todd. I will deal with Master Baines should he object. Wat, find Todd a lantern and something warm for his hands."

While Wat went on his search, Alyssa knelt down in front of Todd so that he could see the seriousness in her expression. "Do you know the midwife, Mistress Fender?" The boy nodded, solemn with the importance of his mission. "Tell her that my sister's water has broken and the pains are coming fast."

Todd drew himself up. "I know about babes, my lady. I have six brothers and a sister, you know," he told her.

He's had more experience than I. "Hold the lantern close so that the flame will not blow out. I don't want to lose you on the moor." She shuddered at the thought. "Stay to the road—no shortcuts. 'Tis longer but safer. Promise me."

"Aye, my lady."

Wat returned with the lantern, a knitted cap and a pair of woolen socks that Todd slipped over his hands. "Off you go, scamp!" He guided the younger boy toward the back door.

"May Saint Michael protect you!" Alyssa murmured as Wat pulled open the door. The white storm howled into the kitchen.

With a cheerful swing of his lantern, Todd pushed his way into the wind. Alyssa and Wat watched his retreating form until he disappeared in a swirl of snow. Then Wat slammed the door.

"Todd's a sharp lad, my lady," he assured her. "He'll return in a tick."

Alyssa wasn't so sure. Putting Todd's fate in the hands of the Almighty, she turned to her more immediate problem. "I want a pitcher of red wine and a cup." She tried to think of what else would be needed. Why hadn't she paid more attention when Mamma gave Gillie all sorts of advice about babies? Jealous at the extra attention her twin had received, Alyssa had distanced herself from anything to do with Gillie's confinement. Alyssa cursed her selfishness and stubborn nature.

Wat drew a large measure of wine from the barrel in the corner. With quick efficiency, he got down a tray and put the pitcher, a cup, a bowl of water and a clean cloth on it. Then he set a small kettle of water over the fire to boil. "Smile for Lady Gillian, for I expect she is sore afraid."

Alyssa stared at the boy in amazement. How old was he? Thirteen? He possessed a maturity far beyond his years. Together, with Wat carrying the heavy tray, she hurried up the wide staircase to the birthing room. Gillian's moans greeted Alyssa when she opened the door.

Averting his eyes from the writhing figure on the bed, Wat set the tray on a low table by the fire. He added a few more logs then quietly withdrew. "I'll be nearby," he said before he closed the door behind him.

"Where's Mamma?" Gillian asked as Alyssa wiped the perspiration from her face. "Has the midwife come yet?"

Alyssa smiled as Wat had advised and lied through her teeth. "Soon, sweetling, soon. 'Tis nearly dinner. Hunger will drive our family home."

Time seemed to have stopped. Alyssa held Gillian when her pains came, then washed her face afterward, fed her spoonfuls of wine to heat her sister's blood and some chicken broth that Wat fetched warm from the kitchen. She massaged Gillian's neck and shoulders and said prayers under her breath as her twin's cries grew louder.

At length, Gillian fell into a light sleep. Alyssa, sitting beside her, cradled her sister's head in her arms. Wat's tap on the door roused her. Full of hope that the midwife had finally arrived, Alyssa sped to the door where she found the boy alone, holding a fresh candle.

"The storm grows worse, my lady," he whispered. "The snow is drifting in heaps about the walls. Methinks that the midwife cannot come."

Alyssa leaned against the door frame as she began to tremble. Summoning up more strength from her near-depleted reserves, she asked, "Any news of the hawking party?"

Wat shook his head. Looking down at his feet, he said, "My lady, I am the eldest of nine children. I have seen my mam give birth. Last time, I even helped to catch my little sister."

Alyssa gaped at him. The boy's ears reddened. "Beg your pardon, mistress, but we cannot stand on custom at a time like this. I am fourteen and nearly a man and…ahem…I have seen a woman's nether parts. I can help, if you give me leave, my lady."

Alyssa gripped the door. How could she allow a mere potboy to touch her sister and yet— She glanced through the window across the corridor. The whirling snow blotted out the clock tower. Since no messenger had arrived, she presumed that the hunting party had been too far from the castle when the snow had first began to fall. She prayed that her parents and Hoodwink had found shelter. Alyssa was well and truly alone except for this boy.

She put her hand on Wat's slender shoulder. "I cannot let Gillie die. She is far more than a sister. She is my other half—the better half," she added without a trace of her former rancor. "We must save her and the babe. Come." Taking him by the hand, she led him inside.

Gillian had awakened during Alyssa's absence. When she saw Wat next to her bedside, her eyes widened.

Alyssa smoothed Gillie's forehead. "'Tis snowing very hard, my sweet. Methinks 'twill take a bit longer for the midwife to come. But you are safe. Wat here is skilled in birthing." She squeezed the boy's damp hand. "The three of us will deliver your little slugabed."

Gillian gave Wat a weak smile, then she gripped the bed ropes and stiffened as another contraction took hold. Wat flinched but didn't flee. Alyssa waited out the torment; the pain in her heart mirrored the physical agony of her twin. When Gillian relaxed, Wat told Alyssa, "Take the candle and look between Lady Gillian's legs. If you can see the top of the head, we must get her onto the birthing stool." He pointed to a solid piece of furniture in the corner that Alyssa had not noticed.

"How will I know if I am looking at its head?" she whispered out of the side of her mouth.

Wat gave her a little grin. "You will know it, I promise." He handed the candlestick to her.

"Don't be a goose, Lissa," Gillian whispered. "Quickly, I beg you."

Alyssa rolled up her sleeves, tossed her hair over her shoulders and steeled herself to the task. Suddenly events happened in a rush. Alyssa found herself sitting on the floor at her sister's feet holding a wet, squirming baby in her blood-drenched hands.

"A hearty boy," Wat told the new mother as he caught the afterbirth. Over his shoulder, he instructed Alyssa, "Smack him sound on the bottom so he'll cry strong and send the devil packing."

Alyssa blinked at the very idea of doing anything so cruel to such a tiny bundle of love, but the thought of the devil inside her nephew prompted her to turn him over and spank him. The baby hiccuped, and then gave a lusty cry. Alyssa wiped the child with scented oil and wrapped him in the swaddling blanket that Lady Celeste had left in the cradle by the fireside. A huge lump filled Alyssa's throat as she stroked the child's fiery red hair. Would she ever have such a sweet child of her own? With a sigh, she gave Gillian her son.

"You did right well, my lady," Wat whispered as he wrapped the afterbirth in a rag. "I'll bury this so no witch will find it."

"Wat," Gillian called from her bed. A tired but beatific smile lit up her face. "I will name my son James after his father and Watkins—little Wat—after you, if it please you."

The boy blushed to the roots of his hair. "Aye, my lady, it makes a fine sound in my ear." Then he hurried down the corridor.

No one returned to Snape that night. Wat kept the fire in the birthing room burning bright and brought the sisters some meat, bread and more wine. When the clock tower chimed eleven, Alyssa bedded down on a pallet next to Watkins's cradle and fell instantly to sleep.

The snow stopped after midnight. The following morning, anxious servants returning from the village filled the castle. Mistress Fender, the midwife, was very surprised to discover Wat asleep across the threshold of the birthing chamber, Lady Alyssa asleep near the ashes of the fire and Lady Gillian peacefully nursing a healthy baby boy. The midwife was even more surprised, and greatly shocked, when she heard the tale of young Watkins's unorthodox delivery. Assuming her authority, she dispatched Wat back to the kitchens and sent for Molly to help Lady Alyssa to her own bed.

Shouting and the ringing of handbells awakened Alyssa as the feeble sun lowered into the west. She didn't remember returning to her room nor changing out of her blood-stained shift. Just then Molly poked her head through the doorway.

"Waked ye, did they, m'lady?" She bustled in with a mug of light ale, a half loaf of bread and some cheese on a tray. "'Tis m'lord and lady returned from the hunt—and none the worse, too." She set the tray on the side table. "They just heard the news of Lady Gillian's boy. That rogue Hoodwink found them bells to ring. He offered to light fireworks, but Lady Celeste feared 'twould wake the mother and child."

Alyssa bit into the cheese. "How fares my sister?"

Molly laid out her mistress's favorite red gown across the chair. "Glowing and full of wondrous stories. She said how brave you were, m'lady. And Wat delivering the babe! Think of that!" She shook her head.

Alyssa stopped chewing. *Wat* delivered the babe? No, it was she who had borne the harder part of that ordeal. "My *sister* told you this?"

Molly fluffed Alyssa's sheer veil. "Nay, 'tis the talk in the kitchens. Wat is so proud that his buttons threaten to fly off his chest. And Lord Campbell rewarded him with a fine new dagger made of Spanish steel and a fat pouch of coin."

Alyssa sipped her ale. Leaping at this opportunity to capture the golden opinions of his peers, the lowly potboy had preempted Alyssa's rightful share of the celebrity. Her mouth tightened with anger. Where was praise for *her* role in Gillian's delivery? But before Alyssa worked herself into a full-blown rage, she checked herself. Poor Wat was only a kitchen drudge. With luck, he might become a footman, but nothing more. And admittedly Alyssa had needed his help and advice during those dreadful hours. What if this day was Wat's only moment of glory in his life? She would be churlish to snatch it from him. Keeping her injured feelings to herself, Alyssa dressed and then descended to the hall.

The Yule log blazed high as cups of frothing wassail circled among the Cavendish family, their guests and retainers. Everyone toasted the birth of James Watkins Campbell, the health of his mother, the pride of his father and the family's safe return home from their adventure in the storm. Smiling and nodding as she moved among the company, Alyssa searched for the Lord of Misrule. Voices buzzed around her.

"If you ask me, my Lady Disdain had nothing to do with the child's birth," sniffed the mayor of the village.

"Aye," the gamekeeper agreed, swilling his ale. "Methinks she fainted at the first sight of blood. 'Tis a good thing Wat was at hand."

Alyssa's cheeks burned. Biting her tongue, she glided away before the speakers realized that she had heard them. Not even her parents had sought her out. The old familiar self-pity rose in her throat.

"You have deep circles under your eyes, my lady," remarked Hoodwink in his melodic voice.

Alyssa glanced over her shoulder. This man could creep up on a rabbit unawares. "Oh, la-la," she said in imitation of her mother's French accent. "You do know how to compliment a lady, Master Misrule."

He touched her cheek with the pad of his thumb. "I do, indeed, when these circles tell me that you had a long day yesterday."

"Aye, a little of this and that," she replied as if nothing had happened.

He gave her another one of his special heart-stopping smiles. "You *are* a wonder," he murmured. "I know of no other gentlewoman who could have delivered a babe under such conditions."

She arched her brow. "In faith, I heard that I had merely *helped* the kitchen boy. How do you know that I didn't faint?"

Hoodwink framed her face between his large, gentle hands. "Your sister praised you to the rooftops when I visited her, though I must admit that I *am* surprised that you have not protested Wat's story."

Alyssa shrugged. "People have grown weary of my vain posturing and would never believe the truth. Besides, 'tis the boy's moment in the sun. I will not snatch that from him."

Hoodwink whistled under his breath. "It seems you have grown from a spoiled child to a mature woman overnight."

She gave him a wry smile. "True, I have learned a great many lessons since Christmas morn."

He lifted the wassail cup from her trembling fingers and kissed the rim. "I salute you and your courage, Lady Alyssa Cavendish." He offered her the cup with his kiss turned toward her.

Tears of joy welled up in her eyes. She lowered her head so that he would not see them and took the cup. She drank the toast; his warm regard cheered her like a tonic. When she looked up, he had disappeared. The chamberlain announced the dinner.

Tonight's feast was greeted with loud cheers and lusty appetites. When the trumpet fanfare once again blared from the minstrel's gallery, Sir Hoodwink strode to the center of the hall and raised his hands for silence. Alyssa sat up straighter, wondering what he was going to say.

"My lords and sweet ladies," he began, "thanks to forces beyond even *my* command—" the hall erupted with prolonged laughter "—the usual parade of gifts and wonders from the Twelfth Knight has gotten a little behind." With a flourish of his peacock-feathered hat, he bowed to Alyssa. "The Twelfth Knight humbly craves your pardon."

Alyssa returned Hoodwink's salute. "When God sends us such a storm, there is nothing we mortals can do *but* to forgive, my lord."

The hall buzzed anew. Hoodwink bowed again, then clapped his hands. The middle-sized page appeared through the far archway, escorting a giant pie that was carried between two lackeys. The pastry appeared to be very heavy. The serving men set it on the table.

Alyssa stared at the pie; its top crust jiggled. Startled, she glanced at Hoodwink. He handed her a knife. "Are you willing to take the risk?"

Alyssa gripped the knife's handle with both hands. Gingerly she sliced through the crust that crumbled at her touch. Ten extremely agitated frogs leaped out. The head table dissolved into good-natured pandemonium, much to the hilarity of the lower tables. Many of the guests stood on their benches to get a better view. The frogs sprang in all directions at once. One bright green fellow jumped onto Sir Jeremy's bonnet. Several frogs took refuge in Lady Celeste's empty trencher and refused to move. A bolder amphibian belly flopped into Sir Guy's goblet of wine, much to the lord's amusement.

Over the din, the Lord of Misrule shouted, "Behold! I give you ten lords a-leaping."

The last frog had remained at the bottom of the mock pie, goggling Alyssa with its large yellow eyes. Finally making up its mind to jump, it sprang onto her bodice, then looked confused at what to do next. Alyssa shrieked with both surprise and laughter.

"Oh, most fortunate of frogs!" Hoodwink murmured, looking at the creature planted on Alyssa's bosom.

"Please, Sir Hoodwink," she begged with tears of merriment rolling down her cheeks. "Rescue me!"

"With great pleasure, my lady." He deftly removed the frog, allowing his hand to brush against her skin.

Alyssa quivered at his touch and at the gleam in Hoodwink's eyes. Just as the serving men retrieved the last of the frogs, the drapes parted again. The nine little girls dressed in their holly and ivy finery skipped hand in hand with the eight boys in their milkmaid costumes. Following them was the ungainly cow, clearly the company's favorite. It ambled up to the head table, made a bow, then the front half took off his head, revealing Wat. The chamber broke out with louder applause for the hero of the day. Meanwhile the pastry swans, goose eggs, whistles, golden rings, hens, doves and candy tree arrived beside Alyssa in quick order.

She rose. Hoodwink rapped his staff for silence.

"Good friends," Alyssa said after the hall grew quiet. "Tonight we celebrate not only the eleventh day of our Christmas revels but the added joy of my nephew's birth." She lifted her goblet. "Please join me in a toast to my sister, her husband and their new son, James Watkins Campbell."

"A health unto them all!" Hoodwink shouted.

Alyssa was gratified that everyone joined in her toast. She replaced her goblet on the table and smiled at the potboy. "Wat, I don't know what I would have done without your good work. Please accept my most grateful thanks and these as a token of my appreciation." She handed him the velvet pouch of rings.

Though the boy looked stunned for a moment, he quickly recovered himself. Turning to face his friends and fellow servants, Wat cleared his throat. "For this gift, my lady, you have my thanks. All today I have heard many among you folk say that Lady Alyssa fainted in the birthing room, or that she screamed with fright or that she puked in the corner. In truth, this good lady did none of these things, though I must confess that I did. 'Tis *she* that caught the babe and she that thumped its bottom right well. She was strong enough for the three of us in that room and I'll bloody the nose of the next one among you who says contrary."

He blushed, bobbed his head at Alyssa and her parents. Then, with the back half of the cow trailing behind him, he exited, clutching the precious pouch to his chest.

The silence in the hall was almost a physical thing. Hoodwink broke the spell by shouting, "What ho, I say! Three cheers for the Lady Alyssa!"

His command was obeyed with lusty shouts from the wide-eyed revelers. For one of the few times in her life, Alyssa felt embarrassed, especially when her parents embraced her.

"This is all true?" Celeste asked in wonderment.

Instead of taking this heaven-sent chance to boast of her deeds, Alyssa merely nodded. "Aye, Mamma. Ask Gillie. I must confess to you that my heart was in my mouth most of the time. I truly *did* wish I could faint when I first saw the babe's head."

Guy and Celeste hugged her again, then resumed their places at the table. Alyssa made short work of dispersing her gifts, sending the capons upstairs for her sister, her husband and Watkins's new wet nurse.

Much later that happy evening, as Alyssa returned to her bedchamber, she encountered the Lord of Misrule waiting at the top of the staircase. Taking her hand in his, he planted a kiss in her palm. "Once again you have given away all," he murmured. "And once again, you have received a hundredfold. You are the heroine of the night."

"'Tis only *your* good opinion that I crave," she whispered.

Hoodwink swung her into the circle of his arms. His lips feather-touched hers with a tantalizing persuasion. She welcomed his caress with her own soft kiss. A warm shiver ran through her as he deepened his kiss, turning it into one of passion. Her mouth burned with his fire. She pressed herself hard against him.

"Tell me, Sir Hoodwink, would you dare to take a risk—with me?" she asked, staring deeply into his eyes. Even as she uttered these bold words, she could not believe her audacity, yet she hoped that he would say yes.

His dark eyes glowed with a savage fire. "I am but a common man."

"A most uncommon man." She massaged the back of his neck.

"You are a lady," he said in a low husky voice.

"You once told me that I wasn't."

He nibbled her ear. "What of the Twelfth Knight?"

She laced her fingers in his hair. "He is a will-o'-the-wisp."

He planted a lingering kiss in the hollow of her neck. "The Knight has showered you with riches. 'Tis not easy to keep frogs healthy in this cold climate, you know," he added with a chuckle. "He has wooed you well."

She traced the contours of his face with her fingertip. "But I desire him to woo me better. Methinks that the Twelfth Knight is very near—even in sight."

He caught her wandering fingers. "What do you mean?"

She smiled at him, savoring the situation. *Now* she knew the truth. "Mayhap I should ask you whom do *you* hoodwink?"

His face softened. "You are as wise as you are beautiful."

She unfastened the top two buttons of his garish doublet. "They say I am a hellcat."

He dipped his tongue between her breasts. "Even in bed?"

"I am not sure about that." As he continued to lave her skin, Alyssa's passion rose within her like a hot flame, clouding her brain. "But I am willing to find out, if you are, my lord Twelfth Knight."

He pulled down one of her sleeves, baring her shoulder to his lips. "'Tis not yet the sixth of January. How can you have the Twelfth Knight on the eleventh night?" He chuckled in the back of his throat.

Alyssa's body flooded with desire for him. "It lacks but an hour." She rubbed his inner thigh with her leg. "And I have always liked to open my presents early."

He groaned. "You are a minx." He freed one of her breasts from her bodice. With exquisite tenderness, he touched the tip of her nipple.

She nearly swooned in his arms. "You are the master of your art," she panted, offering herself for more.

"And you, sweet Alyssa, are the mistress of my heart." With that, he swept her into his arms and carried her to her waiting bedchamber.

The following morning, her mother remarked how glowing Alyssa looked.

"A good night's sleep," she murmured, her head demurely lowered to hide her satisfied grin. Sir Robert Maxwell was a very *good* knight, indeed.

She looked around for him and felt a sudden stab of panic at his absence. Of course he would be true to her after all that they had said and done in the warmth of her bed. He had even confessed to his ridiculous wager with Lord Falwood, but what of that when it had brought them together? She loved Max and he loved her. He had told her so in many delightful ways. Yet where was he now?

Guy gave his daughter a quizzical look. "Alyssa, just what have you— Hoy day! What the devil is that noise? Thunder in January?"

Music and a great deal of drumming impeded further conversation; guests and servants ran toward the courtyard.

Picking up her skirts, Alyssa raced after the others, glad she had been able to avoid the question that she knew was on the tip of her father's tongue. Disregarding the cold, she joined the crowd that thronged the steps outside Snape's front door.

Led by the littlest white-clad page astride a donkey, a dozen drummers thundered through the gatehouse in rhythmic chorus. In three rows behind them, eleven pipers played a cheerful martial air. As the musicians stepped to the side, Alyssa saw all the village boys wearing paper coronets and playing leapfrog in the snow. Close on their heels were the nine little girls, well bundled against the cold.

Wat the cow pranced after them, the poor rear half slipping and sliding on the icy patches. The milkmaid potboys still wore their skirts but with woolen nether hose under them. They pelted the onlookers with snowballs instead of the usual comfits. Behind them marched two more pages, carrying huge platters heaped with pastry swans, gilded eggs, a mound of blackbird whistles for everyone, roasted hens aplenty, and dozens of marzipan pears and figgy partridges. Two more pages followed, both laden down with fresh-baked dove pies. All the treats were passed among the revelers, creating a most unique alfresco breakfast.

Then the drummers began a long roll. When the babble ceased, Tom Jenkins, wearing new livery with the crimson-crowned *A,* rode to the center of the yard.

"My Lord and Lady Cavendish," he shouted. "Good lords and fair ladies, villagers of Snape, lads and lasses, good wives and husbands, poppets all—give ear unto me. I take great pride to introduce my lord and master, lately known to you as Sir Hoodwink who now reveals himself to be the Twelfth Knight—Sir Robert Maxwell of Mordrake Hall! He has come to seek the hand and heart of Lady Alyssa Cavendish to be his beautiful, wise and most loving wife—if she will have him!"

Alyssa's heart swelled. Though she had prayed Max would proclaim himself after such loving bedsport last night, she could not believe that it was really happening. Her toes curled inside her thin slippers.

Sir Robert Maxwell rode into the courtyard on his magnificent charger. Gone were the motley trappings of the Lord of Misrule. Instead he was dressed in a fine suit of white velvet and satin. The crowned *A* blazed from his cape. Though the yard was filled to overflowing with people, Max had eyes only for Alyssa. He nudged his horse through the crowd, reining him to a halt at the foot of the steps.

He doffed his scarlet-plumed hat. "Good morrow, Alyssa!" He bowed from the saddle. Then he winked at her. "I note that you still have no golden ring upon your finger."

Alyssa glanced down at her hands. They shook, though not with cold. "I am glad that you possess such good eyesight," she bantered.

Max shook his head with mock seriousness. "Alas, I have only one ring left to give you." He pulled off his glove and then removed a ring from his little finger. The single ruby and twin diamonds sparkled in the morning's sunlight. "Pray, will you keep *this* one?"

A lump swelled in her throat. Max looked so fantastical, as if he had ridden out of her most secret dreams. "'Tis the only one I want."

Max turned to Sir Guy. "My Lord Cavendish, will you give me your leave to marry this most sweet lady?"

As her father nodded with a laugh, Max returned to Alyssa. Opening his arms to her, he asked, "Do you dare to take one more risk?"

Alyssa gathered her skirts in her hands. "Aye! Now and forever!"

With that, she leaped into his arms—and her new life.

* * * * *

CALL THE ONES YOU LOVE OVER THE HOLIDAYS!

Save $25 off future book purchases when you buy any four Harlequin® or Silhouette® books in October, November and December 2001,

PLUS

receive a phone card good for 15 minutes of long-distance calls to anyone you want in North America!

WHAT AN INCREDIBLE DEAL!

Just fill out this form and attach 4 proofs of purchase (cash register receipts) from October, November and December 2001 books, and Harlequin Books will send you a coupon booklet worth a total savings of $25 off future purchases of Harlequin® and Silhouette® books, AND a 15-minute phone card to call the ones you love, anywhere in North America.

Please send this form, along with your cash register receipts
as proofs of purchase, to:
In the USA: Harlequin Books, P.O. Box 9057, Buffalo, NY 14269-9057
In Canada: Harlequin Books, P.O. Box 622, Fort Erie, Ontario L2A 5X3
Cash register receipts must be dated no later than December 31, 2001.
Limit of 1 coupon booklet and phone card per household.
Please allow 4-6 weeks for delivery.

**I accept your offer! Enclosed are 4 proofs of purchase.
Please send me my coupon booklet
and a 15-minute phone card:**

Name: _____

Address: _____ City: _____

State/Prov.: _____ Zip/Postal Code: _____

Account Number (if available): _____

---

097 KJB DAGL
PHQ4013

Travel to the British Isles
and behold the romance and
adventure within the pages of these
Harlequin Historicals® novels

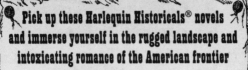

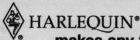